Canvas Carvers
The Death of Matilda Brew

Written by
Maegan Alexandria

WILD REMARKS

Contents

For my Marmee,

who taught me to embrace my liberty.

PROLOGUE

Four figures, one hunched over and the others upright, gathered around the strange newcomer lying on a tarnished bench. A nearby street lamp, its candlelight waning in the thick gray sky, would soon yield to the rays of the unwelcome sun. The night was done, and everyone had travelled back to their luxurious rooms to await the welcoming night. That's what time had become... no more than endless waiting.

The four stood there, each more unusual than the next, as they looked upon the plain boy with utter disdain. Collectively, they appeared calm, but if one were to look into their eyes, one would see a certain frenzied madness. They all looked down, eyeing him as though he were prey, but they wouldn't devour his flesh... they would just bear witness as his soul yielded to the rising swell of the city around him.

They looked at his charred clothing, the ash upon his pallid face and hands, and noted his wild black hair with possibility. This was a boy, not more than twenty, who had escaped from somewhere. This was a lost youth - searching, as they all did, for a future far removed from his past. This was the next guest, and they all beamed, regarding him as a great find.

"What a strange face!" an older man observed with a sneer. The other, a tall woman with blonde hair and a hooked nose, tilted her head.

"Looks like the sun is no friend of his," she spoke dryly, observing his powder-like appearance.

"They get younger and younger, don't they?" a tall, broad shouldered man spoke. They all nodded; never taking their eyes off the boy for fear that he'd vanish. In his unconscious state the boy breathed in and out slowly, his hair moving gently with the cool street wind. Nothing, not even the sounds of the trotting horses nor the distant accordion, played by a man in a satin suit, could wake him.

The woman noticed an object propped beside the boy, which even in the dim light, sparkled and shimmered. It was a mirror, roughly three feet tall and two feet wide. She picked it up and held it directly in front of her face, examining her shrewish looks with glowing optimism. Her visage looked actually pretty reflected in this mirror, and held a certain glow. After a long, deep gaze at her new found beauty, she finally pulled herself away.

"Family heirloom, perhaps?" the woman sneered, and held the boy's sole possession carefully.

Relatively ornate, she felt it a peculiar object to bring along if one was escaping. There was, however, something about it that led her to believe this was a spectacular find. Her eyes could scarcely be drawn away from it. While she was coveting it and questioning its worth, her thoughts were interrupted by the voice of the short, hunched man who snatched the object from her grasp and returned it to the spot by the boy's feet.

"Really, Henriette! Contain yourself!" he scoffed, and Henriette withdrew in embarrassment.

"What should we do?" asked the older man, wearing a deep green suit. He gripped a cane with a glowing ruby attached to the end of it, the rings on his bone-like fingers clinked against the jewel of his pikestaff. He had the cavalier arrogance of one who only interjected to hear the sound of his own voice. The other man, stout and thick-necked, spoke up.

"I say we tell him *about it,"* he said, *looking skyward, or rather, to the top floor of the towering, elegant edifice that stood in front of them. They knew the large, lone window high above them was draped in thick velvet curtains. They also knew what these curtains concealed from the world.*

No one needed further explanation. They all knew and, together, the remaining three followed their friend's gaze to that singular window with devoted reverence for the man behind it.

They stared upward with wonder and unexplainable awe. The beauty of the boy's mirror now forgotten, they watched the window with both fear and admiration, each recalling their first day.

For the woman, she remembered a white dress with a ripped hem. And a bruise.

The thick man recalled the moments after his last train ride, briefcase still in hand.

And for the old man, he was fleeing from the memory of his son who had been fighting abroad and returned home... in a pine box.

The short, hunched man could hardly remember the day he arrived in an alcoholic stupor. It had been so many years since then.

"Ooh! Let me tell him! Let me!" the blonde woman exclaimed, jumping up and down with excitement.

The hunched man again looked up to the window, smiled thinly, and spoke a single phrase that cooled and prickled their skin.

"No need," he spoke, continuing to stare at the window. "He already knows."

Chapter One
Black Umbrellas

It had been two hours since Gunther Doyle had delivered a message that would change my life. It was a cruel irony that as Matilda lay enveloped in the darkness of death; my memories were only of the vivid light and color she had brought to my world. The time we'd shared had been all too brief. Pain filled my soul.

Gunther was known as a vexing man with a blatant history of stretching the truth. I left the house immediately disbelieving.

I had loved her from afar, yet she lived not more than three streets down and around the corner to be exact. Matilda, my Matilda, was leaving this world? Had she not been collecting lilies for Mayday just this past spring? Had she not just danced under the tallest noble fir in the village during Christmastime? Had she left this world, without knowing of my love for her, the love I felt, and yet so guarded?

Racing toward her house, I made my way, desperate and out of breath. A crowd was gathering and making their way into the house to say their last goodbyes. They stood with sullen expressions, shielding themselves from the rain with their newspapers and black umbrellas. Those who came to offer comfort stood there, forlorn and shivering to their very bones, allowing the rain to drench their sorrow.

If you knew her like I did, you'd feel our loss with the same pain that crushed everyone's heart that day. Matilda's smiles lit up this dull town of Howell Village. She brought joy to every street. She *loved* life and my soul ached to know it was leaving her. The rain had taken away our sun...

***

"There was an old woman.
Her name, it was Peg.
Her head was of wood
And she wore a cork leg."

My brother, Anvil, and our mother and I all sat around the table quietly sipping on the broth. It was the same thing we'd eaten every day for the month of December. Anvil and I called it Stone Soup, a fable favorite, but a name that equally described the broth's dull taste.

I was born a Godfrey, into a poor and an unhappy household that despised my very existence. My older brother fared better. The family treasure, he received the only second portions to be had for any meal. His birthday was the only one celebrated, and his curfew was extended on special occasions. As for myself, such favors had never been in question. I'd long been forgotten and, for a while, I preferred it.

As we sat there, a sort of chanting began outside. A small group had gathered, oddly combining song and laughter. My brother and I sat upright with excitement and craned our heads to better hear the noise outside. Our mother sat in silence, tightly gripping the spoon she held in her hand. The singing continued:

"The neighbors all pitch'd
Her into the water.
Her leg was drowned first
And her head followed after."

Anvil and I laughed and my mother slammed her spoon on the table, an action which silenced us both. Suddenly, there came three knocks on our door, each followed by more singing and frivolity. Mother sprang up and nearly threw her chair back as she marched to the door. My brother and I both followed, wide eyed with curiosity and feeling terribly sorry for the poor fool who would soon be torn apart by our mother's fury.

Mother opened the door to a short girl wearing a coat with tails and a worn top hat. She was surrounded by three boys all wearing similar clothing. They all sported painted mustaches and sideburns, and a single carrot stuck out of the girl's mouth. She removed it and jammed it into her pocket.

It was Matilda Brew, the girl with the biggest and finest house down the street. I caught my breath and my face flushed. I was sixteen then, and she was the prettiest girl in the world to me.

"Good Morning, Mrs. Godfrey!" She said, trying to conceal her girlish tones by lowering the pitch of her voice. "We come from the lofty village of Hoover-Kenting-Estonia offering the finest pies that the world has ever tasted. Care you to sample apple or blueberry?" Matilda said, as she held out two pies. My mother looked at her as if she'd just been punched in the stomach. My brother and I hid behind her, trying not to laugh.

"What is this? Where are your parents, Miss Matilda? You ought not to behave so foolishly," my mother scolded. Mother's words did not deter the girl. She held out a pie, which my mother, as poor as we were accepted, reluctantly.

"Sour Apple, then," Matilda smiled. The boys around her all chuckled with a strange admiration.

"Hello, Anvil. Hello, Andrew. What'cha been doing these days? Hiding away from the sun?" she asked. Neither one of us answered, both frightened of our mother's inevitable wrath should we play along in Matilda's silly game. "Here. Take a pie, too," she said, handing Anvil the blueberry pie. He blushed, a reaction I'd rarely seen from him. Matilda was good at charming people, even stupid oafs like my brother.

"Go home, girl, and get out of those ridiculous clothes. I'll speak to your father about this." My mother's cold voice cut through the warmth of the pies. Matilda smiled and pulled out the carrot from her pocket.

"No need, Mrs. Godfrey. My father loaned me this hat to wear," Matilda replied, kindly. The boys behind her chuckled at mother's stone faced expression. The girl stuck the carrot back in her mouth and waved goodbye.

"Enjoy the pies and have a pleasant rest of your day!" Matilda said, as she balanced on our swinging gate and then skipped off with the rest of the group, an action which nearly gave my mother a heart attack.

"Oh! And by the way, you've got a rabbit on your roof!" Matilda called out. My mother turned red and spun around, making her way back into the house.

Matilda. I couldn't help but smile. There was *no one* like her.

My mother closed the door and bolted it shut. We knew to be quiet about what had just happened, but the smell of the pies made that all too difficult. So beautiful were they, each one decorated and woven with leaf shaped crusts and a sprinkle of cinnamon, I could hardly wait to try one.

Suddenly, my mother jerked the blueberry pie away from my brother and headed to an open window in the kitchen. In one swooping action, she dumped both pies outside, providing a feast for the stray dogs. My blood boiled, as I watched her shut the window and dust off her hands on her apron.

"We don't take hand outs, especially from such rude and outlandish creatures," she said, harshly.

Anvil took his seat beside our mother and resumed eating the Stone Soup, ever subservient to her rages. As for me, I was caught between dutiful obedience and the anger that I often suppressed. Anger won, as I stormed out of the kitchen and into my room. I heard my mother call out.

"If you feel differently, Andrew, you are always welcome to leave!"

I fell back onto my bed and stared at the wooden planks above my head. Leaving this place seemed like a dream, but to leave also meant I would never see Matilda again. I'd never see that funny face with a painted mustache, never hear her sing or watch her parade around the town, so carefree. She was a small piece of heaven in this miserable little place called Howell Village, and I knew I'd never find another person like her. I laughed to myself at the memory of her swinging on our gate, the tails of her tattered coat moving with the wind.

I thought of her last words. Rabbit. Rabbit. Rabbit. She said there had been a rabbit on our roof. What did she mean?

Quietly, I opened the window leading to the garden and climbed out, gripping stones as I climbed my way to the top of the house. On tiptoes, I peeked over the ledge and saw a small stuffed rabbit sitting on the roof. Looking around me, I grabbed the rabbit and made my way back inside.

Still gripping the soft doll, I shut my window and flopped back onto my very hard bed with a thud.

It was a small gray rabbit with long ears and button eyes. Tenderly, I held it in my hands, amused by the strange gift. It felt oddly heavy and, upon turning it, I inspected loose stitches running down the animal's back. Easily, I undid them before a small brown package, no bigger than a packet of cigarettes, fell out of the rabbit. A note came along with it:

"For the boy who never speaks, but always draws."

The note was enough to tell me that the rabbit had been left for me. I'd been known to daydream and was frequently spotted using my pencil to create small sketches along the edges of my desk in school. That was many years ago, and I'd since decided, or rather my *mother* decided, that drawing was a foolish waste of time. My heart raced at the thought of Matilda knowing something so secretive about me, so intimate.

Upon opening the package, I discovered six charcoal sticks. My hands shook as I held them with excitement. It was the most precious gift I would ever receive. In truth, it was the *only* gift I would ever receive.

Matilda never visited our house again. Not that I blamed her, but I watched and waited for every moment I could see her. Embarrassment prevented me from thanking her for the gift, but I mentally promised her then that I would always be there should she need me. In Howell Village, I'd remain... if only for a chance to see her again. I loved her then and three years later, I loved her still.

It was evident to me that Matilda had been ill. Weeks had gone by and we saw less and less of her. She hid it well enough, but not too well to fool me. I studied her features and her amiable expressions. They were better known to me than my own mother's, yet there she was slipping from my fingers without having ever shared more than an hour together. The line of sorrowed spectators inched slower than I could bear and I knew I would have to beg and plead my way through it. Solemn laments passed back and forth from the gathered townsfolk, as I pushed my way through.

"Poor girl, not much more than nineteen."

"Her mother is terribly distraught, beside herself with grief, and her father never leaves her side, I hear."

The words they spoke only frightened me as the reality of Matilda's possible death seeped into my boiling veins. The rain poured harder and I looked down at my sopping shoes and drenched pant legs, not caring if I tasted tears or the earth's showers.

With a heavy heart, I saw the remnants of a chalk drawing on the sidewalk; the very one I had a hand in creating a few days before. Large droplets fell from my bowed head, running down the image, wiping away the portrait in all its majesty. The rain had nearly washed it away, taking not only the portrait of Matilda, but Matilda herself.

***

"Old man, what on earth are you doing?"

The sidewalk in front of the Brew house was occupied by an old man kneeling on it, drawing on the pavement in blue chalk. He looked up at me and then resumed his artwork, carefully shading in portions of what looked like the ridge of a nose.

"I'm drawing a portrait of Miss Brew. She's not well, poor girl," he remarked.

On my way home from work, I often took my time as I walked past the Brew House. I'd seen the town doctor walk in and out from time to time. Occasionally, I'd see the local parson make his way inside, and my stomach would turn. It seemed a bit drastic to call for a parson, I thought. I looked up at the window of her room. No one told a boy my age anything. There were whispers around town about Matilda falling ill, but the symptoms always varied. Some said she had a cold, others said it was rheumatism, but often it had been a fever that was mentioned. Her diagnoses never were confirmed or denied, but it had been weeks since I'd seen her and I was growing more and more anxious. My own family knew nothing about it. As far as my mother was concerned, she cared little for Matilda and even less about her condition. So, I'd walk about town, too shy to ask, but desperate to know.

The curtains were only partly drawn, and I could see Mrs. Brew bringing linens into her daughter's room. The old man coughed, pulling me out of my thoughts.

"So I've heard. A cold, that's all. Nothing too serious. She'll get well soon enough," I said, managing to convince myself. The old man kept drawing, focused and quite determined.

"She loves the drawings I often do on the side of my house. The colors, she says, are the most beautiful in the world," he smiled, and I nodded in agreement.

"They certainly do stand out amidst all the gray around this town," I said, closing my jacket around me. "Just like Matilda herself."

"She hasn't been by to see my drawings lately. I suppose she can't go out these days. So, I thought I'd bring some of my artwork to her. I'd like her to look out the window and have something beautiful to see besides the gray skies," the old man said, his face and overalls covered in dirt.

"It's all I can afford anyway," he shrugged, as I smiled and observed the sweet portrait, now recognizable as Matilda herself. It captured her spirit well. Her face was bright, her lips full, and her eyes seemed to sparkle. Her hair had yet to be finished, and I looked up at the sky, with worry. It seemed to be full of heavy clouds, a looming possibility that there would be an unwanted weather change.

"You best hurry. There may be rain soon enough," I observed, and the man looked up at the sky with acknowledgement.

Awkwardly, I shuffled about with my hands in my pockets, eager to help. I looked around me, careful to check the street for my older brother or mother who might catch me slacking about.

"I fair well with my own drawings. Allow me to help you?" I asked, sheepishly. The old man, who's name was Morgan, nodded and handed me a piece of light chalk.

Together, we worked quickly. For the next twenty minutes, each was careful not to smudge any piece of the portrait. We tossed ideas to and fro, passed the bucket of chalk back and forth and, finally, finished within the hour. We stood up and admired the work on the sidewalk with pride.

"It's a masterpiece, old man. You should be proud!" I beamed. He hunched forward and patted my back.

"Couldn't have done it without your help, son," he said, never taking his eyes off the ground. With an anxious sigh, he then headed toward the front door of the Brew House and knocked. In a panic, I ran behind a neighboring tree and watched. This was the old man's gift and I wanted Matilda to know it.

From a distance, I saw Mrs. Brew answer the door, look at the picture outside the gate of her house, and smile. Morgan bid the woman adieu and walked back toward his creation. He stood beside it, smoothing his hair, and waited. I imagined that, like me, he grew nervous as he anticipated Matilda's appearance in the window. Then, the old man smiled, as from behind the window, Matilda looked out, searching for the old man. When she saw him and saw the portrait beside where he stood, she smiled. She waved weakly and set her hand on the window, as if to show extreme gratitude. The old man dipped his head down and waved goodbye. It was a sweet moment, but I stood stunned. Matilda looked pale, seeming to stumble as she turned from the window. I barely recognized her. Why did she appear that way? She was alive and rosy cheeked, always, yet this girl was not the Matilda I last saw. Her frailty sent hot tears of anguish to my eyes. I didn't like seeing her like this and the way the old man had quickly left, made me sense he felt the same.

***

In desperation, I pushed my way through to a low window. A number of children were beside me, all peeking in, anxious to see her. Pressing my forehead against the downstairs window, I imagined her father upstairs, standing vigil. Surely, he held his daughter's small hand in his, giving her the only comfort he was able.

People who had only a *passing acquaintance* with Matilda came to pay their last respects. It didn't seem fair. Why would those who had no strong connection to the girl be allowed to share her final moments? The treasured time seemed to be meant for those who loved her deeply, those who knew her well and, like her father, I felt that I belonged by her side. It was precious time that I needed to say all that I never could.

I wanted to tell Matilda what she meant to me. I needed to look upon the eyes that I had so often seen before, bright and open. I yearned to feel the soft raven hair that had fallen about her face when she visited my father's watch repair shop, the very last time I saw her.

Shy as I was, I knew nothing I could ever do would capture her attention, but there was always the hope that I clung to. Long had I dreamt that I would burst from my shell of soft spoken timidity and take her for my own or, at the very least, speak to her without stumbling over my words. There were confessions that needed to be spoken, and memories still to be made...

***

Something happened the night of my eighteenth birthday. I'd spent the day alone without as much a command to "fill the trough" from my mother. It was to be expected. That was the way birthdays usually went. They were depressing days where, I'll admit, I intended to lie down and do absolutely nothing at all.

The aging part, the part that everyone hated so much, didn't faze me. What bothered me most was that, on a day set aside for the sole purpose of acknowledging someone's existence in the world, I'd always felt so completely removed from anyone else on the planet. Until then, I'd never existed.

The sun had gone down. After drawing in a sketchbook I'd managed to commandeer for myself a few months back, I hid my charcoals in a nook under my bed and headed toward the window.

Nightfall was my favorite time of day. Anything was possible then! It was that feeling that propelled me from my room, out the window and toward a small stream, not too far away. I'd gone there many times to escape, to be away from the house for a while. I found it my solace as the years went by. Mother didn't know anything about it. Had she discovered my sanctuary, I'd be sporting a large welt across my left buttock.

"Godfrey, is that you?" a voice sounded from behind a nearby hedge. Matilda stood under the pale moonlight dressed in the most peculiar get up. She wore a white ruffled collar and a long tulle frock that likened her to a circus performer. In her hands, she carried three small oranges. Her cheeks were painted pink and her face was powdered white. Upon her head, she wore a small red hat.

"I'm so glad I saw you. I meant to head over to your place," she smiled and, unbelievably, threw her arms around me! I stood stiffly. What was happening?

She released me and smacked my shoulder with a grin. "Happy Birthday, you loon!" she laughed. She must have seen the confusion on my face because she quickly added, "We sang to you once at school. I remembered the date. Birthdays are wonderful, aren't they?"

I stood there, stupidly, unable to speak. Here was Matilda, dressed like some sort of fanciful ballerina under the moonlight with *me* on my birthday, and I could say nothing. I cleared my throat.

"You came to celebrate m-my birthday?" I smiled, and she shook her head.

"Actually, I came to juggle for you," she said, and she walked over to a bridge and set her oranges on the ground.

"Have you ever been to the circus?" she asked me, and I shook my head, making my way onto the bridge. "Well, neither have I, but I read in a book once that some performers juggle knives and flaming torches. Lucky for you, I have access to neither one of those things! These oranges - stolen from the finest palaces in northeast India - shall have to do."

"India?" I spoke, disbelieving.

"Imagination, Andrew!" she exclaimed. With a graceful, artistic step forward, she began her introduction.

"In honor of our good man Godfrey's birthday, the palace sends its finest juggler across the sea to Howell Village. Enjoy!" she announced.

She took a step back and picked up the oranges, then took a deep breath, and sent the fruits into the air. In seconds, they had all fallen to the ground. "Let's try that again, shall we?" she suggested, and I laughed as she fumbled again, nearly losing her balance.

"I practiced, I promise you," she giggled, and I laughed harder. "You're laughing at me?" she chuckled. She tossed the fruits up again, only for them to come crashing down.

"You're terrible!" I said, before covering my mouth and concealing my laughter. She threw an orange at my head and I quickly caught it and held it up to her.

"Can we just *eat* these instead?" I asked, and she laughed.

"If the birthday boy commands," she mocked, with a low bow, and I began peeling the orange. It was the first thing I'd eaten all day. When the orange was peeled, I handed her half and we sat on the edge of the bridge eating in silence.

"Thank you for traveling all the way from India for me," I said, rather bravely. She shook her head.

"It wasn't for *you*," she said, with smiling sarcasm. "I was headed this direction anyway. Errands from the palace. You understand," she mumbled, through a mouthful of orange.

At that moment, I wanted to tell her everything. I wanted to taste the orange on her lips and run away with her. A stillness came between us. At length, she spoke.

"It's late. I've got to get home before they find me out," she said, reluctantly. Before I could help her, she jumped down from the ledge and made her way off the bridge.

"Allow me to walk you?" I asked, hoping she'd say yes, but she didn't.

"You should go home. I don't want your mother to be angry with you," she said. She was right, though it broke my heart to see her go. We stood there in silence for a moment, and then she walked up to me and gave me the smallest kiss on my cheek.

"Happy Birthday, Andrew," she smiled.

She left after that, leaving me stunned… and with something to dream about. I'd often walked by her house after that, hoping to share the last orange with her, but it seemed hopeless with one young man after another seeking her attentions and, though it didn't appear that she fancied any of them, I knew that one day she would. One day, I'd run out of time and by then, it would be too late.

***

My palms were moist with sweat, as I walked back to the line of visitors. A single tear caught at the corner of my eye and suddenly, as despair overtook me, I began shoving my way through what felt like a sea of bystanders.

Time seemed to stand still, and I seemed to be running in slow motion. I could not get there fast enough.

Sympathy and a sudden understanding of my frantic behavior seemed to prevail, however, as strangers behind me whispered,

"Let the lad through. He seems to be yet another one of her many admirers."

True as it was, being called a mere *admirer* stung, as if casually tossing my love pathetically aside with all the others who sought her attention. *My* love was real. Couldn't the townspeople, so cloaked in the gloom of the storm, see it? My fists clenched, as my soul ached.

There was the small thought that things *could* be different. The power of love was strong and it was with hope that I clung to the possibility of *curing* Matilda. Foolishly, it was my belief that in my profession of love, she would miraculously recover and the people of Howell would see that I was so much more than a mere admirer.

It was a relief, however, to be acknowledged as one who deeply and sincerely cared for her. I took the stairs, two at a time, and burst into the room. Her father turned to me, tears of overwhelming grief filling his eyes. His daughter had passed. Her body lay limp and pale. The town doctor held the arm he had bled just moments before, tears and lost hope in his eyes.

Somehow, only by her apparel and location, I recognized her as my Matilda, but her spirit was so far removed from her that she was hardly recognizable. Matilda was gone from my world. She had entered another, and I became instantly envious of the angels who now attended her. As beautiful as ever, it would be the last time I looked upon her face. All my life, Matilda seemed to float above me on a cloud. Now, she was truly among those clouds, and I could not even weep at her passing. Even the agonized wailings of her mother could not release the grip of shock that consumed me.

I saw her. I saw my life without her, and the world turned black. I collapsed to the floor.

Chapter Two
Stop the Clocks

What happened next is somewhat humiliating. I woke to find myself on a bed, in an unfamiliar room, with a sea of faces staring down at me as I regained consciousness. I shot up like a cannon from the comfort of the soft mattress.

"Matilda! I had - that is I dreamt - this dream - this nightmare, really-" I sputtered. My rambling was silenced by the cold, harsh tones of my own mother's voice.

"Matilda is gone, boy!" she snapped. She stood in the corner, her expression reflecting the embarrassment she felt at her youngest son fainting. Anvil stood beside her with his usual arrogance. There was no sympathy for me, the son who had just lost the love of his life.

"Get off that bed!" she hissed, "This town has enough to worry about without you fainting like a woman."

I dragged myself from the bed and Fester Davies, the local bookshop owner, escorted me out of the room. I barely glanced at my mother. I knew she was secretly glad that I could no longer waste my time and energy on Matilda Brew. Possessing neither warmth nor compassion, Mother had never encouraged her sons to marry for love. She would never accept Matilda's free and uninhibited nature. It was *Rigabella Newt*, the banker's daughter, that mother thought was worthy of her younger son's affections.

Rigabella. I despised the name even *more* now that marrying the wretch seemed to be my inevitable fate.

I walked from the bedroom to realize that I had just come from another room in the Brew's home. The house was quiet and most of the visitors had gone. The remaining few were talking among themselves, completely ignoring me.

"The wake begins," one woman spoke.

"My sons will see that the clocks are stopped in every room," my mother's emotionless voice sounded.

"Why, look at that! We've forgotten to cover the mirrors!" Mr. Davies exclaimed.

"Don't give any thought to that old superstition, dearest!" Mrs. Davies replied, "Matilda's off to heaven now. We'll see her soon enough," she comforted.

The conversation grew distant as I took off in a determined hunt for Matilda's room. Her spirit was still in the house. I could feel it, and I wondered how long it would take before she left toward the sky and the heavens beyond. I had no doubt in my mind that an angel like Matilda belonged nowhere else but heaven. She had glowed, even on earth.

When would it become real? My Matilda? Dead? When would I fully grasp this? Right now, she felt close beside me, as if she were not gone. I knew, however, that this feeling wouldn't last. One morning, I would wake up and realize there was nothing - no one - to live for. At last, I reached the door to Matilda's room.

"Where are you off to, Andrew? Don't you have and manners, boy? Common decency?" a woman scoffed.

It was my mother standing behind me, her hair so tightly pulled back, it left a bulging vein protruding at the edge of her forehead. With great embarrassment, I walked from the door, following her out of the house. It was my shy, usual way of conducting myself as my mother's personal lapdog and the villagers all knew it. They returned sympathetic stares to my whispered farewell. I'd seen that collective look of pity a million times before.

The streets were dark and empty. All the mourners had gone and resumed their lives, not yet realizing that the days would now shift to a darker shade of the dull gray we all lived in. I knew this with certainty and, as we walked back home in silence, I reviewed that day's sequence of events countless times.

It would always be with me. Turning on the kettle, hanging the sheets to dry, opening my father's shop in the morning... all regular responsibilities of a normal day, masking what was to become the darkest of my life. How did one prepare for death, I wondered. My own father died too early for me to remember how it was then.

We reached our house and I looked around. Was I simply expected to return to my normal life, just as before? It didn't seem possible. Nothing would ever be "normal" again.

"Don't just stand there, Andrew! Start peeling the potatoes!" my mother ordered.

My mother was impossible. If you looked for her heart, you'd find a piece of coal in its place. I clenched my fists as my brother smirked, but dutifully began peeling the small potatoes, slowly at first, then faster under her watchful eye. Every movement I made was scrutinized. Every word was dissected, and then dismissed, as if I'd never said it. Feelings and emotions were not acknowledged in this house. It was something I struggled with time and time again. I heard Anvil sigh as he set the table, and I restrained myself from hurling one of the spuds at him.

"He's broken hearted ma, can't you see?"Anvil jeered. He started laughing and I peeled faster, ignoring the familiar taunting. He acted as if nothing had changed, as though Matilda had not just passed. He teased relentlessly, callous and uncaring that she would be in a casket soon enough. In vain, I struggled calling him *brother*.

My mother, who had finished sweeping, grabbed the potatoes from me and quickly pealed the remaining three. "We won't speak of her anymore, Anvil. She's gone and she'll not be coming back!" she shouted. The words struck me like a slap as I gripped the edge of a chair, avoiding Anvil's smug smile. My mother, with her customary harshness, continued:

"As for you Andrew, there will be no moping about. This will *not* affect your chores and duties to your family. Is that understood?" she pecked, and I nodded. I only wished to have the courage to tell her that I did *not* understand. How could I? She expected me to go on as if nothing had altered my life, but altered, it *was*. I would dread coming home. I would dread going to work. There would be no purpose without the hope of seeing Matilda.

"Ma!"

It was Anvil who called out to Mother. She turned to him, expectantly.

"Did you stop the clocks at the Brew's place?" he asked. My mother's eyes widened.

"Why do you ask me? You and your brother were supposed to tend to that!" she scowled.

Anvil picked up his bag and put on his coat, our mother heaving a great sigh.

I had forgotten all about the old custom of stopping all clocks at the time of a person's death. It was a stupid custom, I thought, brought on by some strange superstition, but I, too, got up and put my coat on. Anything to leave this place.

My mother called out to us, as we headed for the front door. "Best apologize to the Brew Family, Anvil," she reminded. We were almost out the door when my mother snapped at me,

"Don't linger, Andrew!"

Don't linger? I inwardly cringed at that. Perhaps, she didn't remember that there was no longer a reason to linger.

My brother and I headed back to the Brew House and found it still bright from within, the candles not yet dimmed. The door was ajar for those who still wished to pay their respects. Shivers crawled up my spine. I didn't want to enter her house. Not again. It would become real if I saw her, and I wasn't ready for it to be real. I followed closely behind my brother as he took the steps, two at a time, and nearly collided with Matilda's father, Baxton Brew. His eyes were red, and he wore an expression combining anger and fatigue.

We met eyes for a moment before my brother spoke up. "My apologies, Mr. Brew, we forgot to stop the clocks earlier," Anvil muttered. Mr. Brew's eyes widened in horror, his nostrils flaring.

"You boys have one job to do and you can't even get that right," he said. Walking away, he took a sip from his flask. "5:53," Brew continued, his voice slicing through the thick cloud in the room.

"Sir?" Anvil asked, whilst I cowered behind him.

"The time was 5:53. That time will forever haunt me," Mr. Brew said softly to himself.

He was right. The time, down to the last second, would be forever etched on my heart. It would be engraved forever in my memory, just like her smile.

"You take the rooms upstairs," my brother commanded, as he interrupted any further thoughts. I watched him as he began the task in the first floor dining room.

There I stood, in a panic that left my mouth dry. I couldn't stop the clocks upstairs - especially the one located in Matilda's room! That's where she had slept and awakened in the morning. In that room, she had dressed for Sunday school, and fixed her hair for the Bloomington Ball. How could I step into the room that once held the movement of her life, but was now merely a prison of memories that would torment all who loved her...?

I was not yet ready to go upstairs. As I wandered about the place, prolonging the inevitable destination, I found myself envisioning her about the house. There she was at the window… and then, at the piano, playing softly.

With a heavy heart, I stopped the small clock on the mantle above the fireplace, imagining her running down the stairs in the morning, glancing at this very clock so as not to be late. She would cast one last, lingering look at it before ending her day and going to the haven of her bedroom. My entire being was filled with images I had never seen, but could only imagine. These imaginings were my constant companions throughout my workdays at the clock shop.

Upon the occasional encounter with Matilda, I learned much. I knew she was well loved by everyone who met her. She was kind and giving and could make conversation about anything. This was a colossal difference between us, as I often sat timid and quiet behind a book or my sketches, watching her dance by with a free spirit and an open heart. My admiration for her had grown over the years and, as I walked around the house, I remembered the day I last spoke with her. Fondly, I recalled her cheery manner as she brought the last payment for her father's watch.

My own father had passed years before, when I was but an infant. His shop was left to my mother, who passed it on to Anvil and me when I was twelve. Mother was determined that the shop would fare well after our father's death. To that end, Anvil and I spent more years in the watch shop than in a classroom.

Despite our sacrifice, Anvil and I rarely showed a profit. If the people in our town wanted to fix their watches, it was difficult to be paid for our service. We scarcely ever sold a *new* watch. Most of the time, I sat in the back of the store, teaching myself mathematics and the basics of geography.

Anvil arrived home quite drunk one evening, and my mother insisted he spend the next day in bed. There was always a strange tenderness she had for my brother, and an equally bizarre hatred for me. Regardless, I was usually left to run the shop alone, as I had many times before, and await business that rarely came.

Matilda entered the shop that day. Beautiful and vibrant, she spoke to me with ease. I, however, could barely stutter out a thank you when she handed me the last payment. She laughed and asked if I was alright, but what could I say? My throat was dry and words weren't easy to come by when she drew near.

"No," I shook my head. "You make me nervous," I admitted. She laughed at that and I was glad I could take her beyond a smile for a real laugh.

"Why is that?" she asked, as she twirled about the room. I covered my mouth to hide my laughter.

"I think I'm quite the silliest person you'll ever meet. You shouldn't be nervous," she said, tugging her ears and crossing her eyes to make me laugh. When it worked, she left the shop, singing a goodbye, and skipped down the street. I ran to the window and watched her, wishing I could have spoken more courageously.

Perhaps, I still lacked the courage, but death made everything so real. So final. Everything ended, and just as my father's life had ended years ago, so had Matilda's. The sweetness of that memory was embittered by the reality of it all.

Stirred from my reverie by a nearby visitor's sneeze, I resumed my duties and stopped the old grandfather clock in the parlor, before heading upstairs.

There was one clock in Mallory's room, which I stopped first. Matilda's younger sibling, Mallory, was a sweet, small girl, whose looks somewhat resembled her sister's. She was wide eyed and frail because, unfortunately, she bore the curse of being born with a clubbed foot. When she was out for a walk, she found it necessary to stay in her sister's shadow for fear of ridicule. Matilda, with tender cheerfulness and courage, was Mallory's protector, shielding her from any jeers or taunts. It was yet another reason to love her.

I stopped the small ticking clock on the dresser beside her bed and set it down. Taking one last glance around the room, I breathed a sigh, desperately battling my nerves as I prepared for the next room.

The hallway just outside Matilda's room was decorated with small dangling frames, most of them slanted and askew. I straightened them as I passed, using the gesture as an excuse to examine the photographs. The dread of entering Matilda's room, mingled with curiosity, and the overwhelming desire to view these captured glimpses into her life.

There she was, in a family portrait beside her mother. Mallory, an infant, then, was cradled in Mrs. Brew's lap. They looked well and much livelier than any other family in Howell Village.

Our family photograph, by contrast, looked as if we had all been nailed to the stools which we sat on, uncomfortable with such nearness to each other. It also seemed that we had a great aversion to any source of light, chalk-pale as we were. Then, of course, we were missing a father figure, which evoked a sense of pity as one looked at our picture. My mother wasn't one for photographs, but she found it a necessary precaution in the event my brother or I ever needed to be identified. Always mere practicality, I thought. Our family portrait was not taken with a wholesome spirit of loving togetherness.

A few other pictures revealed relatives unfamiliar to me, so I quickly scanned them before approaching a silhouette portrait of Matilda. It was perfect. Had she moved in it, I would not have been surprised, for it was so like her. I wanted to speak to it. I wanted to say all that I never could while she was still alive.

My brother's heavy steps made their way to the foot of the stairs and I heard him call out to me. "Hurry up, chowder head... I'm starved!"

Rolling my eyes at his loud crudeness at such a time, I bravely made my way down the hall toward Matilda's door. *You can do this. There's nothing to it.*

I walked into her room. It was still alive with Matilda, even though her body had already been removed. Her soul would not come back, despite my deepest wish that it would.

Her bed was neatly made and a small bundle of wild flowers lay in the center of the pillow. The night stars shone brightly through the window and I had to remind myself that she was now a part of them. My heart ached as I found her locket on the small nightstand by her table. She wore it everywhere. I opened it and discovered a picture of her parents on one side and Mallory on the other. She loved her family dearly which, to me, was incomprehensible.

After my father died, a black cloud descended upon our house. I was but a baby, too young to remember the details, but deep inside I felt that our family had been much happier before his death.

It was at that moment that something caught my attention. I noticed a *mirror* on the wall. It hung, framed in bronze, and reflected a dismal looking young man in a worn out jacket, black hair askew and unbrushed, and a face so pale it blended in with the white walls. I walked closer to the glass and saw the dark rings under my own eyes.

Suddenly, taking me completely by surprise, I realized I was sobbing. In my head, I could hear my mother's harsh criticism of those tears, and my descent into abject sorrow. I sobbed even more. In a whirlwind of self-pity and loss, I shielded my eyes from my own reflection in the mirror. I felt like a fool whose emotions were betraying him. The sobs I heaved were foreign to me.

I had occasionally seen people cry, but I was unaware that I, myself, was capable of such profound emotion. Empty and alone, I knew that my only chance for happiness was gone all too soon.

Looking back at the mirror, I sobbed even louder. Tears blurred my vision as I saw my face transform slowly, as in a mist, from a pale weakness to a warm healthy complexion. My hair seemed to be lengthening and, while I found this extremely odd, I was incapable of making any sense of it.

"You cry like a girl, Andrew Godfrey," a high pitched voice sounded.

Quickly, I wiped my face and turned toward the door. No one was there, and I turned to the mirror again, feeling not only foolish but delusional. I buried my head in my hands.

"Andrew, pull yourself together! You're such a baby," the voice sounded again, and I kept my head buried in my hands. I knew the voice. It was *her*, haunting my thoughts. Is this what happened when people cried? Did they hear voices? I decided it was only a dream, but I chose to answer it.

"I can't. Not when you are dead," I replied between sobs.

"Oh yes. *That*. Dreadful, isn't it? Dead and stuck," the voice responded.

My mind had not answered as I thought it would. My sobs ceased, as I urged the voice to continue.

"Pardon?" I replied to myself.

A dramatic sigh sounded, and a sharp chill enveloped me. The sigh did not belong to me.

"I'm stuck! You see? In this mirror," the voice nearly shouted. Quickly, I brought my head up and faced a hauntingly beautiful reflection. *Matilda!*

She was staring right back at me, waving! Just when I felt the room start to go black again, I heard her speak.

"Oh please don't faint again. Last time was an awful mess!" she exclaimed.

With trepidation, I reached out and touched the glass. It was warm, as a strange heat seemed to emit from behind it.

Was this some sort of trick? I touched the reflection, but felt no flesh, only glass. I moved my hand slowly across what appeared to be her face. My mind was taunting me with this rather disturbing game.

"Do you mind? I can't see anything," she said dryly, and I quickly removed my hand.

"*Matilda*?" I whispered, "Matilda Brew?"

"Oh, hello, are we on the same page now?" she asked, rolling her eyes at me and my disbelief.

"But how is this possible? Are you a ghost?" I asked, and she shrugged in reply.

"It seems so. I remember everyone crying, and then 'poof!' I ended up here," she said. The unthinkable worked its way into my thoughts. I gulped as I prepared to ask my question.

"Were - were you not allowed through the gates of heaven?" I asked, and Matilda scoffed.

"Allowed? I didn't even have my judgment day! I'm stuck here because someone forgot to cover the mirrors in the room," she sulked.

I recalled the old custom of covering any mirror with black cloth so that the soul of the deceased could not enter it. I had always thought that was simply superstition and nothing more.

Seeing Matilda, who had just taken her last breath, stuck in the large rectangular mirror before me, was proof that this was no mere superstition. This was *real*! I thought of the moment of her death. I had fainted, so there was not much to remember. Then, I felt a pang of guilt and spoke my thoughts aloud.

"This was my fault. None of this would have happened had I not fainted like a woman and created such a distraction," I nearly began blubbering again. Matilda sighed.

"You mustn't blame yourself. It's not your fault you're... *in tune* with your emotions."

I always felt it improper to roll my eyes at a lady, but I did so then. She laughed and I could not help but smile at my foolishness.

The doorknob rattled and I watched as Matilda faded away and my own reflection reappeared. At the door stood Anvil, looking aggravated with my lengthy absence.

"What's wrong with you? Can't you hear me? Hurry up, jackass!" he said, as he grabbed my collar and pulled me from where I was standing. I turned back toward the mirror and cleared my throat.

"I said, I'm hungry!" Anvil yelled.

"I-I'll be there in a m-moment, Anvil," I stammered. His face looked puzzled, but he turned and began crossing the room toward the door.

"She's not coming back, Andrew," he tossed back over his shoulders.

"Serves her right, too. She never accepted my offer to take her to the Bloomington Ball," he scoffed, slamming the door behind him and Matilda giggled.

"Sorry about that," I apologized.

"He's still sore, I see," she smirked, and I shrugged, grateful she didn't linger on the fact that Anvil had nearly just ripped my collar in two. Then, I stepped up to the mirror, desperate to be the hero.

"I will get you out of this Matilda! I solemnly swear it," I vowed, placing my hand on the glass.

She brought her own hand up to mine, and I could imagine the feeling of our palms pressed together, even though it was cold glass that I felt beneath my fingertips.

"Good. You got me in this mess after all," she smiled, and I winced back, remembering the gigantic distraction I had caused near her deathbed. "Please, hurry back. It's frightening being all alone like this."

"You have my word. May I see you tomorrow?" I asked.

It felt peculiar to pose such a question to a girl any day of any week, but even more peculiar to ask a recently deceased girl whose spirit was trapped in a mirror. It would be nothing more than a lie, however, if I were to tell you that my heart did not race when I asked the question, and that my insides did not nearly explode with her reply. A silent, smiling nod of her head was all the response I needed to affirm that she would receive me the next day.

I left her, my face beaming with excitement, not caring that I would have to walk home nearly half a mile in the dark, as my brother had gone off without me. I, Andrew Godfrey, had begun a tryst with Matilda Brew.

Chapter Three
Transparent

Matilda is waiting for me, I thought. She waits for me.

All too excited, I must have spent more than an hour preparing myself for my meeting with Matilda. My hair, which hadn't seen a comb in weeks, was swept to one side, as best as I could manage. My only jacket, despite the patches and missing button, was all that I had. It would have to do. I was awakened early by the morning announcements being shouted by a young boy of no more than twelve years.

"Matilda Brew, eldest daughter of Baxton and Joanna Brew, dead yesterday at 5:53 in the evening!" he loudly announced.

His uncaring tone angered me, but I calmed as I remembered my secret. Matilda, though she wasn't quite alive, was still very much present. It took me a second to realize the absurdity in that thought. How did all of it happen? Why was she still there, in her room?

Panic set it as I thought about the possibility of our interaction being nothing more than a dream, a highly imaginative delusion brought on by grief and desperation. But it couldn't be! I believed in what was happening! It felt so real - beyond even my wildest imaginings. This, however, did *not* come from my imagination. This *really* happened, I reassured myself. Someone - somewhere - had given me a second chance.

I bounded down the stairs and nearly collided with Anvil, who had just finished chopping wood for the fire.

"Where are you off to in such a hurry?" he yelled, bothered by my avoidance of our daily chores. On any other day, his tone would have unsettled me, but no such intimidation from my brother could mar my happiness today.

"The bookshop," I lied.

It would be known all too soon that I had visited the Brew house again. I slid past him before he pulled the collar of my shirt. Despite his primal behavior, I almost recognized the gesture as an act of suppressed brotherly affection, though perhaps that was wishful thinking. His breath smelled of whiskey and stale bread.

"Why do you look so... clean?" he questioned me, not truly believing my story of visiting any place that sold paper with words on it. Slightly offended, I refrained from cowering before Anvil, and tried to remain passive.

"It's called a bath Anvil, you should try one," I said, half under my breath.

Angrily, he shoved me to the door. I took the opportunity to run out of the house and make my escape, managing to tiptoe past my mother in the garden.

As I quickly made my way down the street, Rigabella spotted me. *Blast*, I inwardly cursed. It was too late. She would *not* be avoided.

"Dearest! You look sublime today! Have you missed me?" she squealed. I dodged her open arms and continued walking much faster than I intended.

"My apologies Rigabella, but I have no time today," I panted through quick strides. She followed, huffing and puffing as she tried to keep up. She picked up her skirt and petticoat, trampling behind me.

"Where are you off to?" she inquired, tugging at my right arm.

Anxiously, I increased my pace, hoping she would fall behind, but her strides somehow quickened and became even longer than mine! After all, she stood a whopping five inches taller than my five foot nine inch frame. Her fuzzy red mop gleamed too brightly in the hot sun, as her sausage like fingers, reached for my jacket.

"I have business to attend to, Miss Newt. Good day!" I called out.

Managing to escape her grasp, I looked down at my feet and realized I was actually jogging. With that, I launched into a full sprint to the Brew house, Righabella's high pitched squawks becoming distant. As I turned the corner, I knew I was clear of the spider and her web. Slowing down, I heaved a sigh and continued toward the house.

A few guests were leaving the front door, and I realized the Brew family was still receiving visitors. My spirits lifted as I climbed the steps of the porch, trying to hide my excitement from the grieving Mrs. Brew. They didn't know the truth, I had to remind myself, and I wondered if I should reveal my secret to her family or keep it to myself. No time was spent on the thought, however, as she took note of my appearance and smiled sadly.

"Young Godfrey, didn't you visit us just yesterday?" the woman asked, "Matilda's body is no longer with us. It's been sent off to the mortuary" she informed me, then she pulled out a handkerchief to wipe the tears from her eyes.

"If it's alright with you, ma'am, I'd like to revisit her room and pay my respects. I didn't exactly get to say goodbye the way I wanted to yesterday," I lied. It had been the excuse I had been devising all morning and she seemed to believe it. She placed her hand on my shoulder and gave it a tight squeeze.

"That's certainly kind of you. Go on in, Andrew," she said, as she moved away from the door.

I straightened my collar as I walked into the house, making a direct path toward Matilda's room. The steps seemed to never end and I was positive that my anticipation would be the end of me. The door to her room was shut, so I slowly turned the doorknob and peered inside.

The room was empty, just as I'd left it the day before. Quietly, I shut the door and turned toward the mirror. Matilda was waiting there with crossed arms.

"I wondered when you'd come," she chided smiling, and I suddenly felt fear take hold of me. It would take time to grow accustomed to seeing a reflection other than my own in a mirror, I thought as I exhaled much louder than I intended. Trying, with great care, not to sound like a bumbling fool, I spoke slowly.

"I got here as fast as I could," I began. She looked at me with disbelief and my eyes widened. "Did you think I was doing something else?" I continued, "Some mischief, perhaps?" I asked.

Silently, I prayed Matilda would one day learn what she meant to me, but at that moment she only pursed her lips and rolled her eyes at my tardiness.

"Of course not, Andrew. You're too good and quiet to be mischievous," she sulked.

I sighed with great exasperation. Was it wrong of me to wish for Matilda to see me in a different light? It was evident to me why Matilda never looked my way, but I had always hoped that I appeared to her more *mysterious*, than merely homely and good natured. I stiffened and shrugged off the pitiful hope that had begun to build in my chest. It *was* possible to shake off Matilda as easily as she dismissed

61

me, I tried to convince myself. But as I sulked, from the corner of my eye, I noticed Matilda eyeing the old suit I wore.

"Well, don't you look nice," she smiled, and I felt my skin tingle.

"Oh, this old th-thing?" I stuttered. I had to mask my excitement over the fact that Matilda thought I looked 'nice'.

Discretely, I covered the hole where the missing button was with my hand, only to notice an even bigger hole on the wrist of my jacket. I blushed, angry that my mother spent more time mending the suits my brother wore, than mine. She claimed that Anvil, the manager of our humble store, should be dressed properly, thereby excusing her partiality. I had never been one to require nice things, but I knew that a fine suit would have been a sheer joy on such an incredible day.

"Do you have a plan or what?" Matilda asked peevishly, and I was grateful for the sudden change of subject.

"No," I admitted, "-but I'm still thinking."

She lifted an eyebrow in disbelief. "Still thinking?" she exclaimed, "Well, that's just peaches! The fate of my eternal life rests on your time for thinking!" she sulked. I couldn't help but chuckle, and she crossed her arms at my amusement.

"Well, look, these types of situations don't really happen every day," I reasoned, but her eyes only grew wide as she stared at me.

"Oh! So, this is funny to you? My misfortune is your game?" she said, her eyes narrowing. I could see things rapidly taking a different and unpleasant tone. Things were *not* going as planned.

"No, Matilda, I'm simply trying to it figure out -"

"Are we forgetting whose fault this *really* is? Because of your little fainting spell, whoever was supposed to cover the mirrors got sidetracked and -"

"Hold on now!" I interrupted. "Technically speaking, it's *your* fault for dying," I responded.

I quickly realized the stupidity of my statement, but it was too late. Her lower lip quivered, as she stared at me with defeat.

"So you think I wanted this?" she cried, and I rushed to the mirror to comfort her.

I would be lying if I told you this didn't make me entirely uncomfortable. You see, I'd never really witnessed a woman cry. My own mother, whom I believed was not only devoid of human emotion, but tear ducts as well, *never* cried. Anger was her only emotion and she was ever ready to display it. If I had ever seen a woman cry, it was from a distance, and there were others there to comfort her.

Standing before Matilda as she bawled out her grief felt strange. Shifting from foot to foot, I waited and looked everywhere but her face. If I looked at her puffed, red eyes - tears streaming from them - I knew I might possibly cry as well, and I couldn't cry in front of her again.

It felt wrong just to stand there, however, so I quickly decided to apologize. That always seemed to cheer women up, I'd noticed.

"Matilda, I am so sorry. I did not intend to hurt you," I pleaded, but she turned away and I could see her image fade. "It was a stupid thing to say!" I beckoned again, but she was gone.

I sat down on the corner of her bed wondering how things could have gone so horribly wrong so fast. I didn't have to wonder long, because I already knew. My wretched tongue had done the trick. Matilda, who was so much more upset with me than I would have thought, both surprised me and riled me. She awoke in me this odd yearning to fight back. I hardly spoke at home, yet with her, the words poured from me freely, like water from a pitcher. I felt the embroidery of the quilt on her bed and sighed.

The strikes against me were piling up by the minute. There was nothing to lose, so I spoke what was on my mind. The only memory that came to me was a painful, but necessary one.

"When Father Joseph died, I saw you, your mother and father, and Miss Mallory at the wake. You all came dressed in black. I remember you accompanying me as we stopped the clocks together. We didn't speak. I was too uneasy being so close to you then.

"When we reached the base of the chapel, you looked at me and asked why I didn't cry for our dear priest. I told you I couldn't until I felt that he was alright. The voyage to heaven was what worried me. Would he make it there, or would he get lost? If there was not a heaven, would he be some place nearby? I had so many questions that needed answers before I could cry. Do you remember what you said to me?" I waited, but Matilda had yet to come back.

"You said that being a priest, he would likely reach heaven before us all, but if he did happen to get lost, he would go where he was needed the most. Perhaps, Matilda, you are needed here. There is some task you need to fulfill before you can be set free. It's possible your parents or your sister need your care. It *is* possible that you are not quite finished with this planet yet."

Slowly, I could see Matilda inch closer in the mirror. Her eyes were shiny with tears - and a hopeful glimmer. "You are very smart, Andrew Godfrey. I have greatly underestimated you," she smiled.

"Glad to be of service, Miss Brew," I said, as I returned her smile and saw her wipe away her tears.

"Find out what you can from my parents. Perhaps, you can discover things that they have not even told Mallory or me!" she urged. I got up from the bed and nodded my head at her instruction. With no idea where to start, I decided I would rely upon Matilda's suggestion.

"I'll be a bother, just like my mother warned me not to be!" I smiled, and she laughed and spun around in the mirror, just as she had in our watch shop that one afternoon. As free as an eagle! I longed to soar with her wherever she went.

"I could dance with joy! This is amazing! I really feel we are making great strides, Andrew," she said, as she clapped happily. "Just imagine, *me*, an angel with wings in heaven!"

"Or you could be going to..." I began, and she quickly interrupted.

"Now wait a minute! Just what are you suggesting? Matilda Brew was destined for the clouds!" she beamed, as she spread her arms wide.

I looked at her knowing she was completely justified in believing that. She was an angel, if I ever saw one. I couldn't let her know I agreed with her, however. Being contrary to Matilda was too much fun.

"A little too full of conceit to go to heaven, in my opinion," I smirked, and she shook her head.

"Nonsense! God likes the people who appreciate his work of art," she smirked, arrogantly. Laughing, I smugly crossed my arms and allowed my eyes to capture all her beauty for a moment.

"So, you think you're a work of - *art*?" I teased. Matilda tousled her hair and posed in the mirror, sending my emotions running through me in a race of pure admiration and delight.

"Naturally," she responded with an impish grin, and I closed my mouth, wondering how long it had been open, as I stood there gawking. "Though I'm nothing compared to your *Miss Newt*," she chirped, and my eyes widened in disgust.

"Do you mean to tell me you think Miss Newt and I..."

"Quiet! I think I hear someone," she said, pausing to listen. "Yes! Mallory's coming. I can tell from the uneven footsteps! You must go! Please, find out all you can. Go!" she whispered.

With her last words, she vanished and I turned, stunned, toward the door. The footsteps came closer, but soon they grew distant again. Quickly, I walked out of the room, and headed downstairs, narrowly avoiding a collision with Matilda's sister.

"Hello, Mallory," I said, a little short of breath. "S-sorry for your loss," I gulped. Her face looked forlorn, and it took my deepest resolve not to tell her of Matilda's new "home". Matilda's presence would be kept a secret. No one would discover it, unless Matilda gave her consent.

"Hello, Andrew. Have you gone by the mortuary yet? Father just came back. He says there are dead bodies and buckets of blood there. Can you believe it?" she spoke bluntly. I couldn't even *begin* to fathom something so horrid. The very thought of Matilda's body lying in a place like that made my stomach turn. Clearing my throat, I was about to speak, when a voice spoke up from beside the window.

"Leave Mr. Godfrey alone, girl," a voice, thick with fatigue, ordered.

Baxton Brew sat in an armchair, looking out through the nearby window at the sky above. The young girl walked toward him and put her head on his shoulder. "Please leave me, child." he said, pushing her away and the young girl left the room, a look of hurt on her face. I started to follow her, before I was stopped by Brew's raspy voice.

"Young Godfrey. Come, keep me company," he nearly commanded. Hesitantly, I walked toward him. His eyes remained directed at the window, as I took a seat.

"Mrs. Brew and I have scarcely had one pleasant conversation since Matilda left us. Everything always ends on a sour note when we realize our loss," he paused, still focused on the window and I felt myself grow uncomfortable. "Tell me, are you in school?"

Clearing my throat, I responded, "No sir. Anvil and I run our father's old business. Well, Anvil does, and I help."

"I'm sorry to hear that. Education is very important," he stated. He was short and direct in his response. The abruptness of it made me uneasy. With a large void hanging in the air, I spoke haltingly.

"It is, sir. I only wish I had more of it in m-my life. Sometimes, I f-feel incapable of answering properly. I somehow n-never quite learned how," I stumbled. Brew massaged his right temple with his hand, then scoffed.

"For that, I blame your maddening mother. You fear her greatly. I saw this the day of the Mayday Picnic. She scolded you - a man of nineteen years - in front of the townsmen! We all felt humiliated as we watched and waited for you to respond like a man. I saw you stumble over your words when you spoke to her, as you do now. Then, you ran home, where you no doubt hid under your pillows like a pathetic child!" he scoffed, and I slowly stood up, no longer wanting to be in the presence of Mr. Brew - no longer wanting to hear the truth.

"Sit down," he ordered, and I quickly complied, realizing I was trapped. I looked up at Brew with stifled contempt. He knew nothing of me, yet sharing his memory of that awful day was crushing.

"Are you married yet?" he asked, and I shook my head. *Marriage*. There was no thought of it now. It seemed only a necessity, a chore, that I would be forced into one day.

"No, sir."

"Would you like to be?" he further questioned, still looking out the window.

"Not anymore, sir," I replied, knowing full well I was entering dangerous grounds. The more he pried, the further I was digging my own grave.

"And why is that?" he asked. His eyes, for the first time, looked at mine and I knew lying would be impossible. I trembled, as the words escaped me, and my hands gripped the sides of my chair.

"Because the girl I love is gone."

His eyes narrowed and his jaw clenched. Pouring himself a glass from the bottle of brandy that sat next to his chair, his next words shattered the air.

"No daughter of mine would *ever* marry a man who hasn't the stomach to stand up to his own mother!" he berated.

His words were poisonous. I sat there, stunned and hurt. True as they were, these words were both painful to my ear and my heart. Drinking the brandy like water, Mr. Brew finished the cup and placed it on the table next to him. He then looked up with a small smirk, "Oh look. The conversation has turned *sour* again."

In my humiliation, I stood up - this time refusing to sit back down - and I headed out.

In his blunt and heartless conversation with me, Baxton Brew had revealed what everyone thought. He had all but called me a coward, insignificant, and unwanted... not a *man*. His words were heavy with meaning, and they pierced my very being. Feeling as transparent as the window Brew had stared through, I headed home.

Chapter Four
With Flames Come Opportunity

It had been a week since my last visit with Matilda. Eight days since she died. My heart was full of guilt, but how could I face her, with all that her father thought of me. To him, I was a lowly coward, and he was right. As long as I stood idly by and accepted my life as it was, it would be difficult to receive any respect from anyone. I knew it, and yet I did nothing to change my life.

Time passed as it usually did, with nothing more serious to think about than how many days my mother could stretch one meager loaf of bread. That was my only concern in this house. As the hours stretched on, I saw my time with this family was dwindling into nothingness.

We lived under the same roof, barely tolerating each other. I sensed that any conversation between us would eventually cease to exist.

My secret visit to the Brew house had somehow become known to my mother, who was quick to forbid me from going there again. Little did she know, I had no plans to return any time soon, but her command seemed designed to take any measure of happiness from my life. Her daily list of household chores lengthened so as to keep me occupied. She was barring me from the light surrounding Matilda's home. And yet I stayed, obeying like the coward Baxton Brew declared me to be.

I thought, for the first time, of the possibility of fleeing our home and never returning, but I quickly reminded myself of the improbability of my desire. With no money and no education, as Brew had so graciously reminded me, survival in a world beyond our small village rendered me helpless.

"Boy, you have some gall lollygagging around my house, dreaming about Lord knows what. Come on! Snap out of it! Go help your brother in the shop," she barked. Unconsciously, I groaned. "If you've got any back talk about it, you can just go without supper. Imagine that, you lazy boy!" she squawked. My mother, small and frail, wiped her hands on her old, torn apron and smoothed away the hair falling over her forehead.

Every time I looked at her - really looked at her - I saw a hidden despair coupled with an anger to which there seemed no end. *Who wronged you in a previous life, Mother?* I thought. I knew it would be better to slice off my own tongue before asking such a question. I must have gawked for a moment too long, because she crossed her arms and scolded:

"Have you something to say?" she demanded. I shook my head, biting my lip unconsciously. "Good. Don't let me catch you standing about," she ordered. I nodded and she picked up the mop leaning against the doorframe. "Life was not meant for the weak-hearted. It never turns out the way you want it to, but you work through it anyway."

What she said didn't surprise me. On the rare occasions she spoke of such things, it was only in veiled sarcasm - not nearly as blunt as now. Still, I let it all go in one ear and out the other. Life *was* what you made of it. It *could* get better, I thought. My mother barked, one last order for me to leave, and I headed out the door.

What bothered me, I thought, was less about the work, and more about the person who kept me company every day. Anvil's domineering attitude toward me made the hours feel as torturous as I imagined stepping barefoot on nails would be. I set down the broom I had been using to sweep up the ashes surrounding the chimney, like some sort of male Cinderella, and put on my jacket with the ripped lining and missing button. Oh yes! I was the catch of the village.

Putting on my hat, I headed out into the cool, evening breeze with my hands stuffed in my pockets. As I thought of it, I dwelled on the constant realization that the work I did at the watch shop was as exciting as waiting for the post every day. It was stale, and nothing new ever happened. There were few watches in the neighborhood, most having been pawned as a last resort by many families. We seldom saw work.

Carelessly, I kicked a silk hat with the top cut out along the sidewalk. A *silk hat...* our town wasn't meant for nice things, I observed bitterly. Was there a place where a lust for life was appreciated - where spontaneous passion replaced orderly behavior, and aimless days replaced routine ones? *Or*, would a place like that be just as distant as our solar system... high beyond the sky, where dreams go to float and dissolve into the galaxy?

No one ever asked me what I wanted my life to be. If anyone *had*, I would have said that I wished for something much more exciting than to live and die in Howell Village. I wanted riches, of course, and love, just like any man. I wanted laughter and smiles to be an everyday occurrence, not emotions saved only for Christmas or Easter Sunday. The gloom in our town and in my family was swallowing me alive, but I believed that somewhere was a world of unspeakable happiness. I dreamed of becoming a part of *that* kind of world.

Visitors, even the homeless vagrants on the streets, were always welcomed into our shop - by me. Anvil always disapproved of having the "scum of the earth", as he called them, wander through our doors, but I saw these visitors as a way to pass the time. They were entertaining and, because I hardly spoke at home, conversations of any kind were always pleasant diversions in my day.

My mind wandered to the only subject that truly made me smile. What was *she* doing? Was she still there? Thinking of my secret, my face softened into a smile, relieved that she was still with me in *some* form on this earth. It was pure magic - knowing she was there, waiting for me to see her. *My* life held a sparkling strand as from a rainbow because *her* soul was trapped in a mirror. I winced at my selfishness, but secretly, I knew I would never convince myself that the mirror's capture was a bad thing. Through it, we had spoken as we never had before.

Certainly, the few times we talked I caught a slight glimpse of what she was like, but conversing with her now was different. Despite being trapped within a mirror, she seemed oddly free. Somehow the constraints of living in such a restricted village had been abandoned and she could say and be whatever she wanted. I envied her open nature, and silently vowed that I would find a way to fully set her free! Well, just as soon as I mustered the courage and the time for another visit.

As I headed to our watch shop down the way, a group of men rushed passed. I recognized them as neighbors of the house two doors down from us.

"Hurry, hurry! You don't want to miss it!" one called out. I watched them run, and took off in a sprint behind them, quickly catching up.

"What's going on?" I asked the shortest one, a window washer named Jesop, with dirty shoulder length curls.

"It's a fire! Didn't you hear the bell?" he shouted, his face broad with amazement. I *hadn't* heard it. Was I so lost in my thoughts that I even missed the excitement of the rarely heard fire bells and whistles?

Suddenly, I lost my breath and my stomach lurched horribly. With a racing heart, I thought about the watch shop! Our father's old namesake might have managed to catch fire - and yet, I somehow knew I would be held to blame for it.

The men weren't heading in the direction of the watch shop, however. My jaw dropped in disbelief, when I saw flames shooting from the roof of the Brew home. The family seemed safe, it appeared, as I saw Mrs. Brew and Mallory tearfully looking up as Mr. Brew flung his family's heirlooms out the attic window. A crowd gathered, and men ran into the house, pulling out as much furniture as they could salvage. The flames were intensifying on the second floor - where the sisters' bedrooms were!

Matilda! Her mirror would be consumed by the flames, it was certain! When that happened, where would she go? I would lose her again, and I was not prepared to relive her death.

Without thinking, I jumped over the picket fence and ran for the house, knowing I might not ever leave it. Screams for me to come back came from the gawking villagers.

"You'll die, you fool!" an old woman spouted, and I *almost* turned back suddenly gripped with terror. The crone was right.

She was right. They were *all* right. I *was* a fool, acting blindly to save someone else when I could not save myself. I will say, however, that it was probably the best show they all had seen in years, as the crowd began shouting for me to come back. I bounded up the stairs and felt the heat from the second floor. Brew and two other men were hurrying down the stairs.

"Time to abandon ship, boys!" I heard him yell, as they all raced down the stairs. Hesitating, I briefly stopped on the landing. Pathetically, I stood, with trembling legs, on the bottom step.

"Godfrey? Boy, you've got to get out of here!" Brew shouted. I shook my head fiercely and pushed past him, not able to restrain myself.

"Not yet, sir!" I cried.

As fast as I could, I made my way through the hallway, already almost completely engulfed in flames. A beam came crashing down, nearly missing me.

"Do not do this, Andrew!" Brew called out from down below. "You're mad!" he yelled.

I was! This I already knew, (but this was *not* the moment to point out my faults). Another man below called out to Brew, who still gripped the railing with terror in his eyes, loudly pleading for him to come back.

"Come, Baxton! The floors will give away soon!" he shouted. Anxiously, they all pulled him from the house.

With some luck, I made it to Matilda's room to find the door radiating heat from the hall, and the doorknob hot to the touch. I put my hand into my sleeve to protect myself from the scorching hot doorknob, and braced myself... fearing what I would find inside. There were a few flames licking the walls, but it was mostly smoke filling the room. I heaved a large, grateful sigh when I saw the mirror and its

81

precious occupant were safe from harm. Quickly, I rushed over to it and pulled it off the wall.

I'm here! I've got you!

Tucking the mirror under my arm, I quickly fled from the room. The fire from the hallway grew instantly, and began to spread to the staircase. Skipping steps, I made it to the first floor. Just then, a large piece of the ceiling fell, as if to mock me - blocking the front entrance to the house - making that way of escape impossible.

Frantically, I looked around. What was my next step? If I found a window to climb out, then what? How would I explain the mirror I carried to Mr. Brew or the villagers. Most importantly, how would I explain this to my mother? She would think I'd gone completely daft and lock me up for good.

Suddenly, death looked like gold compared with the life I was living now. I looked at the mirror in my arms and thought about what death would be like trapped in Matilda's mirror. I could possibly spend eternity with Matilda, couldn't I? Closing my eyes, I waited for the flames to consume me. *Ok, death. I'm ready.*

Immediately, I felt the sweat drip from my forehead. I imagined my skin being melted away like a fleshy candle. Burning to death seemed very painful! I tugged at my collar, the same one I knew Anvil would tear to shreds when he next saw me.

I can do this. Many valiant men had left this world fully prepared to die.

Suddenly, I sought an escape route.

Save my recklessness, I realized something that night. I was far too young to be valiant!

Just then, I spotted a window at the rear of the house. With the mirror in my left hand, I used my right elbow to smash the window. With a bit of a running start, I flung myself through the window and landed on the grass. I guess I wasn't as prepared for death as I thought...

The night had approached, as if conspiring to hide me from anyone who would stop me. I heard people screaming my name from the front of the house. And I saw my chance for escape!

Without thought, I ran from them all - my mother, Anvil, Baxton Brew, the memory of my father... that was all behind me, as I headed out into the night... with Matilda.

Chapter Five
The Curious Carriage

A few hours must have passed when I heard the local newsboy make his calls. I had taken refuge within the tall grass of a field. Nearly collapsing from exhaustion, I fell asleep almost instantly before being awakened by the boy's cries.

"Brew House burned to the ground! Witnesses claim they saw young Andrew Godfrey head into the house. No one can find him. Possibility of death by fire!"

The town crier's voice faded into the distance, so I strained to catch every word. I was at the very edge of the village and hadn't the slightest idea where I was headed. *What to do next...* I wondered, whilst I rubbed my shoes together. Lacking any enthusiasm for life as I'd dressed that morning, I saw that I had completely forgotten to put on socks.

"Have you got a plan?" a voice spoke dryly. Instantly, I turned and saw Matilda appear in her mirror, which was lying on the ground next to me. It was a bit difficult to make out her expression in the dark, but I could only assume she was irritated by my impulsive actions.

"A plan? Of course, I have a plan."

"Oh really? What is it?" she asked, as her eyes widened with possibility. I fell back onto the grass.

"No idea," I admitted.

"Right. Well, then perhaps you should head home," she sighed. I shook my head fervently. I was free now, and even she couldn't make me return to the life that was now far behind me.

"No, no. I can't do that." My heart started racing as I thought about going back.

"Terribly foolish, if you ask me. I'm sure you haven't even a cent to your name," she remarked, and I felt around in my pockets. She was right. All I had was the key to the clock shop. Almost as soon as the idea sprung into my head, I jumped up and dusted myself off, nearly dancing as I stood.

"Stay here," I ordered, trying to appear in command of our situation.

"No, I thought I might take a walk through those trees. Really, Andrew? Where would I go? Stuck in a mirror, remember?"

Oh.

"Quite right. I'll be right back!" I assured her, as I took off running as quietly as possible in a field of weeds. The rush I felt that night was sensational and the most fun I'd seen in years.

"Don't do anything foolish!" Matilda called out in an exaggerated whisper, and I grimaced to no one. What I was prepared to do was very, very foolish.

I reached the street and scanned it for anyone possibly still about. The town crier, with lantern in hand, was a few blocks down, likely headed for home. Hunching my shoulders, I crept across the street, and then rounded the corner where my father's clock shop was. Anvil had most certainly gone home, as all the lights were off. The stairs to the shop creaked slightly when I tried to discreetly climb them, and my heavy breathing roared like a steam engine in my ear, as I fumbled to unlock the door. Realizing that a career as a master spy was out of the question, I unlocked the door and wriggled myself through, panting as I entered.

You can do this, I mentally told myself, though I was shaking from head to toe. The sound of a room full of clocks, at that moment, was the most terrifying sound in the world. With each tick, came panic and with each tock, my nerves jangled as I struggled to retrieve the key from underneath the cash register. My heart began to beat along in time with the clocks, as the sound in my ears grew louder and more deafening. The key was right where it always was and, grabbing it, I made my way to the back of the shop, with short, brisk steps.

Heading into the store room, I felt around in the darkness of the box placed on the top shelf and opened it with the key. There were a few small stacks of paper currency and some coins, as well. I prayed that it would be enough, but in the dark, I could not see how much I was taking.

Hurriedly, I stuffed half of the money into my jacket pocket and the rest into a pocket on the back of my pants, then closed the box. Placing it back on the shelf, I suddenly heard the rattle of the doorknob at the front of the shop. My breath stopped, as I made my way slowly beneath a desk, seeking refuge. I placed a chair in front of the desk to conceal myself. Who was in the shop at *this* hour? I heard the intruder walk briskly about the place. *Could it be, Mother*? I had hoped she would be mourning the loss of her youngest son, but perhaps it was she, coming herself to check on the security of her livelihood. Perhaps, it was Anvil, forgetful as he was, returning to wind the clocks. The footsteps approached the back of the shop and I saw the gleam of a lantern. The intruder was inching his way back to the store room and, slowly, I covered my mouth with both hands, willing myself to stop breathing, as if it were possible. Two feet approached very near my hiding place. The large boots were unrecognizable in the dark, but the intruder was definitely a man. The lantern illuminated a pair of loose dress pants.

Almost as soon as the trespasser had entered, he left, clearly not finding what he was looking for. His heavy steps could be heard as they made their way to the front door. It opened and then slammed shut. A neighing horse, instantly obedient to its rider's harsh command, was whipped into a gallop. Whoever had trespassed was not after money, that much was clear. He was there only to inspect the place. The thought was confusing, but I had to refrain from expressing any worry about it. This was Anvil's problem now. He and Mother would have the shop to contend with from this point on. I was off on my own - completely separating myself from that world.

Briskly, I made my way to the front door, and took one final look around. The only fond memories made in the place had been the imaginings of what working with my father would have been like. The rest was a miserable mixture of arguments with Anvil, or scoldings from my mother. If I told you I would miss the old clock shop, I would be lying.

After locking up, I headed down the street, hating myself for leaving Matilda out in the dark. She was alone and, as her protector, I felt entirely responsible for any misfortune that befell her. The street was dark and empty. I was ready to get to Matilda and take her far away from the stagnant, cruel air of this miserable town to a place that was fresh and alive.

Hurriedly, I ran through the open field, picking up Matilda's mirror along the way. "There you are! I wondered where you'd gone," she spoke, as I ran. I laughed out of no particular reason, being simply excited to be free. "Where are we going?" she asked, and I held the mirror up to where I could see her pretty face.

"Away from this place, Matilda," I said, panting as I spoke.

"Ah, I see. You're trying to elope with me, aren't you?" she smiled, and I reddened a bit. "You should know, we dead girls like engagement rings, too!" she winked, and I laughed again.

"I'll keep that in mind!" I grinned. It was the most intimate thing I had ever said to her and I didn't care. Running away together was thrilling - beyond anything even my wildest dreams could fathom. I was in love and marked this day as the greatest I had yet lived. We ran together, or at least I ran and she was dragged along, and I felt a mutual feeling of understanding between us. It felt indescribable, not to be alone... to have a companion in this adventure.

We reached a small station, just outside of our town, with a few people gathered by the entrance. A black carriage stood parked in front of the station and the driver, who sat eating a radish, looked at my charred appearance as I approached. He gave me a peculiar questioning look and nearly dropped the radish to the floor.

"You look terrible," he stated, and I casually brushed his rude observation aside. Standing as tall and proud as I could, acting as one who travelled often, I spoke up.

"Where does this carriage go?" I inquired. Casually, the driver took another bite of the radish and, with a mouth full, spoke.

"Hotel Larouche."

Hotel Larouche. The name sounded vaguely familiar. If it was mentioned at all, it was always in hushed whispers, as most thought it a "pagan place" - with activities too lewd and sordid for the righteous citizens of our town. My mother never spoke of it. *Why would she*, I thought. We never traveled, so there was never a need to lodge at a hotel.

Since I recalled Anvil once saying that it was not a great distance from our village, I decided Hotel Larouche would do for the rest of the night. Rather loudly, I heard Matilda "ooh" in agreement. The driver looked around to find out where this feminine sound had come from, before returning to another radish.

"When does this carriage leave, sir?" I asked, and the driver passively stated that it would be departing in ten minutes. Taking a seat on a bench, not too far away, I set the mirror down, and the driver eyed me again. I noticed his beady eyes, long pointed nose, and pockmarked face. *Handsome*.

Avoiding his glares, I turned toward a woman in a veil holding a bundle in her arms. The way she coddled and smiled at it, I knew it was her child. She began to hum softly to the infant, and I looked over at Matilda, knowing she was listening.

I wondered how she was feeling about it all. So young... her life was gone all too soon. She hadn't traveled to Paris, or advised her sister on matters of her first courtship. She would never share vows with another; never feel what it was like to be in love with the right person. Did she regret that she would never be able to grow old with someone?

There was so much that I, myself, had yet to learn, that I shuddered as I thought about my impulsive decision not to let the flames at the Brew house consume me. Cowardly, perhaps, but I was grateful I left when I did. If given the choice, I knew Matilda would have chosen as I had. She was so full of life, so full of joy, that naught could take her from this world but death itself.

Of course, the beauty of the unusual situation Matilda and I found ourselves in was remedied by my persistence to see the world and its treasures with Matilda close beside me. She would live through my eyes and see all that she could not see in death, even if it meant viewing life through the shimmering glass of her mirror. Whatever was left unfulfilled at the time of her death was my obligation, even *honor* to complete for her. It was the very least I could do for the girl I loved, and my only way to hold on to her, at least until we found a way for her to escape from the mirror.

So lost in thought, I barely heard our driver call for us to board. As I handed the man a few coins, I took note of our traveling companions. A tall man with whiskers boarded the carriage followed by the woman and her baby. As I was about to board, the driver called to me.

" 'Ey there boy! Don't you want to put that with the luggage?" he asked. His look was directed at the mirror that I held close to me. I shook my head and noticed his nostrils flare with disgust as I entered his carriage, filthy as I was.

"No, sir, I've got it," I assured him. He slammed the door behind me and, to my surprise, managed to elicit neither a cry nor a stir from the infant in the woman's arms.

Along with the mirror, the three of us were somewhat cramped in the confined space. The man with whiskers, his long legs ill-suited for the narrow seats, pressed against one side of the carriage, careful that our knees would not touch in passing. He exhaled loudly with annoyance and resumed his reading. The woman, so taken with her child, didn't seem to mind the crowded condition. I placed the mirror in my lap, and a whip sounded. The carriage began to move and we were off.

We only sat in silence for a minute or two before the woman sitting beside me spoke to the child in her arms.

"My precious angel. We'll be there soon," she cooed, in a high pitched wavering voice. Only the tip of her pointed nose was seen behind the black lace veil she wore. She hummed softly, and I detected a slight quiver in her song. I spoke up, attempting to make light of the awkward situation we all found ourselves in.

"Are you staying at the Hotel Larouche, too?" I asked. The woman rocked back and forth, still looking down at the baby in her arms.

"Oh yes, it will be the best day of our lives. Won't it?" she asked the infant. I cleared my throat and began to relax in the carriage.

"I've never been before, but I can imagine it's much better than anything in my hometown," I laughed to no one in particular. The man didn't budge, so I looked for reassurance from the woman sitting beside me. "I'm sure you know the feeling."

At that, the woman tilted her head at an odd angle and smiled - a smile so wide it seemed humanly impossible! Her teeth had begun to rot slightly, and her breath was enough to repel hell itself. It was the first time I saw her face, and I struggled to keep my expression calm. Her eyes were wide, bulging from their sockets and bloodshot - with something resembling watery black paint streaming down her cheeks. She looked as if she'd been crying for ages, but her gleeful expression said otherwise. Before I realized I was staring, she replied in a high, shrill voice.

"Why yes, we do!" she smiled, looking down at the infant in her arms, and I followed her gaze. The child, no more than six months old, was *dead*. For how long, I wasn't certain, but the eyes and mouth had long been *sewn up* and its tattered, lifeless appearance made me believe that the woman had dug this child up from the grave herself. Small maggots weaved in and out of the blanket that swaddled the baby, and its fingernails were blackened and covered in dirt.

I slammed into the side of the carriage from fright and sheer revulsion. My breath quickened as I saw, in the moonlight, a scene far worse than any of my most horrifying nightmares. The man, still reading his paper, gave me an odd look and then resumed his reading.

"Oh dear, you've got him crying again," the woman scolded, as she viciously rocked her lifeless baby. "Daddy's far from baby now. He won't rock the cradle, precious. If you'd only smile for your mama. Smile, little Alec. Smile."

The faint, dizzy feeling I often felt consumed me. I felt myself regain outward control, but my insides lurched as I saw her spread the baby's mouth wide with her fingers, tearing the stitches one by one. I hardly remember when my head slammed against the side of the carriage and my eyes rolled into their sockets. Darkness veiled the horror and, blacking out, I welcomed the dark with open arms as it barricaded me from a horrifying image that I knew would *never* leave me.

I couldn't say *what* happened while I blacked out, or for how long it happened. I was unconscious and knew that only a combination of fear and exhaustion took hold of me.

In a haze, I awoke on a golden bench some time later to find the carriage *gone*. Matilda's mirror was by my feet. My eyes weary and my vision blurred, my ears at least seemed to be functioning. I listened to sounds I had never heard before. There were smells so heavenly, I felt my senses come alive! The carriage had left me at the place that, unknown to me at this point, would become my sanctuary for the next few days. In a fragment of time, I would be checking into the Hotel Larouche.

Chapter Six
Checking In

Whether one would believe it or not, Mother had, at one brief point in my life, permitted me to attend school. On a particular day, all the students gathered around our professor's new treasure. Mr. Alastair Wick was the only one in our town who had traveled beyond Howell Village, often exploring the world and bringing back his findings from faraway lands. I frequently wondered *why* he had chosen to come back to Howell. I would not *ever* have returned, had I been given the opportunity.

The treasure Mr. Wick brought to the schoolhouse that day was a new discovery from Scotland. He called it a *kaleidoscope*. We each took turns, looking through its funnel, and twisting it around in our hands. We marveled at the assortment of colors compressed within this small tube-like invention. Each one of us imagined the possibility of a world that could capture such spectacular color, light, and movement. Why couldn't life be like *that*? I recalled thinking then.

Looking at the spectacle that currently surrounded me, however, I saw that some parts of the world were very much like that kaleidoscope I peered through as a boy. Sitting on a bench of shined gold, I saw life like I had never - ever - seen it before.

The sky glittered in purple hues, as lanterns and small brightly colored lights dangled high above me. The stones beneath my feet sparkled as if made of bits of amethysts and rubies, with dazzling silver cementing the pavement. The streets were outlined in a gold trim so fine, I felt God, himself, could have painted them! The whole city seemed unreal, as if it were veiled beneath the finest satin that money could buy.

With a firm grip on the mirror, I found it peculiar to see so many people up and about at such a late hour, and dressed so impeccably! My appearance was shameful in comparison. The women wore lace dresses in every color, adorned with such things as feathers and pearls. Their faces were almost as colorful, with bright red cheeks and lips. The men sported neatly trimmed whiskers and wore hats of many colors. The most amazing bicycles whizzed past, and oddly groomed dogs with colored fur pranced along the streets. Vendors lined the large walkways selling everything from decorative parasols to silver and gold pistols, and other various weaponry. The men gathered around in huddles, laughing and firing their weapons off into the sky, while the women shamelessly flirted, cooing over their baubles and trinkets. Some women, I observed, lifted up the hems of their skirts to unveil their *own* brass and pearled weapons neatly strapped to their legs and tucked into the bodices of their gowns. These looked like the people my mother had warned me about.

As accordionists played festive music, young men and women kissed and held hands in the wide open street. I could hardly believe what I was looking at, as I watched a parade of jeweled horses pass by. Slightly overwhelmed by what was before me, I turned around and faced, perhaps the most spectacular sight of all.

It was like something I had seen painted only in pictures. Shining brightly from the carefully crafted colored lanterns that decorated it, the Hotel Larouche stood eleven stories high! Men and women waved out of windows and danced on their personal balconies. Laughter and cheers filled the skies above me, as I marveled at how a city could be so alive! A man balanced precariously on a window sill. Another man swung by his legs from a ladder - upside down - holding his arms above his head, bursting with uncontainable laughter.

The village pastor back home would have immediately declared this a place of sin, but to me, it was a place of *fun*! From the 'oohs' and 'ahhs' coming from the mirror, I knew Matilda felt the same.

These strange and particular occupants were so merry; their cheeks were pink over their broad smiles. It was impossible for me to associate these humans with the ones back home. The people in my life lacked joy and managed to master every frown and grimace known to man. By great contrast, the residents of this place bubbled and glowed! They all cheered each other on in their never ending game, where not having enough wine seemed to be the only opposing factor.

Almost as if on cue, champagne popped behind me, punctuating my observations; I laughed as I felt the light foam tickle my neck. Men celebrated in the street for no apparent reason, except that it was *fun* and *joyous* to be alive. The kaleidoscope had come to life!

Seconds later, a large man with a jolly and booming voice greeted us as we walked toward the entrance.

"YES! BELIEVE WHAT YOU SEE! ALL YOUR DREAMS HAVE COME TRUE!"

He tipped his red hat and roared with laughter so loud that I felt his vocal chords must have surely torn apart. I moved past the man and made my way through tall revolving doors that nearly whirled me into the hotel, quicker than I could imagine.

The lobby was pulsating with dancing couples and men standing about in close groups, engaged in lewd conversations. The miraculous raucous and unfamiliar sound of poker chips hitting the floor after being tossed in the air provided even more frivolity. Girls spun around atop chairs and tables, and men watched and cheered them on, clinking their glasses together as they brazenly looked up the ladies' skirts.

As I turned from the sight with mild embarrassment, I spotted the woman from the carriage who had also entered the hotel. Men and women surrounded the new arrivals, the woman still holding her dead infant. They looked at the child with expressions of awe, each treating him as if he were still alive! The woman beamed with pride while I looked on. It seemed that anything was acceptable - even *normal* - at the Hotel Larouche. I wondered if, perhaps, even an insignificant boy - too shy to be noticed and too much of a coward to be respected in his hometown - could belong in a place like this.

A small man on a unicycle rode up to me, as I stood there lost and completely out of my element. He loudly honked a horn attached to his jacket and jumped off the unicycle.

"Your friendly concierge, here!" he said, standing proudly. He held out his hand and I took it, nearly wincing beneath his firm grip. "Would you like a room, sir?" he asked me, cheerfully.

I nodded, barely capable of speaking. The concierge looked at me, expectantly. I suddenly realized he desired some sort of payment. Confusing as the night had become, I was not oblivious to the monetary requirements of the world.

"How much?" I asked, quickly. Flipping through the sum of petty cash I retrieved from my back pocket, I counted that I had taken a weeks' worth of money from the store. From the looks of it, a place like Larouche was certain to be costly - perhaps, more than I had.

"It's pay what you want friend!" he beamed, and I stared at him blankly, not fully comprehending what he was saying. "You may want to freshen up a bit, however," he suggested, taking in my ghastly appearance.

"Pardon?" I asked. He laughed jovially and patted me on the back, then waddled back to his unicycle.

"Come on! Follow me!" he called out, as he began to pedal away. He wheeled his way through poker tables and smoking parlors. Eagerly, I quickened my pace and followed him, still trying to take in everything that I was surrounded by.

Contortionists and snake charmers mixed together among the rich and elegant men and women, head to toe in finery our family could never dream of. *Imagine what the watches look like,* I thought.

"Do you see what I see, Matilda?" I asked, hoping she saw everything I was laying eyes on. It was a sight I never wanted to forget, and hoped Matilda would feel the same way. In perfect unison, our eyes - our worlds - opened to a door so bright, we momentarily forgot our bleak pasts and uncertain futures.

"It's spectacular!" she fawned and I smiled at her response. 'Spectacular' was the perfect word. It *was* a spectacle that one could not possibly dream, but must actually witness. The small man beckoned to us once more and he stood, cheerfully smiling, by a set of golden doors. The machine's doors opened with a loud ring and we stepped inside its small room. He hummed along with the music the strange machine played as he ushered us completely through the doors and smiled warmly once again.

"This way up. You'll be on the fifth floor. Room number 553," he declared. The doors closed before I could thank him for his help and hospitality. With a lurch from the machine, I found myself clinging onto the mirror that was tucked under my right arm. My other hand embarrassingly grasped a plump woman's shoulder. I quickly yanked it back, as if I had touched a boiling pot. The woman, along with her two female friends, waited silently in the small compartment. They all, with identical purple eyes and big hats, glanced at me then resumed their conversation.

"It really is the liveliest of places, isn't it?" one woman spoke to the crowded room of passengers.

"Very much so! Now, I shall never return to my husband!" another woman hollered. All the women roared with laughter and I chuckled softly at their jests. One woman pulled out a hand mirror and examined her face before sneering slightly at the others.

"Do you notice the rings under my eyes? Ghastly!" she sulked. Another woman spoke up.

"With that creature wandering around all day, how can anyone truly rest? I *do* need my beauty sleep, Zelda."

"It doesn't do much harm. Nothing to fret about, Petra!" the third woman scolded. What they spoke about was unclear, but it didn't matter then, as I knew would be checking out soon enough. The more I thought of it, however, the new world I found myself a part of was too exciting to only stay *one* day. *Another night at the hotel wouldn't be such a bad thing,* I thought. I remained silent and as invisible as possible, as I continued my eavesdropping.

The doors, however, opened with a piercing ring and the women turned to me as I stepped off of the contraption, uncertain if I was in the right place. The numbers on the rooms all started with the number five, so I sighed with relief. As the doors of the moving machine closed, I heard one of the three women speak.

"That boy looks as if he's been through hell and back!"

"Oh! Did you hear about Howell Village? There was a fire there, I heard! The houses there are so horribly old and outdated."

The doors closed shut and Matilda cleared her throat in an attempt to capture my attention. I looked down toward the mirror, and saw her lips pressed together.

"Word certainly gets around fast, doesn't it?" Matilda whispered and I nodded with concern. News of the fire had already reached the ears of neighboring towns. If there was any mention of a slim, wild haired boy lost to its flames, the patrons of the hotel could decide to turn me in when they realized it was most likely me. Interrupting my thoughts, I heard Matilda sigh, and immediately held the mirror to my face.

"Isn't this place wonderful, Andrew? It's so different from our home, so merry and bright. I will say I've never seen such beautiful dresses or such handsome men in my life!" she buzzed. My jaw twitched at her last observation.

"You thought they were handsome?" I asked, trying not to betray my feelings. A massive lump of welled-up emotion bobbed in my throat. She looked past me, clearly not as invested in her last statement as I was.

"I think you've missed the room," she snorted, and I turned back, looking at the door I passed moments before. There was room 553. *553.* The number struck a familiar chord.

"So I have. Well then, here we are!" I spoke, with relief. Something was not right though. I checked my pockets, only to feel bills stuffed within. "Matilda, do you recall the man on the unicycle giving me a *key*?" I asked. She shook her head and I stood, staring blankly in her direction, quickly thinking up a reasonable solution.

"Honestly, there's a sign up above, genius!" she sighed, and I turned around, my head nearly colliding into a hanging sign inches from the door. Clearing my throat, I read it aloud:

"The answer to this question is a one-time permanent key to your room."

I puffed out my chest, prepared to conquer the riddle with ease. "What has hands, but cannot clap?" I asked aloud. With a pause, I re-read the question. "What has hands, but cannot clap?" It seemed impossible to have hands and not have the ability to clap. One came with the other... didn't it? I reread the question. "What has hands, but-"

"Oh, criminy! It's a clock!" Matilda shouted, "I should think you, a watchmaker's son, would know the answer to that one," she said, crossing her arms. The door unlocked and I looked at Matilda stiffly, my ego only slightly bruised.

"Know it all," I sneered, and Matilda stuck her tongue out at me, a gesture which made me laugh as we made our way inside. "That riddle isn't very safe as a door lock," I observed, with some worry. "Anyone could guess that answer."

"*You* couldn't," she retorted, and I stuck my tongue out right back at her. It seemed that I had resorted to childish games, but the intimidation I felt around Matilda was overwhelming and clouded my thoughts and any sense of decorum I possessed. We opened the door to a small and undecorated room. There was nothing lavish about it, though

I will admit that I half expected a school of clowns to pop out at us at any moment.

"Well, this will do. I suppose the people here don't spend much time in their rooms anyway," Matilda commented.

"Right you are, Matilda, and we just need a place to sleep," I spoke up, looking about the room for some sort of a hook. "Besides, what more do you want for a free room?" I asked. A frame with a picture of a black cat hung on the wall next to the door we'd entered. Removing it, I set Matilda's mirror on the hook in its place and closed the door.

"Now listen, tomorrow we will find a way to get you out of this mess. For now, though, this has been the longest day of my life... and I think I need some rest," I said, loosening my collar. Matilda paced back and forth in her mirror, and I sensed she was about to argue with me.

"Tomorrow, tomorrow, tomorrow! That's all you ever tell me. Then you *abandon* me for a week. You know, I had no one to talk to. It was lonely in here - watching life move on without me," she sighed, with frustration. The pain in her eyes revealed a very real envy of those still living. I felt, best I could, what she felt... but I knew that could never be entirely possible.

"Matilda, my sincerest apologies, but I didn't want to intrude upon your family. Your father... I don't think he likes me very much," I said.

"I don't think he likes *anyone* really," she sulked. I wondered why Matilda spoke of her father in such a way, but I didn't want to pry.

"I won't abandon you again, Matilda. You needn't fear," I spoke, wanting desperately to assure her of my sincere intentions.

"Yoooo hooo!"

I heard a knock and I opened the door to find a string of women holding champagne bottles in their hands. A large woman pulled me out of the room and shut the door behind me, shoving me into the group of giddy women. Breathless and in a sheer panic, I felt as if the hands of the women stroking me were the flames back at the Brew house. *You survived worse*, I reminded myself, but the disgusting mixture of perfume soaked feathers was overwhelming.

"We heard there was a new young gentleman at Larouche!" one girl said, with such excitement. The women, with heaving bosoms and giant red lips, grabbed my cheeks and kissed them, as some younger girls giggled.

"Isn't he a handsome thing?" another girl asked the group. The rest of the women tugged at my collar, as I desperately tried to pry them off. In a flash, I felt myself back in Howell Village, enduring Anvil - pulling at my collar - and my anger rose. The memory of his oafish brutality caused me to shove one of the women off so roughly that she nearly toppled into the opposite wall. She roared with laughter.

"Let me have him!" one girl cooed, and another pouted, with false displeasure.

"No, it's my turn!" another yelled. I would never tell, but all this female attention was oddly exhilarating, and I might have been lost in it if I knew Matilda wasn't waiting for me.

"Look at his hair!" they all giggled. I was being pulled apart, as hands ripped open my vest and tugged on my untamed wire-like hair, as if trying to remove it from my skull.

"Ladies, please! Stop this!" I yelled over their laughter. No one was listening, as I struggled to release myself from the heap of women I'd somehow fallen into. Reaching for the door, I felt a little woman, no more than four feet tall, take a mighty hold of my ankles. The woman cackled and then started singing loudly, with the rest of the women all joining in:

"Buckle him down, 'til he can't leave!
Soon we'll be loving, you best believe!"

"Sincerest apologies, ladies!" I shouted, managing to shove the women off - one at a time - before bursting into the room and bolting the door shut. Tumbling onto the carpet, I lay flat on my back, gasping for air, staring up at a disapproving Matilda, who sat in the mirror shaking her head.

"'I *won't abandon you again*' you said. Well, *that* was quick!" she huffed. Panting, I held my hands up in defense.

"I was attacked by a pack of women! That was not *my* fault!" I argued. She laughed and crossed her arms, clearly amused. After a much needed moment to collect my thoughts, I pulled my way up to the bed's soft mattress, much fluffier than my own back home.

"Oh, I'm sure it was one of the most terrifying experiences of your life!" she responded, sarcastically. Crawling beneath the sheets, I lazily smiled at the annoyance I detected in her voice.

"It's not *my* fault they couldn't keep their hands off me," I yawned, and she laughed again, with greater force. I cocked an eyebrow at her, slightly offended. It wasn't *that* ludicrous that I should be found desirable, *was it*?

When her laughter diminished, the silence in the room grew heavy, as the awkwardness of our current situation began to dawn on me. Clearly, it was entirely inappropriate to be sharing a room with a young lady I was so little acquainted with. Seeing, however, that she was recently deceased, the matter of propriety was insignificant... *was it not*? Would she mind being so unusually close together as we shut our eyes for the night's rest? About to ask this necessary question, I turned to her and noticed a rather sad look on her face. She seemed lost in thought. In an effort to be sensitive, I asked what was wrong.

"They will all forget about me soon, won't they? Mother and father, and little Mallory.... they won't even remember me in a few years," she said, staring at the wall opposite her mirror, looking pitifully desolate. I understood her fear, but quickly dismissed the thought with a shake of my head.

"Never! No one could ever forget you, Matilda. You are a bright light that shines everywhere you go," I spoke truthfully, and she smirked.

"I *was* a bright light. That light's gone out," she said, resolutely. I sat up from my place in the bed and she continued, "You know something, Andrew? I never got the chance to say goodbye to you while I was living, yet here you are, carrying my soul in your hands. Do you hate me for it?"

"Who was *I* in your life, Matilda? You had no reason to say goodbye to me," I responded. Though her kindness was always apparent, I knew that my existence in her life was no more important than the wallpaper in our room. She was under no obligation to think of me, and I had come to accept that. But she smiled as if that was not the case.

"Of course I did. You convinced your brother to give me a fair price on my father's watch, a kindness I will never forget. He still wears it, at least he was the last time I saw him pass through my room," she recalled, tenderly.

I remembered the watch she bought Mr. Brew for his fiftieth birthday. It was bronze, not one of the best models, but uniquely different from all the watches we had in the store. There was a small image of a dove carved into it, with an olive branch in its mouth. The symbol of peace, it had come to us by way of train from many miles away. My mother thought it distasteful - too odd to capture anyone's interest. I loved the watch, but knew its intricate designs wouldn't be appreciated by many - until Matilda arrived - and chose it instantly from the array of other watches in the shop.

"There! You see!" I smiled, realizing that hope was not lost. "He still wears it! He can't forget his daughter with such a watch in his pocket. It will *always* remind him of you," I reassured her. At that, Matilda grew giddy.

"I suppose you're right. Besides, I'm much too memorable to forget!" she quipped, "I was the top student at Mayfield, you know," she gloated. We all knew of Matilda's academic achievements. At the end of each school year, a ceremony was held where the top scholars were given special medals, along with baskets of various breads and fruits. Matilda was *always* awarded the highest accolades. I watched her approach the stage, yearly, to a brief, slightly unenthusiastic round of applause. It certainly wasn't that Matilda was unloved, but more that the children and parents of Howell Village were incapable of expressing enthusiasm over *anything*, least of all education.

"I remember," I smiled, recalling my hiding place at the back of the crowd, where I stood trying to catch a glimpse of Matilda.

"And I was the only girl to fill up *two* dance cards at the Bloomington Ball," she continued.

"Yes. I know," I responded, fully aware of that small detail. Everyone loved her.

How could I forget her appearance at the Bloomington Ball? She had been sick for weeks and no one thought she would be able to attend the dance. She arrived, radiant as ever, in a pink gown that turned everyone's head on the dance floor. I admired her from afar as young men rushed at the chance to dance with her.

Though beautiful, her most attractive qualities were her pure zest for living and her bright smile that lit up any room. I yearned desperately for a single dance with Matilda, but my knees shook and my palms became soaked with

117

sweat at the mere thought of asking her. I feared that out of all the men asking for a dance, my offer would be the single one declined. Then, of course, there was-

"Henry O'Shea! Do you remember him? Oh, he loved me so," she reminisced, as she clapped her hands excitedly. My jaw tensed with jealousy. Henry O'Shea was rich and well versed in the ways of the world. He courted women daily and dangled their hearts on strings. Matilda continued, "Mallory and I stirred dirt from the garden into his coffee last time he visited. It was terribly wicked of us!" she laughed. My brow furrowed in confusion.

"But why would you do that? Didn't you like Mr. O'Shea? All the girls did!"

"Good lord, no! Do you know what he did when he first sampled the coffee? He cringed and then, maintaining composure, sipped the entire cup out of politeness. What an idiot!" she laughed again, while I sat in complete confusion.

"But I thought *everyone* liked Henry. Henry the Handsome? He's rich and well groomed-"

"And a bore. Oh sure, maybe Sarah Beth and a few of the others like him well enough, but not me. He nearly put me to sleep with his talk about what a woman should be like.

He spoke of how women in other villages obeyed their men at all times. Frankly, I think he may have been politely throwing me under a carriage the whole time. My mother always felt the need to scold me after one of his visits for not behaving in a more ladylike manner."

"You always seemed-er-well behaved to me," I spoke, only lying a little. Matilda gave me a look.

"Oh, I was awful. I gave my parents great pains. After some time, they gave up and went along with my games... and believe me, I took full advantage of it. It doesn't matter anymore, though. I suppose that's one benefit of being dead. You can be whoever you want to be. You are free," she sighed, as she looked around at the frame that surrounded her. "Except here I am, stuck in a mirror... with you," she said. My heart fell a bit and my shoulders slumped in disappointment. She continued, "Oh please don't misinterpret me. I'm very grateful to you."

Realizing I was still fully dressed, I took off my jacket and started pulling up the covers of the simple bed, avoiding all possible eye contact.

"I just know you must be wanting to see Miss Rigabella, and I feel awful having you go through all of this for me," she said. I pulled the sheets back and crossed my arms.

"*Miss Rigabella?* I don't understand. What makes you think I like *her?"* I asked, quite befuddled. Now, it was Matilda's turn to look confused.

"But she's your bride to be," she said, pursing her lips together, and looking away. My jaw dropped in astonishment.

"BRIDE TO BE?" I shouted.

Soon, I began pacing around the room. "Now look here, Miss Matilda! Anything you may have heard from that-that cackling hyena is a lie! I've been trying to avoid her grasp for years, but do you know how difficult that is? She's incredibly persistent, and I'm not at all sure why. I don't encourage her pursuits, I have nothing to offer her - and - I'm almost a foot shorter than she is!" I argued. She looked upon me with disbelief, and I saw that she was truly misinformed.

"Is that the truth? Are you absolutely sure?" Matilda asked. She looked puzzled, then oddly sad. A range of emotions flashed across her face, and I tried to interpret them. Then, after a moment, she looked up and smiled.

120

"Poor Mr. Godfrey! Had I known, I wouldn't have encouraged her advances toward you. It seemed like something you would want!"

"You did *what*?" I walked to the mirror and saw her place her hands up in defense.

"Now Mr. Godfrey, realize I did this only because I thought you loved her," she said, holding up her hands apologetically. She tried to appear serious, but a slight smile betrayed her. I approached the mirror, not really prepared to do anything more than allow her to see my frustration over the entire matter. *Gossip* was the devil of devils, to be sure.

"Break this mirror and you'll get seven years bad luck, Andrew! I'll make sure of it!" she warned. After a moment, Matilda shrugged, "Serves you right anyway... you were never really talkative at parties."

The girl's meddling was questionable, even downright intrusive, and I saw my hot breath cloud the mirror. The more I grew to know her, the more I discovered that Matilda was no saint. She could be quite the mischief-maker! She, too, often did and said the wrong thing, just as I did. She frustrated me, angered me, but often surprised me - and I found I liked it.

A thought sent me easing back from the mirror, however, with a smirk. Though I should have been offended, I remembered that she *had* thought about me, even if it was in the hope of arranging a courtship with *another* woman. It was enough to make me laugh at her failed attempt at matchmaking.

"Matilda Brew, you are what the New World calls, a 'pill'," I said, as I walked away and blew out the lamp.

"A *pill*?" I heard her whispered question in the dark.

"*Pal.* I meant '*pal*'. Goodnight, Miss Brew!" I smiled.

It wasn't a bad thing - getting better acquainted with the meddling, stubborn girl. To know Matilda, *really* know her, was quickly becoming a great privilege. In fact, it was a very wonderful thing. For years, had I not put Matilda on so high a pedestal, I would have had the courage to approach her. I would have gotten to dance with her. Matilda was an angel... with a crooked halo. She was a spoiled and flawed human-being. She meddled in some people's affairs, and tricked others... and that made her all so *real* to me. It was her faults and her insecurities that were turning into *perfections* before my eyes. She angered me and thrilled me all at once. I cannot explain what I felt as I entered dreamland. This person, about whom I knew so little, had made herself known to me as she never had to anyone else. I felt privileged - even in awe - of this flawed being. I loved her for it... and was falling even more for her wild spirit. Madly in love, was I, with a dead girl.

Chapter Seven
A New Friend

I awoke the next morning to a booming thud on the door. With a yawn, my eyes opened slowly.

Matilda was in the mirror, running her hair through with her delicate fingers. My *own* hair was of little importance - and I was *alive* - so Matilda's meticulous grooming made little sense to me. If *I* was dead, I wouldn't give a second thought to the way I wore my hair. Still, she brushed her raven curls, unaware that I was watching. Lost in a trance, I removed myself from the sight of Matilda and her magnificent hair, and got out of bed.

"It's a good thing I don't sleep anymore," Matilda remarked, as I yawned with a stretch. "I never would have gotten any rest with your *snoring*."

"You're an absolute hoot," I replied dryly, while I made my way to the door. Upon opening it, I peered down the hallway and saw that it was empty. Looking down at my feet, I spotted the daily paper rolled neatly in a bundle on the doorstep. As I picked it up, I heard a faint whizzing sound. I looked up to find a *different* man on a unicycle, hurling newspapers at various rooms as he went.

"Is that really necessary?" I called out, and he grinned.

"Of course not!" the man said, after turning around on his unicycle. He rode his way back to me and jumped off the contraption with ease. "How was your stay, Sir?" he asked, and I yawned in response.

"Excellent," he said, "If there's anything more I can do for you, just holler!"

As he spoke, his eyes scanned me, and then swerved back up to my hair. "Oh, and you might want to schedule a haircut, sir... *and a bath*," he advised. Chuckling, he jumped back on his unicycle and sped away. *Everyone is so direct here,* I observed. I went back into my room, with a slightly bruised ego, and unfolded the newspaper in my hand.

"He's right, Andrew. You look like death!" She paused, then she added, *"I* should know!"

I rolled my eyes at her tasteless joke.

Taking a seat on the edge of the bed, I opened the paper to the front page and scanned it quickly. A headline in bold lettering read:

"LOCAL HOUSE BURNED TO GROUND"!

Quickly, my eyes raced over the article, as fear took hold of me.

It seemed that no person was held responsible for the fire, and the fire department had determined the disaster to be the result of a fallen candle in one of the upstairs rooms. The Brew family, the article stated, had been moved to Basil Quadray's house along with most of their belongings, and restoration of the house would take place in the weeks to follow. Many villagers had also given their accounts of the sequence of events as they had witnessed them. Each account ended with seeing a young man - a boy they'd seen pass through the village now and then - willingly run into the flame ridden house like a madman. Others swore it was Andrew Godfrey - the quiet boy from the watch shop.

The end of the article was punctuated with a small drawing of a young man. Even without much detail, my hands shook as I recognized the face in the sketch as my own. A short statement pronounced him *dead*.

Unknowingly, I twisted the paper in my hands as I felt familiar panic grip me. *I am dead.* I repeated the words over and over in my head. *I am dead!*

In the event that I *was* to be discovered as truly being alive and residing a few short miles away, I knew my mother would wallop me to death, herself! Being pronounced dead gave me a new found freedom! In my false death, I could finally *live*!

Each time I repeated the phrase, it became more of a blessing than a curse. *I. Am. Dead.*

"What does it say?" Matilda interrupted my thoughts with her anxious question. I looked at her, as she peered from the glass.

"Seems you aren't the only dead person around!" I smirked, mischievously. She raised her eyebrow at me.

"*I've* been declared deceased!" I waved the paper above my head, as if it was a flag. "The authorities have decided to pronounce me dead, not having recovered my body from the fire. Naturally, my mother sanctioned this," I said, sarcastically. With excitement, I showed her the picture, recreating the same face from the paper with my own.

"I always wanted to be invisible. I guess being a dead man will have to do!" I chuckled.

"That won't last," Matilda rolled her eyes. "Someone's sure to spot you. Whoever that artist was got you down exactly!"

I looked over the portrait again. The sketch, I felt, did more justice than my face deserved.

"You mean he captured my roguish charm and good looks?" I said, quite boldly. Daringly, I threw a wink her way. She returned it with a look of disgust and I laughed.

"I mean that you best find some sort of disguise or you'll be escorted straight back to Howell, in a criminal wagon with your tail between your legs," she warned, and I nervously gulped.

"Vivid picture. Thanks for that," I retorted, but she was right. If I wanted to make a clean getaway, desperate measures had to be taken. I put on my jacket and shoes, concealing as much of myself as possible, and quickly grabbed the mirror off the hook before heading out.

"Where are we going?" I heard Matilda ask, but I couldn't respond to her question. I realized I had not a moment to lose.

"Hello there!" I hollered.

In no time, the man on the unicycle rode up to our door, out of breath.

"You called, sir?" He stood at attention with his hat in his hand.

"Yes! Where is the closest barber? I'm in need of a good haircut," I admitted, desperately trying to pat down the untamable mess upon my head.

"Third floor, sir. Glad I persuaded you!"

With a wave of my hand, I sent the man off as if I was accustomed to such service. It felt odd, almost wrong, to behave in such a way, and I wondered where that sudden confidence had come from. Quickly, I dismissed my behavior and together, Matilda and I headed down the hallway into the moving machine.

We arrived on the third floor. Plenty of accommodations lined the hallway. Walking past various specialty shops, I spotted residents entering and exiting doors for nail care, shoe shining, barbers, and poodle primping.

Discreetly, I hid Matilda's mirror behind a nearby divan and followed the signs leading to the bathing stations.

I turned toward the gentlemen's bathing area and walked into a room full of men lounging about. Some were disrobed, while others only sported towels around their waists. Most of the men there were trim and muscular, but a fair amount stood proudly, admiring their large, oversized bellies and extra chins. I walked in, bathed quickly, and averted my eyes from anything but the water that surrounded me. Feeling vulnerable and much more *worldly* than I was when I *first* arrived, I left the bathing stations in a hurry. They really *did* come in all shapes and sizes, I observed as I headed out.

Clean, and dressed in a new suit purchased from a shop along the way, I pressed on... feeling fantastic! I felt lighter from the water that had washed away not only pounds of dirt, but - I hoped - my sins as well! I picked up Matilda's mirror and made my way to the barber shop, bracing myself for the next step in my transformation.

A painted sign on a tall glass door read Buster Barber's and I entered, rather apprehensively.

About twelve barbers, all in white coats with finely groomed mustaches, snipped away at the tops of heads with precision. Shying away in embarrassment, I knew my hair looked ridiculous in comparison. A tall, thin man, with an equally thin mustache, approached me and sneered as he looked at my hair. He immediately called out to a nearby barber.

"Charles! This boy needs a haircut immediately!" he exclaimed.

Charles, looking almost identical to the man calling to him, waved me over. His station was empty, and the surrounding floor gleamed with an open invitation. I took a seat in the swiveling chair, feeling quite like a small child.

Haircuts were foreign to me. Occasionally, I snipped away at the hair that had fallen over my face. Only out of the sheer necessity to *see,* were scissors ever in my hands. The whole notion of a haircut was unthinkable to me, and it made me nervous. Wanting Matilda to have a front row seat, I held up the mirror to Charles.

"May I use *this* mirror?" I asked, and Charles looked at it flippantly.

"But of course, sir," he said, as he returned to my hair, his fingers twitching with delight. Setting my mirror in front of his, I stepped into the chair, tossing a wink at Matilda. Charles washed and shaved my face clean. The smell of soap, scented with lemon and lingonberries, was simply divine.

"Let me have a look at you," the barber observed as he circled me slowly, then he snapped his fingers in the air. "I've got it!"

He got to work almost immediately, turning my chair away from the glass. "It will be a surprise!" he beamed. He worked and worked, wiping sweat from his forehead with a crisp handkerchief. Snip after snip, my black hair was being tamed by a man who, I believed, could make me appear as rich and as polished as the others. I took a look at the men that surrounded me with their slick, shiny hair and thick mustaches. They looked mature and sophisticated. They were cultured men, who almost glided as they walked. It would be delightful to start a new life looking as elegant as they did.

What I faced in the mirror when Charles turned me around, however, was anything *but* elegant!

"All finished!" he sighed, with relief. I sat there, petrified.

My hair was twice its height! It looked as if it had survived many hurricanes and a bout of lightening! Patches of white were spotted across my bush-like hair, appearing as if my head had been used to clap the chalk dust from erasers. My hands flew to my hair, with terror.

"What, in God's name, have you done to me?" I cowered from the horrifying creation I faced in the mirror. The barbers all bent over with laughter as the room went wild. A small feminine laugh, that I *knew* must have belonged to Matilda, joined them. Humiliated, I stood up and faced Charles.

"I can't go out like this!" I shouted. In a panicked effort, I began erratically combing my hair through with my fingers, willing it to rest flat. Charles doubled over in laughter.

"Just a parlor trick, boy! Take a seat, I'll fix you up." he assured me, then he motioned to the chair.

Angrily, I sat back down and crossed my arms over my chest, glaring at Matilda. I knew she was enjoying my complete humiliation. I turned to the barber and pulled his coat so that his face was inches from mine.

"And see what you can do about *this*," I demanded, pointing to my bare upper lip. Fearful, Charles nodded.

"You'll be a fine looking young gentleman when I'm through with you!" he said, assuredly.

A few hours and a bottle of adhesive later, the chair swiveled back toward the mirror again, for what I *hoped* was the last time.

My reflection *was* vastly different! I could scarcely believe it. My appearance was so altered that I began to search for myself behind the neat hair and whiskers that created a face so similar to the other men at Larouche. Who was this *man* I saw in the mirror? I turned to Charles, who placed his scissors down, as he gaped in awe.

"My work is done," he said, as he stood back to admire his masterpiece.

In truth, I looked nothing like the Andrew I was accustomed to seeing in a mirror. I looked like what I had always *envisioned* my appearance to be, but could never attain. That boy hiding in a darkened corner of his room, or sweeping the floors of his father's watch shop was *gone*. The mustache had been so expertly applied; I completely forgot it wasn't mine! My hair looked so perfect I feared making any sudden movement. Was this what it felt like to imagine yourself one way and actually see it reflected back at you?

Heads turned to look at me and I waited for the familiar embarrassment to set in, but it never did. I was proud of what I saw and what others would see in me. I looked normal, like *them,* and any trace of the Andrew that *was* would be swept away with the scraps of hair on the floor.

Charles swept the tiles clean. Still, I sat there, waiting to see if any of my old insecurities would find their way back.

Free yourself, Andrew, at long last! Let your past be washed - the storm of your old life is over! Happily bewildered, I wondered what my mother and Anvil would say if they saw me. What would my father say had he been alive to see me now?

"Come back when your real whiskers have grown in. I will fix you up free of charge," Charles whispered. I only nodded in response, still in awe.

Minutes passed, and I realized I had overstayed my welcome at the barber shop. I got up, taking the mirror with me, and headed out, quite stunned. It was amazing what one haircut could do! No one laughed *this* time, as I headed out, leaving a few bills behind.

Passing the hallways and noticing unaccustomed stares and winks from women, I barely heard a small voice call out to me.

"Psst, psst - Andrew! Hey, you've got some dirt on your face!" the voice whispered. I looked down to see Matilda waving her arms to get my attention.

"Can't you see they love me?" I gloated, and she scoffed at my outward conceit.

"Love you? Honestly!" she laughed, and then she grew quiet. "I liked your old hair better."

"This certainly is a different feeling!" I continued. A surge of confidence burst from me. "I wanted to dance with you Matilda. That night at Bloomington... I wanted, just once, to dance with you, but you didn't notice me. Why would you? I was a peculiar nobody with nothing to offer?"

"You wanted to dance with *me*?" she asked. I continued strolling along the crowded hallway, feeling as though I was floating on elephant sized clouds. The amount of confidence in me was extremely unusual, but not unwelcome.

"You know something? I think I *am changing*, Matilda. I feel *alive*! More alive than I've ever felt before!"

136

"Really?" Matilda asked, flatly, "And what's *that* feel like again?" I looked down at the mirror and saw her face start to fade from me.

"Matilda, I didn't mean it like that. I'm sorry-" but she was gone, and the confidence within me dwindled a bit. *How could I say such a thing?*

The sulking returned, as I dragged the mirror down the hallway and into the moving machine, making my way to the fifth floor. Where and when would my verbal outbursts come to an end? It seemed that I always spoke before thinking. The doors opened and I stepped out, holding the mirror up to my face.

Before I could plead for Matilda's forgiveness, I was interrupted by the arrival of two large men wearing long black winter coats. Their pupils, I noticed, were almost white - as if they'd been cursed with cataracts. Each held a firm grip on a leash that was attached to a black Great Dane, much larger than any dogs I had ever seen. They pushed past me and bounded down the hallway, each dog racing ahead of its master.

An older man - a priest - hurriedly followed behind them. He was much smaller in stature, but just as serious and intimidating as the two men who accompanied him. Together, they made their way down the hall - quite determined, as their boots trampled across the velvet carpet. I turned and felt myself drawn in their direction. It was as if strange, invisible strings pulled me to the door they had just gone through. Before I could reach them, it slammed shut and a long piercing shriek that sounded like neither man nor woman, blared through the hallway. Just then, a *different* man on a unicycle sped past immediately. He quickly stopped and turned back toward me.

"Can I help you, sir?" he asked, through shallow breaths. I shook my head, still looking in the direction of the door where the scream had come from. The unicyclist took me by the arm and led me to the moving machine, as a wide, unnatural grin spread on his face. "Why don't you come along *this* way, sir?" he urged me away from the scene I just witnessed.

"What was *that*?" I asked, my eyes never leaving the end of the hallway. The small man shoved me inside the open doors of the moving machine, still cheerfully smiling.

"Perhaps, you'd enjoy a walk. The streets outside the Larouche are quite lovely," he assured me. I nodded again,

138

before realizing that the man had closed the door of the machine. I was heading down to the lobby before any of my questions could be answered. I shrugged, dismissing the event as none of my business and decided to move on with the rest of my day. That's when I remembered Matilda, locked in the mirror and upset by my earlier inconsiderate remark.

"Matilda? Are you still angry with me?" I asked, but received no answer. "Please, speak to me. Show me your face," I pleaded. The doors of the moving machine slid open before I could ask again. They opened to reveal a picturesque scene of people enjoying themselves. A woman strode by and placed a piece of chocolate cake in my mouth and another placed a glass of champagne in my hand. *Did the amusement ever end?* I wondered.

Loud laughter echoed throughout the lobby of the hotel and I found myself lost, once again, in the distractions. Grown men flipped and tumbled past me. One strange gentleman paraded around the room, festooned in floppy ears and a tail, acting like an untrained dog! He howled and barked at all who passed by him, some encouraging his bizarre behavior by tossing small treats his way. The scene was otherworldly, and the characters were outwardly outlandish, simply because they *could* be. There were no rules at Larouche. *Anything went.*

The way of life at Larouche was one I had always wanted to live. I wondered why my family had never thought to move to this town and say goodbye to the daily struggle of our life in Howell Village. All the money earned there only went toward the hope of better food, or the donation box at the church. We continued our efforts in vain, longing for something we would never achieve. Yet, at Larouche, happiness was a *guarantee!* None of it made any sense to me.

After minutes spent eavesdropping on conversations that weren't mine and watching a race between lavishly decorated pygmy pigs, I made my way out of the lobby.

Stepping outside, I squinted as my eyes became offset by the sun. The streets were empty, with the exception of one drunken man stumbling along as he sang a nonsensical tune. I felt the urge to return to the hotel and its pleasures, but pressed on in search of - I know not what. At night, the streets had been so full of life, but it seemed that the daylight only spoiled the people's excitement. It was odd

- in complete opposition to my village back home, where the people thrived in the daylight, and remained behind locked doors at night.

I passed multiple shops displaying a number of goods my family would have deemed unnecessary. A shop called Kiss Me Corsets sent a deep scarlet blush of embarrassment over me and I unconsciously turned Matilda's mirror around. Cake shops, silk shops, pipe shops, and many others lined the streets, each individually styled with decorative window displays.

The last shop we passed was a beautiful gown boutique called Madame Luelle's. Elegantly embellished with red trimmings, it featured a whimsical display so captivating it was difficult to look away. A mannequin caught my eye and I inched my face close to the window. The small hands of the mannequin were clad in white gloves and - unbelievably- attached to *real* arms! Likewise, a pair of real eyes adorned a face with a wistfully sad expression. A girl, no more than sixteen, stood frighteningly still in the display, adorned in a scarlet red tulle dress and white slippers. Her hair, thick and auburn, was swept upward from her face in an elegant fashion and her lips were painted to match the dress.

I waited for her to move even an inch, but the only movement I saw was the soft rising of her chest, as she almost imperceptibly drew an occasional breath. She was remarkably brilliant at being still, and I knew she wouldn't bother to look at me, so I reluctantly moved on. Still, the thought of the girl in the window lingered in my mind.

"Did you see that, Matilda?" I asked. There was no answer and I immediately flipped the mirror back around, realizing that Matilda hadn't seen a thing since we left the hotel! "The streets of Larouche aren't as lively as I thought they'd be," I continued, but there was *still* no answer.

Curiously, I scanned the wide street, running my eyes over all its pleasures. Anxious, was I, to discover all I could about my new surroundings.

I caught sight of a sign a few doors down that read, *The Social Hour*. Never having heard of such a place, the simplicity of the wooden sign compared with the others called to me. Its entrance was merely a wooden door with a simple brass knob. On the door, in faded golden lettering, hung a sign from a protruding nail. It read:

"Thieves, Gunmen, and Havoc Seekers Welcome!
If you wish to reflect upon your sins, find a church."

I knew it had to be some sort of joke, but hesitated regardless. What sort of place was this? With a sudden burst of courage, I pulled open the door to find a long downward flight of stairs, ending in a pool of soft light in front of a green door. I crept down the steps, wincing as the wooden planks emitted a terrible creaking noise. Unable to make a discreet entrance, I boldly opened the door and walked in.

A few poker games were in session and one pool table dominated the center of the room. Dark green velvet covered the chairs that circled rich mahogany tables, creating the interior of a gentleman's lounge. Only a few men inhabited the room, smoking cigars and drinking whiskey. They gave me a hard look, but only for a moment, then spoke to one another quietly and resumed reading their newspapers or playing cards.

One man, tall and middle-aged with a light brown mustache, waved at me from his relaxed position in a chair. His legs were draped over one of the chair's arms and a fat cigar hung casually from the corner of his mouth. He smiled smugly and the men watched his every move.

"Welcome, friend!" he said, taking the cigar from his mouth. "We love newcomers, don't we boys?"

The men grunted and resumed their activities. The welcoming gentleman, who stood as I approached the table, was clad in a sleeveless undershirt topped with suspenders attached to loose dress pants. He extended his hand and I shook it, looking directly into his steel gray eyes. Smiling widely, he said, "Take a seat, dandy. You play poker?"

I shook my head, remembering what pains my mother took to keep my brother and me away from bad gambling habits.

He continued, "Well, that's alright. Just as long as you don't talk politics. What's your name?"

"Andrew," I responded, quietly. The talkative man waved his cigar in protest.

"Don't disgust me! You're Gunshot and I'm Patch," he said, pointing to three burly looking men sitting across the table. "That's Rage, Filth, and Anguish over there," he said. Lost in confusion, I had an urge to run from The Social Hour, but the thicker man named Filth spoke up.

"Don't let Patch fool you, Andrew. He's a jobless mongrel with an uncanny knack for getting his ass handed to him in Rummy," Filth teased, as he raked the poker chips to his end of the table.

Patch smirked and blew the smoke from his cigar out in rings.

"Jobless? As if anyone in Larouche has a real job!" he laughed. He said it so casually, but the notion of unemployment was unthinkable to me.

"How *does* Larouche stay afloat? It seems like an expensive place to keep up," I inquired. The three men didn't bother addressing my question. They didn't need to. Patch spoke up, leaning back in his chair with his arms folded nonchalantly behind his head.

"Remember when all the *good* people were helping all the other good people out and all the *bad*, wicked people were hoarding everything for themselves? Well the bad blokes finally got smart and decided to do things for the other bad bastards and here we are! The mayor himself sits in his suite, as we speak, with a prostitute in one hand and a pistol in the other, giving away hotel rooms in exchange for the company he's keeping. Ah, 'tis a dangerous place. 'Tis a dangerous, *glorious* place!" he laughed, then he reached for the bottle of whiskey on the table, and took a swift swig.

"Larouche seems like a wonderful place, though," I spoke up, not fully comprehending the danger they all saw - and loved - in it. "It's alive and bustling with smiles and laughter!"

"And it's a perfect place for escape, if I so myself may say," Patch hiccupped. His words slurred slightly, but I understood his meaning. I, myself, had escaped and found refuge in Larouche, but I had taken it as a sign of *good* fortune.

"*Galileo*... have you heard of him?" Patch looked at me, as his cigar came inches from my nose. I nodded and he continued, "Galileo... loved the stars so much, he had them tattooed on his chest in a constellation. Can you believe it?" he asked. I looked around at the furrowed brows and shook my head in response to Patch's nonsensical assertion.

"No, I can't. I don't actually think that's true," I replied, and he cocked one eyebrow at me with genuine concern, sheer disbelief contorting his face.

"Are you certain?" he asked. I nodded, as he crossed his arms. "That's unfortunate. I took after his example and had the key to my *own* heart tattooed to my chest."

He placed his whiskey on the table and pulled down his shirt to reveal a set of female eyes tattooed in the dead center of his chest. "What a pity that Galileo did not do the same," he sulked, releasing his shirt with such sadness, as a weary gloom washed over him. I sensed he spent many nights this way. I looked on, as despair settled on his face and he became lost in it. With a sense of heightened curiosity, as well as feeling a need to be sociable, I resumed our conversation.

"Whose eyes are they, if you don't mind me asking?" I pried. The men around me all groaned, but Patch's eyes brightened at my question.

"They are my lady's. They are my love's. She is the most magnificent creature you have ever seen, Andrew. And she dances... oh, how she dances!" he smiled. I looked at the table for clues about who he might be referring to, but no one spoke. Patch picked up the card deck in the center of the table and placed it directly in front of him, then plucked a card from the top and tore it in two, tossing the pieces behind his head. He repeated the card mutilation while the man called *Anguish* spoke up

"He's talking about *Tansy*, the dancer from his hometown," he relayed, with a hint of annoyance.

Patch smiled widely. Nearly half the deck was gone and scattered around him. "She is more than a dancer," he stood, and circled about the table. "She moves like the wind and sculpts the air with her figure, fine and elegant," he said, looking at me. "You have not experienced a love like *I* have," he declared. Arrogantly, he sauntered behind me as my temperature rose. He knew *nothing* of the life I led. Without thought, the words slipped from me.

"I *have*, though perhaps I have not professed it as openly as *you*," I scoffed. His eyes widened at my response. Harshly, he jammed his finger into my chest and I winced from the pressure.

"*That* is more unfortunate than I can even *begin* to tell you. Find your lady love and never stop telling her what you feel... and even if it seems that you cannot get through to her soul, keep trying, Andrew. She will come around someday. I *know* she will."

With that, he made his way out of the room, grabbing his hat off a hook on the wall. As I heard his footsteps hit the creaking wooden stairs on their way out, I made the decision to follow him. Even in his drunken state, he made more sense to me than anything that I had seen during the past day. With a small farewell, to which no one responded, I was out of the Social Hour. In no time, I caught up to Patch, who was calmly walking down the street.

"Do you live at Larouche?" I asked. He shrugged, as he drank from his small bottle of whiskey.

'I'm just part of the scenery, really," he admitted.

"Well, what is there to *do* here?" I asked.

Patch smirked, still looking straight ahead. "So much... and yet *nothing* at all," he smiled. As I walked beside Patch, I saw him eye the mirror in my hands curiously. "What's that?" he asked. I didn't bother hiding the truth of the mirror as Patch, in his drunken state, would most likely forget.

"A friend," I replied and, with a shake of his head, he took yet another swig of his whiskey.

We entered the Larouche hotel and all its liveliness, as the women draped themselves over Patch, fawning over his presence with the same overwhelming admiration I received at my door the previous night. The reception that welcomed Patch, however, was *twice* as large.

149

"Patch, stop by my place tonight!" a beautiful blond woman spoke. "I've got a present for you," she cooed. At her demands, Patch merely brushed her aside. A full red headed woman pulled at his suspenders, as he tried to slip past the girls.

"He's mine tonight, aren't you, Patch?" she baited, but the woman was also dismissed. The leader of the group, a svelte looking woman with red lips, scoffed bitterly at the girls.

"He'll never stray from Tansy, ladies. Don't even bother!" she nearly spat. Patch stopped walking and turned to the small group of young women as if prepared to give a speech.

"I'm afraid she's right, ladies. It's best to send your affections elsewhere. There's only *one* woman I want in my life," he spoke passionately, but the leader responded with a shrieking cackle.

"If only she wanted you back!"

All the girls howled with laughter and took off in pursuit of another gentleman, leaving Patch stung by the cruel woman's words. I searched his face, trying to determine if her outburst held any truth. If it *did*, he hid it well.

Clearing his throat, he shook off the sour exchange and turned to me as he pushed his way through the crowded lobby.

"Hurry Andrew! You won't want to miss the fun!" he shouted, smiling devilishly. An accordion and multiple fiddles played a lively song that had the guests in the lobby cheering and singing along. Patch briskly made his way toward a raised platform surrounded by the denizens of the hotel.

Atop the platform, danced a magnificent looking woman with wild, magenta hair. Wearing a colorful sea of fabrics, she created a twirling vision of delight. She danced with all the grace and passion a single body could express. Her eyes, bold and alive, held a strange familiarity. She dazzled the audience who, in return, chanted a name I had heard earlier.

This was the woman Patch spoke so highly of! The fine eyes tattooed to Patch's chest were *hers*. I saw him watch her with both admiration and lust, as he slowly approached the platform step by step.

I began to see what he saw in the woman. Though she may not have returned his love, she was a treasure to be pursued, even if only to be entangled in just one dance with her. Fashioned not *exactly* like a goddess, she exuded an aura that was not common among the sea of feminine faces. Her features were broad, her skin pale, and her hair blazed with a life of its own. I must have stood there, as awestruck as all the other fools, by the vision before me. Though she was not *my* love, I could see why Patch was so captivated.

Like a wild mare, he charged the stage and leapt atop it, joining the girl in her movements. Struck with surprise, she didn't turn him away, as I thought she would. He took her hand and pulled her toward him in one swift action. They looked as if they had danced this way millions of times, and together they were femininity and masculinity in perfect harmony. His arms wrapped around her waist, strong, yet gentle, as if her form would shatter under the weight of his hands. As the music blared, their steps aligned in unison. Beads of sweat formed at the very top of his forehead. Great fervor filled his eyes, which never drifted from his partner.

If someone asked me to describe passion, *this was it*. Noticeably heated, dancing with complete abandon, I saw that she appeared as much in love with him as he was with her. If it was only an act, then I was as fooled as Patch was. The way she looked at him, with a small curved smile, told me much went unspoken between them. I saw the love I never had with Matilda, but *always* dreamed of.

They ended in each other's arms as the music finished. Patch's mouth moved to hers, but she quickly pushed him aside and dipped into a crowd pleasing bow. I saw Patch's eyes return to normal from their dreamlike state, as the pair made their way off the platform.

In seconds, they were flocked by the excited patrons that gushed praise over their talents. Yet something seemed wrong. The young woman pushed and shoved her way from the adoring attention, stopping just before the moving machine. As the gates opened, she stepped inside and the crowd began to disperse. Patch was left alone, and out of breath.

Anxious to comfort my new friend, I approached him and placed a hand on his shoulder. "That was amazing," I said, in awe. He looked at me, and I saw the depth of his longing.

"That was Tansy."

Chapter Eight
Unaltered Confessions

When you believe, you see.

What I saw on that first day at Larouche marked me so ardently, that my world was not what it once was. If you had told me the planet was pear shaped, I might have believed you. Nothing was predictable, and my life had become a wonderful mixture of eccentricities and excitement. I didn't think returning to my hometown would ever be possible! The grayness of it was no longer appealing - as if it had ever held any real appeal in the first place. I always felt it was where I *should* be. My life, I once believed, would start and end in the small, quiet town where nothing ever happened. Looking around me now, however, I knew that it would definitely not.

Patch invited me to share a meal with him in the dining hall, after he had used up his energy dancing with

Tansy. I refrained from mentioning her again, as I sensed it was a delicate subject not to be breached carelessly.

Instinctively, I looked down at the mirror resting beside me and wondered if Matilda was still sore at the *careless* words I had spoken earlier. Knowing I had hurt her was the worst feeling in the world, and I anxiously yearned to correct myself.

"If you have the duck, I'll take the goose," Patch started. "A slice of chocolate ribbon cake may suffice, as well."

Patch had been poring over the menu for the past fifteen minutes, changing his mind for the fourth time. After our waiter's fifth round to our table, we finally agreed upon mutton and horse steak with jelly. The waiter left with an unconcealed eye roll and Patch began peering into the menu again.

"Perhaps, I've chosen the wrong thing," he sulked, but I didn't give much thought to his indecisiveness. I was just happy not to be having Stone Soup again! Everything on the menu looked spectacular; I could hardly choose just one thing! It was a relief to have Patch decide, but his indecisiveness produced large rumbles from my empty stomach. When he finally decided upon a dish, I sat back in my chair. Behind him, however, someone caught my eye.

An older woman at a nearby table, dressed in black, looked at us curiously and I shifted, uncomfortably, in my seat. Her hair, white as the clouds, sprouted messily from her head in a wild knot of twists and tangles. She wore a golden monocle in her left eye, and nearly a dozen rings on each hand. The woman's eyes locked upon my own, her gaze leaving me shaken and unnerved.

"That woman keeps staring at us," I informed Patch in a whisper, and he raised his eyebrow with curiosity. He looked over his shoulder at the old woman, then turned back with serious look.

"*That's* Widow Sherrigan. She's a peculiar sort," Patch said, inching in closer.

The widow stood up and approached the table. Quickly, I averted my eyes to the vase of blue orchids set as a centerpiece on our table, but it was too late. A thin bony finger, adorned with large rings set with ivories and emeralds, rested on the edge of our table. I looked up to find the widow peering down at us, her skinned cracked like powder.

"Patch, your friend sees through me," she spoke in a raspy voice and Patch rolled his eyes at her strange comment. Across from them, I shrunk in my seat at the accusation. Fearful, was I, of making enemies with the guests of Larouche.

"Nonsense, Widow. He is just mesmerized by your... *charms,*" he said, throwing me a wink and I feigned a smile at the woman. She whispered in Patch's ear softly, but not so softly as to be unheard by my own set of ears.

"He mixes with *death*. I can feel it!" she nearly shrieked. The manner in which she spoke was so matter-of-fact, I felt my breathing quicken. In vain, I struggled to dismiss the woman's mystic opinion of me. *What did she mean?* Patch looked at me oddly and then waved her off with a smile.

"You are mistaken, Widow Sherrigan. My friend is good and fresh faced, and no possible gloom surrounds him. I solemnly swear it."

Mockingly, he crossed his heart and quickly changed the conversation's course. "When shall I come and play your harpsichord?"

The widow reluctantly withdrew her eyes from me and gently set her hand on Patch's shoulder.

"Soon, young man. You should stop by very soon. Most certainly before Tuesday!" she warned. Patch looked up at the woman with concern, whilst I squirmed in my chair, inwardly wishing the old crone would leave us alone.

"Why is that?" he inquired. The old woman stood up straight, her frame rigid and stern.

"Because I will be *dead* on Tuesday," she spoke, resolutely. Patch lifted his eyebrows and I sat, stunned by her words and casual tone.

"My word! Is it that time already? And they say time stands still at Larouche!" he chuckled with amusement.

I sat, lost and not entirely able to decipher what I was hearing. Was this a strange game the pair played? Did they mean to frighten the new guests with their tricks? Either way, I was completely baffled by the manner of conversation between Patch and this woman. Nothing made sense to me.

"You are *joking*, aren't you?" I intruded, disbelieving. Patch and the Widow turned to me. Their smiles were gone quicker than the descending blade of a guillotine.

"Death is *not* a joke, young man!" she said, quite vexed with me. The widow looked disappointed in my choice of words and Patch spoke up.

"Forgive us, Andrew. I forget you have just arrived!" he said, through nervous chuckles. "The widow has predicted many deaths, including her own husband's! She has a *gift*! But it's a heavy price to pay for her readings. Nothing that *I* could afford, that is," he shrugged. The widow clucked her tongue at him.

"I'd offer *you* a discounted price, naturally!" She ran a crooked finger down his jaw and Patch smirked, taking her hand in his. He looked at me with a small shrug.

"Is it strange of me to say that I'd rather *not* know when my unfortunate demise will be?" he said, as he lifted his hands apologetically. "I've cheated and robbed death many times. I'm sure he's no friend of mine!" he joked. Patch and the widow shared a laugh, but my mind was still swirling with the notion that *anyone* could predict death. How could such a thing be done and, if it *was* possible, how is it that I had never heard of Widow Sherrigan before?

"So, you say you are going to -" I cleared my throat, "- *die*... this Tuesday? Are you afraid? Can anything be done to stop it?" I had so many questions for the Widow, but they were all dismissed as she picked up her gown and spoke stiffly.

"When Death comes knocking *no one* can stop him." She started to leave, then turned back to Patch and myself. "I'm not afraid to die. There are worse things to be found among the living!" she scoffed. With that, she left the dining room. I saw Patch smile as he watched the woman leave. My head fell into my hands, heavy with thought and mingled with confusion. There was *one* thing, however, that was certain.

"I don't think she likes me," I sighed. Patch leaned in, playfully swatting my shoulder.

"Well then, cheer up. She'll be dead on Tuesday!"

He turned back to the menu still stuck in his hands and left me with unsettled thoughts. If the widow *had* predicted many deaths before, it was luck and nothing more, I reasoned.

The waiter set our plates down and Patch excitedly tossed the menu in his hands back over his head. Suddenly exhilarated by the cooked meat set before him, he carved into his steak, its juices leaking out and flooding the plate.

"Dig in, Andrew. You've got a lot to digest!" he spoke, with a mouthful.

His words were doubled with meaning and accuracy on both accounts. There *was* much to absorb at the Hotel Larouche! There were new people to meet and new philosophies to absorb. Everyone lived so differently here. Absent-mindedly, I stabbed a roasted potato with my fork and took a bite.

At one end of the room, I noticed two girls sitting at a table, sipping tea. They moved as one, swiftly and elegantly, but what struck me most of all was their outward appearance.

Covered, head to toe, in what appeared to be red clay smeared across their bodies, their haircuts were short and as ruddy as their skin. They sported short fur coats, concealing even shorter dresses, and wore long pearl necklaces around their necks. They moved gracefully when they talked, engrossed completely in their own world. A person couldn't help but stare.

"Terra Cotta Twins, Tammy and Tessa," Patch spoke. He didn't need to look back to know what I gawked at. He took another bite and then continued. "The clay, they believe, wards off evil spirits. They're also, coincidentally, on Tansy's team of dancers," he spoke, with a hint of annoyance, so I returned to my meal.

After scanning the rest of the dining hall, I noticed a tall, gaunt man walking out of the bustling lunch room. He wore a long black coat and a tall top hat. A thick dark mustache topped his mouth, and a white scarf was casually draped around his neck.

I didn't catch a long enough glimpse of the man to make out his expression, but his hurried departure caused me to sense that he was a man of great importance with pressing matters to attend to. Many of the hotel patrons even tipped their hats to him as he passed. I wondered where he was off to in such a rush. What business was conducted within the walls of such a place? Patch, I began to see, was right. The Hotel Larouche was a place of fun and relaxation, free from any laborious work and duty.

I ate my meal in silence, listening to Patch quickly sum up other nearby diners.

The scrawny man sitting at the next table, he confided, made his living by pretending to have an injured leg. He often pleaded for money from good hearted Christian folk for his "pending surgery".

Another man and his wife had lived off feigned titles their whole lives. They were currently the "Duke and Duchess" of Treasure Falls, an island unbeknownst to anyone! They deceived and tricked others into treating them as if they were royalty, a nasty game they'd been indulging in, even *after* others had caught onto them.

As we consumed our dinner, I learned that some guests were dishonorably discharged military men and others were ostracized political figures. Still other residents were retired thieves and pimps who had "seen the light" within the walls of the Hotel Larouche.

I asked Patch if it was possible to become an *altered being* while at the hotel, and he determined that it *was* and happened frequently. Most of the time, however, many alterations made to a person's character were in the *opposing* direction, blatantly away from goodness. With that, we shared a good laugh, but the entire time we spoke I thought that he could be wrong. I felt that, already, in my first day as a resident of the hotel, I was *better off*! I felt oddly stronger and more decisive than I was back home in Howell Village.

It was not true, I thought. A person *could* change for the better at Larouche.

Turning to my new friend, I watched as he busily gnawed away at his food. Occasionally, he stopped eating and applauded the musicians playing at the far end of the room.

Desperately, I wanted to inquire about Patch's past. Who *was* he? Who was Tansy? How did they find Larouche? Questions about his previous life hung in the air, but there was no time for it. He spoke up first, pointing the end of his fork to my chest.

"So, why are *you* here? Did you get lost along your way to church?" Patch sneered.

I laughed and took a drink of the red wine I had been served. Patch continued, not even close to finishing his interrogation of me. "Don't you have family? Friends that will miss you?" he pried. I shook my head and finished off the green, leafy vegetable on my plate.

"You've not been away from home before, I gather," Patch observed, another jeering smile spreading across his face. I felt that he enjoyed my torment entirely too much. "Don't be surprised, Andrew. You're like a school girl in a brothel," he teased, and my cheeks reddened. After a moment, I nodded in agreement.

"I lived my life in a cage and now I'm free, you could say," I said. It was little information, but I couldn't bring myself to reveal any more of my history. After all, we'd just met! Patch rolled his eyes, unsatisfied with the answers I had given.

"Yes, but how did you *get* here?" he said, growing aggravated with me, so I set my utensils on my plate and nervously drank down my entire glass of wine. I shifted in my chair, uncomfortably.

"I ran away, like anyone does," I shrugged, and Patch leaned in closer.

"From what?" His fingers drummed along the table, anxiously. I knew his questions would be never ending, but I hoped to conceal as much of my life as possible. Not *everyone* could be an open book as easily as he was. Worry over the published article in the morning's paper also plagued me. Though I sensed Patch was a free bird, with little respect for the authority of the law, I knew enough to be apprehensive around strangers. Without revealing too much, I spoke in a bit of a whisper.

"I ran from my mother... and my brother... and perhaps, the memory of my father," I admitted. Patch smiled and clinked his half empty cup with mine, playfully toasting my rebellious decision to depart from my uncaring family.

"What took you so long?" he asked, with a smug grin, and I smiled. Knowingly, I felt the cool framed mirror underneath my fingers. *Matilda*.

"I guess I was waiting for a miracle... but then she was gone."

Matilda was so close, but she felt miles away. She was angry with me, and I knew I had to beg her to look at me -to speak to me. Amidst the glamour of the hotel, I had nearly forgotten all that I really wanted. I nearly forgot that nothing *really* mattered without *her*.

Patch sighed, and a wistful look spread across his face.

"I think you and I should commandeer a boat and leave those finicky females behind for a while," he smirked, and I chuckled in agreement, though my heart was not fully in it. I wanted to think I was different from Patch regarding matters of the heart. My love, though unreturned, was clear and chaste. It was constant and readily available should she have ever desired it. With all my might, I didn't want to appear manically enamored of Matilda like Patch was with Tansy. Admittedly, I didn't want to be humiliated, and caught in a hopeless *one sided* love affair. I forced myself to believe that I, Andrew Godfrey, had more dignity than *that*.

Just then, my attention was drawn to a commotion at the end of the hallway. A serious looking man with spectacles and tufted brown hair rushed passed all the diners. A pencil, tucked behind his ear, bobbed up and down as he went.

Following immediately behind him, was a man wearing a baker's uniform. His eyes were strained and his face was red as he argued with the first man.

"We're low on so many things, Nicholas! There's no sugar, no milk, no strawberries! Honestly, where's your mind been these days?" the baker fumed, as he shook his hands irately above his head. The first man, undeterred by the baker's rage, stopped walking. Standing no more than a few feet from our table, the man responded, calmly.

"Careful, baker, or do you forget *who* you're talking to?"

The baker, his chest heaving with anger, looked down at the man with narrow eyes. The first man inched closer to the baker, looking about the room as he spoke.

"You know how difficult *it* can be, so I wouldn't go barking demands if I were you!"

"Just get it done, Nicholas, or the people around here will start to worry!" the baker whispered to the man, the steam from his nostrils nearly curling the ends of his whiskers.

After a moment, the baker pushed past the diners, quite infuriated. The man the baker identified as Nicholas, stood flustered and remained there in an uncomfortable stoop. Taking an opposite route, the man, with the pencil still tucked behind his ear, darted from the room.

Patch and I turned toward each other, and my eyes all but pleaded with him for an explanation. My friend, on the other hand, relaxed in his chair, indifferent.

"Who was that?" I asked, at last.

"That's the only man with a real job around here!" Patch replied sarcastically, as he pushed aside his finished plate.

"Really?" I asked as I sat back, wondering what the man's occupation could *possibly* be. Patch leaned in close.

"That, Andrew Godfrey, is God's architect. Or, maybe, he works for the devil. I can't *really* tell sometimes. They call him *Harvey Nicholas*."

Harvey Nicholas. The name was shrouded in mystery. Before I could ask any further questions, Patch removed the napkin tucked into the collar of his shirt and threw it on the table with a yawn. He was finished with his meal, and getting ready to head on. I looked at my own unfinished chocolate mousse and quickly shoveled into my mouth. It was sensational.

My questions regarding Harvey Nicholas, I knew, were best left unasked. I would have to wait before I could ask Patch anything more about my peculiar surroundings and the even stranger people that lived there.

The afternoon ended pleasantly, I felt. Elated was I, to have met my first real friend at Larouche. Despite his prying questions, it felt wonderful to know Patch. He was confident, I saw, and had many acquaintances. He knew most "ins and outs" of the hotel and I sensed that he had been a resident there for some time. Before we departed, we agreed to meet at the Social Hour the next day for gin and rummy.

The next day. I hadn't planned on staying another day at the hotel, yet there I was making future arrangements with Patch. Surely, I felt, another day wouldn't be *such* a bad thing! It would give me time to think about what my next steps would be. As I felt that familiar lurch twist my insides, I realized *more time* was an excellent thing. The both of us headed off in different directions.

After riding the moving machine up to the fifth floor and rushing to my door, I entered the small chamber and set the mirror down on the hook. I locked the door, subconsciously.

"Matilda? Are you there?" I quietly pleaded. A bright face appeared in the reflection.

"Hello," she spoke, with pursed lips. Tenderly, I placed my hand up to the mirror.

"I'm so sorry, Matilda. I am so, so *very* sorry. Can you forgive me?" I asked. Reluctantly, she smiled and placed her hand up to mine. I took the gesture as a sign of forgiveness, and was relieved that she chose to pardon my actions.

"Dearest Andrew," she sighed, wistfully. "You've carried me around all day. I should not have overlooked your kindness. After all, having a dead girl as a companion is no *easy* task," she spoke, mildly embarrassed. I shook my head, not wanting her to feel badly about our situation.

"I do it gladly," I smiled. We stood for a few moments in silence. "Did you enjoy everything you saw today?" I asked.

Matilda nodded, as if lost in her own reverie. "I thought Patch and Tansy danced beautifully. It was as if one was created with the other in mind," she sighed. I nodded in agreement and removed my hand from the mirror. She saw exactly what I saw. "I wished all my life to be in love like that... and now -" She bit her lip, as her voice trailed off.

"Matilda, you mustn't think those things!" I nearly begged her to stop, not wanting to be reminded of all the things she could no longer attain. Quickly, I searched for some sort of reasoning that would appease her. I searched at length, before I slumped into a crestfallen stance. Love was fickle, and for me... *unrealistic*. I sighed.

"What's the point, anyway? Most of the time love is hard to come by. You can love someone, but what if they

172

can't love you back?" I admitted, shyly. Uncomfortable, I began pacing. I did that sometimes.

"*Unrequited love*. I know it well," she confessed, as she bit her lip again. It appeared that she revealed more than she planned to.

"You do? But you're *Matilda Brew*," I said, in my astonishment. Curiosity got the better of me, as my pacing subsided and my eyes locked onto hers.

"Yes, well, let's forget all that," Matilda blushed, then she perked up. "I've always wanted to run away with a circus! I read about it in a book once. It sounded quite romantic! Could you just imagine it? What would my circus name be?" Matilda began rambling, and I couldn't help but smile.

"Matilda?" I pressed.

"Brew The Bold! Blazing Brew! Or how about Matilda the Magnificent? I do like the sound of that!"

"Matilda!" I nearly chided.

"What?" Matilda said, looking away with embarrassment.

So Matilda *had* loved someone. Had I met him before? Had we ever crossed paths?

It struck me that the day she died may have been just as bleak for many other hopeful hearts. A young man back in Howell could be sick with grief wondering if Matilda had loved him back, same as I. Desperately, I wanted to know if this young lad saw her and dreamt of her as *I* did. I wanted to know all this and yet, I found I wanted to remain as much in the dark about Matilda's love life as possible. It would only bring about misery for me, as no good news could possibly come from it.

"That day it rained..." I began, almost too terrified to ask. "Did he come then? Did he see you the day you died?" I asked. Deep down, I knew I shouldn't have asked, but I couldn't help myself. Matilda stared at me, a cloud of suspicion floating between us.

"He did, but it was too late," she spoke. Her lips pressed together.

I opened my mouth to respond just as a loud series of knocks and scratches sounded just outside, in the hallway. Sounds of fingernails clawing *my own door* left me stunned. The door rattled violently! Vibrations from the walls shook Matilda's mirror and I ran to it, as a loud howl - then a guttural scream sounded in the hallway. I looked at Matilda, whose eyes were full of fear and uncertainty.

"What was *that*?" she whispered, her voice quivering. I took the mirror down quickly, and pressed it to my chest. Terrified, I leaned my head to the door and waited.

The screaming subsided. Heavy footsteps trampled close to the door, and then moved away slightly. A muffled voice spoke, but my ears couldn't make out what the voice said. The footsteps resumed, loudly at first, then fading. At last, a door somewhere down the hallway slammed, and Matilda and I breathed out a sigh of relief.

The unsettling ruckus was over, but the unknown cause of it left me petrified. I couldn't move. Paralyzed with fear, I could scarcely breathe.

How much more of this could I take? There were twists and turns at every corner, and my poor mind had been jolted all day! The strange event, I convinced myself, was just another instance of the peculiar occurrences at this absurd hotel. I would simply have to accept that.

Still, I felt there was a logical explanation for the sounds at my door. *There had to be*. No human was capable of making those terrible sounds. What exactly was concealed within the rooms of this hotel? I shuddered.

Back home, we learned that the answers to any problem could be found everywhere. Nothing was a mystery and no miracles were ever witnessed. The small town boy was desperate for answers and plausible explanations - but what if there were *none*? Could I accept that some events just happened for no reason at all?

I couldn't. If I wanted to sleep that night, I knew that finding someone who could shed some light on the event would be the only way to calm my shattered nerves.

"I'm going to go find Patch. Maybe, he can tell me where those wails came from," I said, trying to appear as brave as I could. Watching Matilda, as she wrapped her arms around herself with worry, I hesitated before placing the mirror back on the wall.

"This place gets stranger by the minute," she whispered, and a tremor of fear consumed me. She was right. I kept reminding myself, however, that the hotel was a place accepted and *even cherished* by all the people who resided in it. *There was nothing to fear within its walls*, I recited in my mind.

176

"Go, and leave me here," Matilda spoke, interrupting my inner deliberation. Quickly, I dismissed her command.

"Impossible! I *won't* leave you. It's too dangerous!" Desperately, I tried to justify my reason for not wanting to part from her, but she rolled her eyes at me. I continued, "Did you not just hear what was outside the door?" Matilda sighed.

"They can't do *me* much harm, can they?" she replied, and my shoulders slumped. She was right, and I was once again foolishly reminded of the unfortunate situation we found ourselves in. But suppose this *thing*, this *monstrosity,* was of *another world.* Could it not harm Matilda then? I shrugged off the idea. My mind was taking me to far off places, and simultaneously toying with my sanity. There *was* a logical explanation, I believed. Cautiously, I placed the mirror on the wall. I knew Matilda would be fine, but I secretly wished she was coming along, too.

"I'll be back soon. Don't do anything exciting without me!" I quipped, and Matilda crossed her arms.

"Oh, I wouldn't worry about that!" she chuckled, and, with that, I left the room.

The hallway was empty. I breathed a sigh of relief, secretly glad I found myself alone on the fifth floor. Apprehensively, I made my way down the hallway, one step, then two....

It didn't take long before my eyes were drawn to the walls of the long, winding corridor. Outstretched gashes ran along the wallpaper! Slashes ripped and split through the vertical stripes on both sides of the hallway. Those markings, those terrible gashes, had not been there before! The hacked wallpaper could have been produced by none other than the creature I heard at my door!

I touched the torn paper with my own trembling hands. The creature who mauled the wallpaper was vicious and wicked, so why was it kept in such a beautiful place? Why was such a beast, who clawed its way through the hotel, living among us - and not living in a cage far away?

One step at a time, I realized I was close to the moving machine. A part of me half expected to see a ghost - or some flying monster - whiz past, creating even more havoc. I was on high alert, as I fell further into the realization that *nothing* was what it appeared at the Hotel Larouche.

Ghosts. Death predictors. Dancers. Vagrants. *Monsters*. This place was *nothing* like Howell Village.

CHAPTER NINE
THE TURBULENCE WITHIN

A familiar little man on a unicycle sped down the corridor, just as I reached the moving machine. He looked flustered and out of breath.

"No intrusions, I hope..." he drifted off. I caught him looking behind me, wide-eyed, as he took in the ghastly sight of the wallpaper. His eyes examined the corridor with disgust. "Heavens, not again!" he sighed, with defeat.

"There was a scream at my door. It was as if someone was trying to get in!" I said, as I looked around at the other rooms down the hallway. "I'm honestly surprised no one else heard it."

"It's Anais," he grieved, with a quick look over his shoulder. In a whisper, he continued. "You grow used to it." His cryptic expression faded quickly, as a smile plastered itself onto his face. "Can I help you with anything else, sir?"

"Anais?" I questioned. "Who - *what*- is Anais?"

The man's face grew white with realization. "You've not been acquainted with Anais yet, have you?" he inquired, growing pale as he spoke.

The man cleared his throat and shifted nervously. Something tightened in my own throat and I shook my head, suddenly fearful. What was this *Anais*, and what sort of calamity followed it?

"Another time, perhaps," the man said nervously, as he climbed back on his unicycle. "I've got errands to run."

Reluctantly, I bid the man a farewell, but not before asking for Patch's room number. In no time at all, I was headed down to the fourth floor of the moving machine. My mind was still numb from the events of the day. Nothing made sense or, if it *did*, I was as removed from this society as I was from my old way of life back home. Did I belong anywhere? Would there ever be a place where I could be as comfortable with the people as I was with the palm of my own hand? New information was given to me at every turn and, for a young man from a small village, it was proving more than I could handle. *Anais.* I repeated the name again and again, so as to remember it.

Finally, I arrived on the fourth floor and made my way out of the moving machine. I stopped. The sound of someone playing the piano drifted down the hallway. It was lovely to hear such a sweet melody, soft and tender as the keys permitted. I took my time, the gentle notes drawing me toward the instrument that played them. As I enjoyed the music, I passed the first few rooms, seemingly pulled to the end of the hallway by an invisible cord.

Patch's room was the twelfth one on the floor, but as I walked by the eighth room my feet came to a halt. The door was slightly ajar, and the sound of the instrument lured me to it. Boldly, I pushed the door open a bit more and peeked inside.

There was the piano making the beautiful music, and behind it sat both Patch and Tansy, absorbed in their surroundings. Tansy looked at once both wild and elegant, if ever such a combination existed. Her long burgundy-like hair draped over her shoulders like a cape, flowing across the bodice of her fine damask dress. Her brows were strong, and a smile softened her heart shaped face. She sat, as if mesmerized by her own hands as they ran along the keys, playing a hauntingly lovely melody.

Patch stood and walked around the piano, beaming with admiration. Often, he tried to catch her eyes, but she didn't dare look at him. If she gave him an opportunity, he'd take it and never let go. He watched her as if she was the most fascinating creature on earth. Slowly, he moved toward her and bent down to wrap his arms around her waist. His face lowered to her hair, kissing her lightly on the head. When the song ended, Tansy didn't move.

"Did I ever tell you how much I hate you? I despise every part of you, like I've never despised anyone," Patch hummed into her hair.

"I know *exactly* how you feel," she sulked, but after only a slight pause, she turned around on the bench and met his lips for a moment. Then she removed them, the spell undone, and walked away from the piano, pushing her love struck friend to the side.

"You must stop, Patch. Leave me alone!" Tansy demanded in a thick, rich voice. I heard him groan with discontent.

"Not this again."

"*This* is nothing but your pathetic delusions."

He ran his hands through his hair and removed the loose tie around his neck. Then, he walked toward a picture - a portrait - hanging on the wall. It was the face of a *man*, similar in looks to Patch, but much healthier and kinder in appearance. He dipped his fingers in a glass of wine on a nearby table and marked the image's mouth, carelessly staining the portrait.

"Stop that! What's the matter with you?" Tansy yelled. Patch wiped his hands on his pants and stood back, admiring his work.

"He looked like he needed a drink!" Patch howled. Tansy removed the picture from the wall.

"Go home, Patch. You're a fool!" Tansy nearly spat. A flicker of hurt crossed Patch's impish expression.

Realizing my presence still went unnoticed, I knocked on the door. It felt rude intruding, looking into their private lives as if it were a theatrical presentation. Patch looked up at me and forced a smiled.

"Andrew! Good grief man! Didn't I just leave you?" he fumed, then turned to Tansy with concern. She slammed the lid down on the piano with great force.

"Who is this?" Tansy raised an eyebrow, and I felt my skin grow red with embarrassment. We were perfect strangers, but the way her eyes bore into me, I felt as if she held a small vendetta toward me. Perhaps, it was an adversity held toward any of Patch's acquaintances or, to an even further extent, *men* in general.

"This is Andrew. Andrew meet *Tansy*."

I didn't know whether to bow or kiss her hand, for it felt as if I was being introduced to royalty from the way Patch had spoken about her. Instead, I opted for a small wave, which she returned with a slightly bothered look. Naturally, this made me all the more uncomfortable.

"I sh-should go-," I stuttered, but Patch reached out for my arm, laughing.

"You look afraid, Andrew. Tansy won't bite, and if she does it's likely to be in *my* direction." Patch threw her a wink and she dismissed it, taking a seat on a velvet chair next to the window.

"Sometimes, it's not about how well you can take the bite. It's how well you can take the *hint*," Tansy spoke, facing the window. Patch clutched his heart as he walked toward her. He knelt down on one knee in front of the chair where he sat and took her hands in his.

"A hint? Remind me what *those* are again," he grinned. She rolled her eyes, and removed her hands from his grasp. Remembering herself, she bounded from the chair and ran her fingers through the thick hair that fell about her face.

"This is what we do, Andrew. *We fight*. We beat each other down because it makes us feel good. We argue, and your friend confuses the emotion for something more. But there is *nothing more*," she stated, unsympathetically.

She retied the laces of her boots and I froze awkwardly. Patch slowly drifted down into a chair, producing a thin lipped smile that masked his disappointment.

Suddenly, remembering where I was, I shifted from one foot to the other, while Tansy stood up from her seat and smoothed the folds of her dress. Realizing the room had grown stale from the turn of the conversation, Tansy left, closing the door behind her. This left Patch and me alone in the heavy silence that followed Tansy's abrupt exit. His eyes followed her out of the room and he turned back to me with a sigh.

"We have *arguments*. That's enough to show me she cares. When that's gone, then I'll know it's over, but until then..." his voice wavered.

"She seems nice," I lied, and Patch shrugged.

"Tansy? She's alright, I suppose," he said nonchalantly, and I looked away, embarrassed for having witnessed Patch love Tansy earlier. We both knew he thought she was much more than *alright*. Patch shrugged off the remnants of his conversation with Tansy and served himself a glass of brandy. I wondered if it served as his calming medicine for the times when Tansy refused him.

Awkwardly, I walked around Tansy's room looking at trinket boxes and picture frames scattered on cabinets and shelves. Patch lounged on the love seat, lost in his daydreams. Immediately, I changed the subject, to avoid drifting off into some sad conversational ditch over unattainable women.

"Patch, have you heard anything *unusual* lately?" I asked him. My words hung in the air, heavy and weighted. Patch's forehead wrinkled in response, so I proceeded. "Just today, I heard strange noises -scratching on the walls and horrible snarls! This terrible scream echoed through the hallways. I asked someone about it, but he only gave me a very foggy answer," I stopped talking, realizing that my words seemed to be falling on deaf ears. Patch looked on, unfazed. I took a seat beside him, continuing my account of the event. "And then, there was this loud rapping at my door! It was as if someone was trying to dig their way through the wood," I explained. Patch set the glass down and relaxed his head on the love seat.

"That's probably Anais. Just ignore her," he dismissed. *It was the name again*! Anais was the very name the man on the unicycle had whispered earlier. I shifted nervously on the couch beside him.

"That's the same name the man mentioned! Who is *Anais*?" I pressed. The more I said the name, the more it began to embed itself in my memory. It sounded like a foreign yet oddly familiar name that I had heard someplace before. Patch reclined his head on the sofa and sighed.

"Anais is a strange, wicked young girl. Some say she was crazed from birth, but others say the devil struck his sword into her heart and now, forever manipulates her. She's a heathen with no soul and no awareness of anything. Some have heard her speak in languages far beyond a child's depth, and her eyes..." Patch said, as he swirled the leftover brandy around in his cup. "Tansy told me her eyes turn completely white when demons choose to speak through her!" he described. Patch drank the last of his drink and poured himself another glass. He must have seen the fear on my face because he chuckled, lightheartedly.

"Rest at ease, Andrew! She stays locked up most days, and her father watches over her at night. *I've* only seen her *twice* in the three years that I've been here."

Absolutely terrified, I swallowed the lump in my throat and shuddered. I could not imagine a person, so entwined with the devil, existing. The people in my town were all God-fearing participants in the church. Was I supposed to believe that a human residing in this very hotel was in league with the dancing black-hoofed goat?

"What does she look like?" I further inquired. Boldly, I dared to piece the question together. Morbid curiosity struck me, and I found myself both not wanting to hear the answer and inwardly, begging for it. Patch smiled.

189

"She looks like the spittle of the devil himself... like a monster! When you look at her, you see your sins laid out onto a table in front of you. You see all that you are, and the darkness inside you, in the form of a ravenous child."

He finished the next drink, faster than the first, pausing afterward to contemplate his last statement.

I didn't want to think about going home, but my mother's fury seemed like a run in the stream compared with facing Anais. I hoped never to see the unfortunate creature during my stay at Larouche. In fact, I briefly pondered running upstairs and packing my bags immediately.

Patch stood up and wiped his mouth with his arm. I realized I had been gripping the sofa, tearing the threads beneath my fingers. Patch continued with a roguish grin.

"Let's head down to the Social Hour. I'm meeting a gentleman there."

Absent-mindedly, I stood up and made my way to the door, following my friend out of Tansy's room. My body was moving, but my mind was still lost in Patch's detailed description of the wicked girl living in the hotel. Patch gently patted my shoulder, perhaps, to offer me comfort before we headed down to the lobby. Tense as a fence post, I constantly scanned the patrons for any signs of Anais.

Patch had said with *certainty* that they kept her locked up, but I had my doubts. She was at my door earlier. She marked the walls with her nails and tore the carpet. I couldn't believe that someone like Anais was *easily* restrained.

We made our way through the lobby, casually pushing aside multiple hagglers and a few scantily clad women as we reached the revolving doors. Patch, who had thrown on a pinstriped jacket and brown derby to shield him from the strong breeze outside, looked slightly out of style compared to the spit spot nation of brightly dressed residents. He vaguely reminded me of the villagers back in Howell, with their ill-fitted, tattered clothing and their hay-like hair. It seemed that everyone in Howell Village wore nothing but hand-me-downs. The pants I had worn daily came from my great uncle Fredrick Barringer, on my mother's side. He had long since passed, but the pants were *never* put to rest.

The appearance of a moderately current suit jacket or hat would be the talk of Howell Village! Clothing was a necessity, yes, but hard to come by. Patch, however, seemed to deliberately choose a disheveled appearance. There was little time for giving much thought to wearing the latest trends in his carefree lifestyle, I presumed. It certainly set him apart from the well groomed and tailored residents walking the streets of Larouche, making me feel at ease. I had all but forgotten my own transformation earlier.

It was only when I passed the windows of the shops and saw my *own* reflection that I remembered how much I looked like all the other men in Larouche. I looked sophisticated, a sight I wasn't sure I would *ever* get used to. In my mind, I knew I would always feel like Andrew Godfrey from Howell Village, with a torn jacket and his great uncle Fred's pants. It would take time to fully accept the new man I saw in the window.

Patch headed down the street briskly and I struggled to keep up with his long strides. He called out to me, but I was caught trying to pass through the large number of men and women that crowded the streets. Unluckily, I found myself crushed between two heavyset men who tried to squeeze through a narrow opening. That was *one* benefit of living in Howell Village. The lack of food kept people thin and the streets *less* crowded.

We hurried into the Social Hour and anxiously rushed down the steps, the distant sounds of a jaunty piano growing louder.

"Boys!" Patch yelled with open arms.

He took off his hat and cast it aside. It landed on a snoring man, passed out cold, sitting in the corner of the room. The rest of the men were torn in their opinion of Patch's arrival. Their coveted social circle had been disrupted. Some men cheered and pounded on the tables, begging Patch to join them in their respective poker games, while the other half stood up angrily, shouting and throwing their cards on the table.

One particular man, brawny and slick haired, bounded over to us with large bloodshot eyes! He appeared outraged, violently knocking chairs and bottles over as he charged across the room. He pulled Patch by his coat lapels and breathed into his face - nostrils flaring.

"You owe me money, DAMMIT!" he boomed. The man shook Patch by his shoulders. "See that I'm paid or I'll bash your skull in. I swear it!" the man hollered, throwing

Patch into one of the poker tables. Patch collected himself, strangely calm and indifferent. He smiled smugly.

"I don't need to tell you that my presence here tonight is payment enough, Ol' Lox! Since you seek more, send your *wife* my way. I'm sure the payment she'll receive from me will be *more* than enough," he provoked. "Certainly more than she gets every night," Patch ended, half under his breath. A howl went around the room and I tried to conceal my laughter by biting my lip. I didn't need any enemies at Larouche, certainly not ones that were much taller and bigger than I.

Ol' Lox, as Patch called him, clenched his fists and took a step toward Patch with his face red and tight. A few men stood between them, forming a barrier. Nonchalantly, Patch shoved his hands into his pockets, quite proud of himself. Ol' Lox pointed at him, breathless.

"You stay away from my wife, you hear? So help me, you bastard, if I find you near my room, near MY family, I'll put a bullet between those eyes!"

He looked down toward Patch's chest, recalling his enemy's well known tattoo and smiled. Then, he lowered his finger so that it was pointed at Patch's chest."And *those.*"

194

A trace of anger flashed across Patch's face. He quickly shook the feeling off, cracking his knuckles and smiling. Then he turned away and the whole room, including myself, breathed a sigh of relief. The fight wasn't over, however, as I saw Patch contemplate his next move. I should have guessed that Patch wouldn't let the conversation end that way. He casually picked up a few darts and threw them near the center of a target hanging on the wall.

"Don't come near your family, you say?" Patch's voice relayed complete innocence. We all hung onto his next words, half fearful, half admiring. "Best not talk to your *mother* then, Lox, or should I start to call you *son*?"

The men in the room cheered and laughed. Through chants and sing-song howls, Patch was praised as a conquering hero. Now, I'll admit that a jab at one's mother was a bit below the line in my hometown, but the way Patch stood there, calm and collected, was praiseworthy indeed. He was master of his kingdom, and it was something I aspired to. My whole life, I always had a million things to say, but never did. Patch spoke - loud and clear. He had no inhibitions and I, being nothing more than an onlooker at this game of wits - which he had so clearly just won - yearned to speak as freely as he did.

The men gathered around Patch, mockingly bowing to him and giving him congratulatory slaps on the back. Patch acknowledged all this, quite satisfied, then returned his focus to the dart board. Now, he was not just coming *near* the center - he was hitting nothing but bull's-eyes! Meanwhile, I looked at Ol' Lox, whose friends were trying to persuade him from going another round with Patch. They held him back, as his eyes blazed with fury.

Men like Ol' Lox were as common as blades of grass in a field. They were an angry sort, always eager to settle scores with their fists instead of their words. *Mr. Brew* was also a singular blade cut from that same patch of grass, I thought. Angry and ill-tempered as he was, I saw Matilda's father as no different from Ol' Lox. Perhaps my *own* father was like them. It was possible that he was as hungry for a good fight as the men in this club, who led their lives with bitterness in their hearts. Carefully, I approached Ol' Lox and he spat in my direction, his spittle narrowly missing my face.

"Your friend has a mouth on him! You may want to clamp it shut next time I'm around!" he warned. Without thinking, I reached into my back pocket and retrieved a small portion of the money I had stolen from our family's shop. I handed it to him and his eyes narrowed in on me.

"This ought to cover my friend's debt. If not, it's the best you'll get," I spoke sincerely. A voice called out to me as Ol' Lox took the money from my hand. Patch approached us and grabbed my arm. He pulled me away from the menacing Lox. With distance now between him and us, Patch spoke.

"You *don't* have to do that, Andrew. That sad sack had it coming to him!" Patch scoffed. I looked at my spiteful friend, wanting to appear as casual as he had earlier, but my quivering voice gave me away.

"It-it's fine. I want to! Anyway, it will make our lives easier for a day or two," I shrugged. Patch placed his hands on the side of my head, with both gratitude and sympathy.

"You are too good, Andrew. I hate to see that go," he smiled, sadly. Before I could respond, a short, poor looking fellow approached Patch. They mumbled in secret for a moment, then Patch looked toward the entrance of the Social

Hour. Another man, tall and with the same light hair as Patch, waved at him. I saw Patch's mouth twitch. He took a few steps toward the man and they shook hands. No words passed between them, only a long silent stare. At last, they embraced.

Who was he? I wondered. Not wanting to intrude, I took a seat beside the robust drunkard passed out in the corner and looked on as Patch and the man exchanged words. The conversation began, it appeared, with the usual social pleasantries. Shortly, however, the conversation seemed to turn sour as Patch continually shook his head defiantly and, at one point, threw his arms in the air with an incredulous laugh. After a few more exchanges, the strange newcomer placed his hand on Patch's shoulder, consolingly. Patch all but jumped away - as if this man's hand had been as hot as burning coals.

Returning to his place opposite the target, he continued to throw the darts, slightly more agitated this time around. Clearly, Patch considered the conversation over, but the man wouldn't allow him to walk away from it. After more persistent pleading from the newcomer, Patch spun toward him.

"I said 'GOOD DAY', brother!" Patch swung his fist at him, making contact with the man's jaw in one swift motion that sent him tumbling to the floor. After a moment, the man stood up, wiped the blood from the corner of his mouth, and dashed out of the room. He slammed the door shut on his way out.

The room silenced. Everyone stared at Patch in disbelief.

Brother. So *that's* who the mystery man was, I thought. His looks led me to believe that they were related, but *how close* exactly came as a big surprise. No one said anything at first, but eventually the various conversations in the room resumed. Patch turned back to his dart game.

Meanwhile, I sat and took it all in. Where had his brother come from? Did he live at Larouche, as well? There was no point in asking Patch what had passed between him and his brother, however. Having a brother, myself, I knew the bond could be strange between kin and sometimes actually nonexistent. In his animalistic behavior, my friend had revealed his true nature, and it both frightened and intrigued me. Patch had not mentioned his brother, but then again he hadn't mentioned anything about himself at all! The longest conversation we had was a veiled account of his relationship with Tansy. I had no idea where he'd come from or who he was. His independent manner and quick tongue were the code he seemed to live by and I knew no answers would ever be given to me if I asked.

After a few drinks, we picked up our coats and headed back to the hotel. The time was nearly midnight and I longed for the comfort of my own bed. It had been a long day, maybe the longest of my life.

Patch barely spoke during the walk back. I knew there was much on his mind, and I hoped that, in me, he would find a confidant.

He didn't. We spent the evening consuming many bottles of beer. Finally, we drunkenly staggered back to the hotel, hoping we didn't collide with any street lamps. Looking up into the night sky after my first full day at Larouche, I saw the stars and the moon *differently*.

I remembered looking up at them from my window back home. They were meaningless *there*. They seemed like some painting, similar to the one in the Sistine Chapel that only hung above our heads to be admired. *Now*, I felt like I could be a part of those stars. They were the perfect background to the spectacle that I was becoming immersed in.

"It's beautiful. It's the *most* beautiful thing I've ever seen," I spoke aloud, marveling at the brilliant sky and dazzling fixtures of the hotel above us. Patch looked up in turn, beer bottle still in hand. He grinned at the moon and nodded.

"Yes. Yes, it is, isn't it?" Patch swung his arm around my shoulders and led me to the familiar revolving doors. "Come on, Andrew. Let's *enjoy* this sinfully wonderful place!"

That was it. *That* was the moment of my immersion in a new life... my future. Perhaps, it was in the way that Patch spoke, inwardly daring me to play the game. Perhaps, the moment after he spoke those words, I felt *included* and part of a new family. I felt so fortunate to stumble upon this extraordinary place. It only took *one day* at the Hotel Larouche for me to want to stay there always. Magic words, I subconsciously always yearned to hear, opened the gates to never ending enjoyment in a new world. Patch had unknowingly given his stamp of approval and I would so willingly take it.

201

I was a boy, not merely thrown into the wolves den but becoming *one of them.* I couldn't know it then. I could not even fathom the sort of person I would become. I was ready to be just like Patch. I was *ready* to say and do whatever I pleased! Nineteen years had prepared me for the moment that I would take charge of my own life - and there was the *Hotel Larouche* - waiting for me. In my new home full of laughter, joyous music, and spinning tables, I embraced the night.

Chapter Ten
Step in Line

"We're staying?" Matilda asked in astonishment. "For how long?"

"Just for a few days, Matilda, until I can decide what to do next," I lied. It was the first time I had lied to Matilda. A small part of me wanted to believe in what I was saying, but the largest part of me - the part that fed my deep curiosity combined with a sudden love for pleasurable things - knew I was only staying for *one* reason.

It was the same reason most people stayed, I felt. Life was *easy* here, so why should I leave it? There were no worries at the hotel. There was nothing to stress about, except what sort of pâté I was going to put on my toast. Everyone was a part of a single celebration, so bright, I *couldn't* look away.

"I see right through you, Andrew Godfrey. Not that I can blame you, of course," she said. Matilda looked at me sternly. "Just be careful," she warned. Dismissively, I chuckled at her cautious tone.

"If I ever lose myself Matilda, all I have to do is look in your mirror to remember who I am."

My words were true in many ways, but most likely not how *she* interpreted them. Looking in Matilda's mirror, I saw myself. Most importantly, I saw all that I *wanted*. I saw Matilda, the girl who would forever remind me of the old Andrew Godfrey. I'd drawn pictures of her and snuck glances at her in school. She was the girl I had fallen in love with and could never even remotely consider leaving. She was my history - my past and my future - and, as long as I looked in her mirror, I would *never* forget it.

"Don't worry Matilda. I'm still Andrew Godfrey, the boy who loves to draw."

***

The Widow Sherrigan entered eternal rest the following Tuesday. It was all everyone could talk about. She had predicted her death accurately, and arranged her own funeral quiet beautifully. Still, the notion of it all completely baffled me. How *anyone* could predict their life's end seemed unreal!

Hers was a strange and dark sort of magic that gave me chills, as I watched her wooden coffin head out of the lobby, and down the street in a horse-drawn carriage. The Hotel Larouche, for a few hours, fell completely silent. The dancing ceased. The roulette tables were empty. *Everything stopped.*

The Widow's nephew, who claimed he possessed the spectacular gift also, moved his effects into his aunt's office in the days after her death. Business commenced, and a line of eager patrons wanting to purchase death predictions formed outside his door. The whole idea of buying a death date was unnatural, but an alarming amount of curious guests crowded the man's office daily. If they happened to visit between the hours of 12:00 pm and 3:00 pm, he would receive them. The rest of his time was spent in the lobby, involved in high stakes poker games.

I passed by the office as the days marched on. As I continued to reside in the hotel, I found myself realizing two things.

First, death was *already* my friend. Not only had I managed to escape death when I ran through the Brew's house, surrounded by flames, but the only person whose death I truly mourned was Matilda, yet there she was in a mirror. She was in my room, still able to communicate with me as if she had never gone.

The second thing I realized was that death made everything all too real. With death came a great deal of responsibility - responsibility for things that must be accomplished *before* that day dawned. Knowing the date of my own death only made my actions more definite and inhibited - with the certainty that they would be taken into consideration on Judgment Day. Suffocated by the rigid moral code my mother had instilled in me, I wanted to live without hearing the familiar Voice of Reason pinning me down. Tied as I was to that teaching, I couldn't live life as I wanted - free and unguarded, knowing death was just around the corner. So, I ignored it and, for once in my life, I felt truly invincible.

Gladly, I abandoned thoughts of my own uncertain end. I decided there was no need to anger Death. I would not inquire or ponder about my own fated expiration date, because meddling in my own future would be wrong. Some things, I felt, we're best left unknown.

Month after month passed and, over time, I began living under a *new* anthem. I had friends. People liked me. I lived as I pleased, and any thoughts of my mother and brother were so far removed, I could scarcely remember their faces. At nineteen years of age, I saw myself smarter than any of the young men back home. *I* had found my paradise and there *they* were, still slaves to ritual and responsibility.

Admittedly, I attended all the parties and galas at Larouche. Nights became my days as I mingled with the finest members of the hotel, who welcomed me as one of their own. They sang bawdy lyrics and told rude jokes. I loved it. My skin, now constantly engulfed by women's perfume and smoke, somehow gave my whole body a new life. All the layers of the shy boy I once was were being stripped away. Though I had never shared a romance with any woman, I felt temptations continually seize me. There were moments when I thought release from these desires to be impossible!

In the early morning, however, I'd return to my room alone. I'd look in Matilda's mirror and see myself - my face softening into the boy I once was. After a moment, Matilda shined through, eager to converse. We spoke like we did before, sometimes extending the conversation until I, so overcome by exhaustion, collapsed onto the bed. I was, once again, Andrew Godfrey from Howell Village.

The months stretched on in a never ending parade of fun. There was, however, one duty I performed as payment for my stay at Larouche. It was something I found tedious, but necessary. Many of the patrons had advised me to take up a hobby. They were careful not to say the word *occupation*, as the word implied responsibility. A *hobby*, however, was a way that someone could give back to the charitable community of Larouche. A person could serve others if they wished, but no one was forced.

Patch refused to find himself a hobby, as he claimed he wasn't particularly good at anything. From the way he drank rum and played poker, I sensed that there were *many* hobbies that he could exceed at, but none that could benefit the Hotel Larouche!

"It's like this," Patch always began, "If I *really* want to give back to Hotel Larouche, the best thing I can do for it, is to stay out of everyone's hair," he explained. None of us ever questioned his logic. In fact, we *completely* understood it.

Eventually, word got around that I was able to mend a broken watch. There were constant requests to fix clocks and pocket watches, and I wondered how it was that so many of them were broken. Each morning, to my dismay, a bundle of parcels would be brought to my door by one of the men on unicycles. It was the only part of my day that I felt was a time consuming bore, but it was an easy way to earn my keep and give back to the hotel. Though my mind often drifted to my excitement over that evening's festivities, I did my best to remain focused and work as quickly as possible. My nights at the hotel usually began around seven and, anxiously, I knew the ladies and gentleman I had formed acquaintances with would be waiting for me.

I didn't *mind* the work, necessarily. It was apparent, however, that it was not my main priority. The singular benefit of mending watches, I found, were the conversations Matilda and I shared. It was my chance to learn more about her.

Often, when I returned to room 553, stumbling in from the typical soirée, she'd throw me a judgmental glance from her mirror. It would take lengthy conversation to melt away the brewing frustration within her.

"Matilda, you should really come along! Let me take you to the party!" I pleaded one night. Matilda shook her head, fervently.

"I would just get in the way, Andrew," she said, cowering away in her mirror. "Besides, there are some things I just don't want to see," she admitted. I couldn't blame her for feeling that way. The previous night we had watched a man light his eyebrows and eyelashes on fire. The image still disturbed me!

Some nights, I asked Matilda to accompany me, but most nights I went to the celebrations alone. A part of me didn't want Matilda to see her old friend in such a wild and misbehaving light, but a bigger part didn't want her to prevent me from having fun.

"Goodnight, Andrew," she often spoke, just before I closed the door and made my way down to the lobby. *Andrew.* I grimaced. Lately, the sound of my name struck me. Some days I appreciated the sound of it, while other days, I despised it.

If she was upset with my late night gallivanting, I was completely stumped. Matilda loved a good party. Back home, I saw her mingle and dance the night away while I stood stupidly in the corner watching. Yet, here she was, secretly chastising my behavior for "mirroring" her actions. There was no impressing Matilda. I would always be one step behind, never able to meet her expectations.

Nevertheless, I treasured the small conversations we shared whilst I worked away, repairing watches. I felt her temper cool and her hostility diminish as we spoke freely. Often, Matilda dove into a pool of nonsensical questions, so as to keep conversations from ending quickly. I found it was not only her way of passing time, but of testing my values and sense of character, as well.

"Do you prefer *raspberry* or *chocolate* tarts?" she asked. I had been fixing a silver pocket watch when the questions started one afternoon.

"Chocolate," I replied, maneuvering my bifocals so that they rested on the end of my nose. It was the perfect spot for seeing the small screws on the watches. Matilda stuck her tongue out at my answer. "Wrong choice.

Raspberry is *my* favorite!" she smiled. I laughed and turned toward her, my bifocals falling off my face and onto my lap.

"So, if chocolate tarts are not *your* preferred choice, then they're the wrong choice?" I asked, challengingly. She nodded.

"Naturally. I have much better judgment than *you*," she replied, smartly.

"Better judgment than me?" I laughed, slightly appalled.

"*Where,* exactly, were you stumbling in from last night?" Matilda chided, with narrowed eyes. I swallowed, guiltily, and nodded.

"Right you are. Next question," I said, turning back to my work at the desk, avoiding Matilda's smug smirk. We never spoke about what I did during the nights. I doubted she wanted to familiarize herself with my new found drinking habits or my preferred choice of tobacco. Letting the moment pass, I focused on the watch in my hands.

"Do you prefer *straight* hair or *curled*?" she continued. I crossed my arms, fearful of where the particular question was heading.

"Well, I'm at a crossroads aren't I?" I leaned back in my chair, pensively. "If I say that I fancy straight hair, you might become offended, as you often do," I said, looking at Matilda, who rolled her eyes at me. "If I say I prefer curly hair, however, you might call me a liar and accuse me of trying to flatter you! Am I wrong?"

"You're wrong either way!" she exclaimed, flipping her hair with pride. "The correct answer would have been *wavy* hair, as my hair is neither curled nor straight, but wavy," she scoffed, as I threw my hands up in the air.

"Matilda Brew, you can drive a person mad!" I chided, with a chuckle.

Among some of my favorite questions were 'why men grew hair on their chin and women didn't' and 'why our hotel room was so bright even though we had no window'. My response to the first question was that some women *did* grow hair on their chin. If she didn't believe me she could look at my mother for proof! To the second question, I responded to Matilda with sincerity. The room's brightness, I explained, was due to the simple fact that *she* was in it...a response she *quite* liked.

Our interactions always warmed my soul, but in a strange way they filled me with both delight and frustration. They reminded me of who I once was, and it was always difficult to leave our conversations when I left my room at night. I'd shut the door, leaving both Matilda *and* her questions behind.

Patch and I frequented the lobby and dining hall nightly. We made friends and quickly dismissed them, hopping from one social circle to another eagerly. There wasn't a moment that we did not occupy ourselves with cheap thrills and excitement, not wanting to waste a second of the night. Patch's motto of *endless fun* became my own, and I adopted it gladly. I saw that he was as much a culprit in the ongoing shenanigans at the Hotel Larouche as most of the men were.

***

"Patch, come down from there!" I laughed, waving my friend down from a ledge, with the free hand *not* occupied by a bottle of brandy.

Patch had decided to walk along the ledge of one of the balconies that night. It was a bet, agreed upon by two gentlemen who'd been drinking and challenging each other

214

all evening. I stood, helpless and bubbling with uncontainable laughter. Lost in my drunken state, I wailed below to my friend who teetered on the thin railing. His arms were outstretched from his sides as he maintained his balance, drunkenly singing to a small group gathered below. The patrons cheered wildly each time Patch turned back to cross the railing again. They all cackled with excitement at my friend, and the spectacle he was creating.

"The trick is not to look down!" Patch called down to us. Nervously, he looked down, wavering a bit. "Oh, Hellzafire! I looked down!" he laughed, through chattering teeth.

"Patch, you're an idiot!" a portly man yelled, throwing his beer bottle at Patch. My friend dodged it, tipping forward and catching his balance. The possibility that he could fall to his death was not even a thought, as we all became lost in the entertainment. Patch howled with laughter, until at last, he stepped down from the ledge and leaned forward.

"Avert your eyes, mes amis!" he shouted, then he turned around, lowered his pants, and mockingly bared his buttocks. The men and women present all whooped and laughed. *I laughed.*

The following months were a blur of endless parties! Patch didn't step on the ledge again. He didn't need to. He spent his *entire life* suspended on a narrow railing, always wavering - never knowing when he would slip off.

Each night, I stood by him. Each night, I took part in the charade gladly. I felt I was a part of something much bigger than myself.

On another particular evening, a crowd in the lobby circled a man in a white waistcoat. Patch and I immediately made our way over to the spectacle, and we shoved our way through the mass of intrigued patrons. The gentleman, whose name I recalled was Casper Vale, saw me and beamed.

"Andrew!" Casper called out to me. In complete awe, I saw that he held an *alligator* on a leash! "Come and put your hand in my darling Suzette's mouth!" The crowd looked at me expectantly. I looked back nervously to Casper, who motioned to his large, terrifying pet. "Suzette has the best manners, Andrew. She won't bite!"

Everyone around him laughed. I, however, seemed doubtful as I stared at the vicious animal, baring her teeth.

Casper tapped the alligator's head and Suzette opened her large mouth. Patch nudged me forward, laughing along with the spectators.

"Andrew won't do it. He's chickenshit!" Patch teased, and I looked at the arrogant expression on his smug face. I wanted, so much, to prove I was capable of doing anything. I wanted to live in a world where fear didn't hold me back, so I took a sip from the flask in my pocket and approached the alligator.

I was terrified. My hand outstretched in front of me, I slowly moved it closer to Suzette. I felt her hot breath on my skin and saw my hand shake with fright. The crowd was silent. For what felt like an eternity, the entire lobby fell into a spell, captivated by the foolish boy sticking his hand into an alligator's mouth.

At last, my hand was completely inside. Suzette's eyes fell on me, and I almost saw that same judgmental glare Matilda often gave me written on the animal's face! It was as if the animal was saying, "Andrew, what on earth is wrong with you? What has become of the boy from Howell Village?"

I shook my head dismissively and removed my hand from Suzette's mouth. The lobby sounded with thunderous applause.

From that night forward, I was a *hero* among thieves and vagrants. I was respected by the citizens of the Hotel Larouche and accepted as one of their own. Most importantly, however, I was no longer that insignificant boy who followed Patch around everywhere he went. I was my own person, and equal with my friend.

Patch was thrilled with our friendship. I knew that, in me, he had found a close comrade and I was glad for it. Some nights, however, his mind was elsewhere. When Tansy danced, he stood close by, like an artist observing his masterpiece. He fell into a trance at the glowing sight of her beauty, and each day that she enjoyed the company of *another* man, a small part of him withered away.

There was one occasion which left me particularly worried for my friend, and that was the night of the Day Light Savings Masquerade. The hotel guests had found it necessary to celebrate everything, even something as menial as leaping forward an hour. Patch and Tansy spent the afternoon arguing about who would accompany her to the party, each flinging insults at each other as they usually did. It was Tansy's wish that a young bachelor, Charlie Houston, would accompany her. Naturally, Patch flew into a jealous rage!

"I had a pig named, Charlie! And if I had another pig, I would name him Charlie, too!" Patch yelled, as Tansy fled the room. She slammed the door on her way out, and Patch turned to me, frustrated.

"Did you really have a pig named Charlie?" I asked, cutting the silence. Patch rolled his eyes at me.

Both Matilda and I attended that evening's event. Somehow, I managed to coax her into it, despite her objections. She had not left the room in months and I thought the change of scenery would be nice. As the evening wore on, however, I sensed that she began to become more withdrawn. She no longer wanted to see the magnificent sights, or hear the glorious music of the night, and I could not comprehend this.

Tansy went to the Masquerade with Charlie, while Patch stayed in his room, sulking. I watched Tansy drift from her dance partner, casually looking about the room for any trace of her most ardent lover. He hadn't shown up and, after an hour of dancing and dining, she left, feigning a headache.

I stayed seated most of the night, watching others dance on. Matilda seemed tired, and out of sorts, and I gathered that she wasn't having as grand a time as I'd hoped. Not long after Tansy left, I, too, made my departure, mirror in hand. A party just *wasn't* a party without Patch.

I found him in his room, a half hour later, quietly sipping a bowl of beef stew. It was our usual supper, both hearty and filled with essential iron required to help our stomachs battle the alcohol we consumed. I stood there, looking at him, as he fiddled with his spoon.

"Do you think I'm a *bad* person? Do you, Andrew Godfrey, think I am truly *wicked*?" Patch spoke in a whisper. Quickly, I fumbled for an answer... but I could think of nothing to say to him. The man had taken me under his wing and welcomed me, a boy alone in a strange world. He cared more about my welfare than any other person at the hotel had... but did that make him unconditionally good? Were any of us really *good*?

"Why?" I asked, and he shook his head, mindlessly stirring his soup.

"They said *that* would happen, that's all," he stated, without any hint of feeling betraying him.

He didn't say any more. His statement hung in the air between us, as neither of us dared to speak. We couldn't. If we had, I feared we would stumble into something that could ruin the great and exciting life we were pursuing.

Changing course, I mentioned Tansy's early departure from the masquerade. Patch grinned, full of pride. That was *all* he needed to hear.

The rest of the night was spent in strange tranquility, as we played blackjack in Patch's room until midnight. For a second, our lives were still, and we were both fine with just that.

But by the afternoon of the next day, things were back to the way they had always been. The unusual calm didn't last, and we were back to our reckless selves in no time. Patch followed his Tansy endlessly, and I returned to a life spent waiting for what the night would bring.

More time passed at the Hotel Larouche, though to me, it felt like one continuous string of extravagant fashion and exotic food. *How long had it been since my escape from Howell?* I could hardly remember!

Most days, I'd be lying if I said I wasn't having the time of my life. There was companionship at Larouche. There was an overwhelming freedom that I so cherished. Yet, when I remembered Matilda and recalled her shining face, I felt a tugging sensation deep within me. The hotel was perfection on earth, so why couldn't I enjoy it?

One evening, Patch suggested that we head down to the Social Hour for the evening's high stakes poker game. Reluctantly, I agreed, though I felt overwhelmingly fatigued from the previous night's fun. A part of me had even contemplated staying in! The feeling quickly passed, however, as I felt the familiar twitch of my fingers, anxiously awaiting fun.

"Don't go, Andrew. I have a feeling..." Matilda started. Impatiently, I shook my head.

"You don't understand, Matilda," I grabbed my jacket and opened the door of my room. Matilda wilted, like a flower under the rain, and my heart sank.

"I won't be long. *I promise,*" I spoke, with confidence, but Matilda didn't respond. Instead, I heard her sigh ruefully on my way out of the room. The door closed, and I realized I had decidedly shut Matilda out.

I rested my head against the doorframe, guilt plaguing me. Part of my mind was being gnawed away by doubt and worry, like a predator feasting on his prey. The rest of me embraced the new life I had chosen with great desire! My tingling fingers buzzed fiercely as they gripped the doorknob, just as if they were calling out to me:

"Everyone's waiting for you, Andrew! Hurry!"

Chapter Eleven
Pestilent Poker

Patch and I met downstairs in the lobby. I saw Patch, quite distracted, scan the room. His eyes landed on the only person in the lobby *not* mingling with all the other excited guests. *Tansy* was seated in an armchair, quietly reading a Jules Verne novel. Patch's face brightened as he walked up behind her, placing his hands over her eyes.

"Guess who?" he asked, devilishly, but Tansy didn't need to guess who it was.

"The antichrist?" she asked, dryly. Patch removed his hands from her face, as she waved him off.

"Her comparisons are terribly accurate, aren't they?" Patch asked me, and she shifted away from him slightly. With that, Patch yanked the woman up from her seat and pulled her close to him. "Miss me?" he asked.

"No, but does *that* ever stop you?" she retorted. He turned to me again, and smiled.

"And she's funny, too! *And* clever, Andrew! Oh, she's too clever! Almost as clever as I am!" he laughed, looking back at her with all the fondness a man could hold in his heart. Tansy rolled her eyes and shoved him away, then she walked over to the revolving doors and headed out of the hotel. We both followed her, much like pathetic lapdogs, and made our way to the Social Hour together.

Patch tried to grasp Tansy's hand with his own. It wasn't difficult to predict Tansy's irritable reaction to the gesture, as I noticed her twisting fingers try to wriggle themselves free of his grasp.

"Let me go! Don't touch me, you brute! I'd rather hold the tail of a hound," she spat.

"Shut your stupid mouth!" Patch commanded, holding on more tightly until, at last, her fingers relented and entwined with his. The gesture seemed to sum up their existence with each other.

"You can't have your way with me, Patch. It's just like you to be so incredibly arrogant and pig headed!" Tansy scowled, stopping in the middle of the street.

"Are you done?" he asked, pulling her by the roots of her hair. She screeched.

"I'll kill you, you bastard! I will!" Tansy shoved him toward the window of a nearby shop. Patch, his skin turning purple with anger, caught himself in time to avoid falling disastrously into the glass. His balance regained, he walked briskly to catch up with her.

"Would you?" he barked, "I highly doubt it! Who would flatter you, then?"

The argument went on, as insults spewed back and forth. What had started as mere tension between them escalated to outrage, and then, burst into *complete hatred*. It was definitely a different sort of affection, *if* one could call it that.

As we made our way to the Social Hour, Patch and Tansy continued their unrelenting banter. Rushing ahead to give them privacy, I heard the sounds of their bickering behind me, echoing through the street. A few nearby pedestrians merely rolled their eyes at the sight of the pair. It was as if they had witnessed these heated arguments countless times before.

It wasn't long before we all passed a familiar sight. It was the girl in the window. I'd seen her again and again during my stay at Larouche, often in the same stance behind the glass. So impossibly still, the live mannequin captured my attention more than any other display. As I stopped to inspect the window further, Patch and Tansy collided with me.

"What's the matter, Andrew?" Patch said, with a trace of annoyance. Tansy placed her hand up to the window beside me, catching her breath.

"*Valentina,*" Tansy whispered, with a new tenderness. "Poor thing."

"Who is she?" I asked, with overwhelming curiosity.

"Valentina was an only child, and a sculptress, when her father sold her to Madame Luelle. She was forced to leave her home town and all of her carvings behind, as she was dragged from her sleep one night," Tansy relayed. She paused, her features turning rigid, then continued.

"The terrible keeper of this shop is a stingy and a wretched woman. I've often heard others say that Luelle starves Valentina to keep her looking good in the dresses she wears. Madame Luelle wants *her* window display to be the best one on the street, so she keeps Valentina there to bring in the customers. Poor Valentina rarely leaves her spot! Sometimes she sits there for hours, frozen like one of her own sculptures. It's terribly tragic!" Tansy said, as she lowered her hand from the window. Valentina, in her lovely red gown, remained motionless. I felt my heart swell at the girl's story.

"Madame Luelle refuses to fit any dress for *me*. She thinks me common and low, from no family. I suppose she's right," Tansy scoffed, and she pulled her fur collar closer to her cheeks as she pressed on.

Sadly, I looked back at the window. It wasn't beautiful at all! It was Valentina's cage, just as Matilda's mirror was her cage. Valentina let her eyes drift a bit, before I took my departure from the window. She looked at me for a scant moment, her glance speaking a million things all at once. One day, I prayed that Madame Luelle would release the girl from the cell that she lived in. *One day*, I hoped Valentina could feel the freedom *I* was feeling.

It wasn't long before we arrived at the Social Hour. Nearly all the same men were huddled around a circular poker table. We walked in; the air was filled with the familiar smell of whiskey and cologne. Patch pulled out a chair for Tansy, and we took our seats around the table.

"Alright, boys! What've we got?" Tansy asked, and my eyebrows lifted with astonishment. It appeared that Tansy was well versed in the ways of poker! Patch's smile grew wide with pride. He wrapped his arm around her chair and he lit his cigar, as the men all gazed at Tansy. One man, with a thick toupee, looked in the direction of the woman and licked his lips, drawing uncomfortably close.

"I say we add a *new* prize to the pot," the man slobbered, "How's about a dance with Miss Tansy, eh?" he said, as his finger ran up and down her arm. Tansy rolled her eyes as she swatted him off, unruffled by the leering man. Patch, by contrast, exploded! He grabbed the man's shirt so roughly and pulled him so close that their noses nearly collided. Patch, I knew, was moments away from bashing the man's face in.

"Have you something to say, *friend*?" Patch said, breathing hot air into the man's face, who cowered in fear.

"Come on, Patch. Let's play," Tansy softened, lightly tapping Patch's arm with her gloved hand. The gesture eased Patch's rising anger and reluctantly, he tossed the man back into his chair.

"Buy some class, you piece of shit. She's a lady!" Patch placed his cigar in the corner of his mouth, as one of the other men chimed in.

"Yeah, but not *yours*!" the man yelled, laughing wildly.

The room fell silent, and Patch's eyes widened with rage.

Fortunately enough, at that moment, trampling footsteps rumbled down the staircase. A gruesome little man with rat like features bounded into the room, a large satchel swung over his back. His voice slicing through the deafening silence, he stood proudly, as if prepared to make a speech.

"Just you wait 'til you see what I've got!" he gushed. His voice was shrill and loud, and he spoke through yellowed teeth and skin fraught with warts. We all leaned back in our chairs, not expecting much from the scrawny man and his satchel.

"Wallace makes his way around the hotel collecting gems for our gambling pots. Not a lot of patrons are aware of this small fact, so...," Patch put his finger up to his mouth, visibly silencing anyone who dared to reveal the gang's secret.

In truth, I'd seen Wallace before, shifty as he was, running around the lobby with a bag swung over his shoulder. His hobby had not crossed my mind then, but *now* it made perfect sense. Wallace was one of the many thieves residing in the hotel, stealing trinkets and treasures for the poker tables.

Proudly, he set the bag down on the table and opened it slowly. Everyone in the room grew silent, anxiously waiting to feast their eyes on the stolen goods. Even Patch and Tansy leaned forward, filled with growing anticipation.

A pair of women's jeweled shoes were among the first items retrieved from the satchel. Tansy eyed them quietly, their glimmer reflected in her eyes. Wallace proceeded by pulling out a small golden dagger with a matching sheath. Many of the surrounding gentlemen shifted in their seats impatiently, as they all eyed the weapon with favor.

Among the many items were pearl necklaces, binoculars, silk handkerchiefs, and an ivory comb. Seeing the trappings piled in the center of the table, I imagined that most of the goods were some of the resident's belongings, possibly forgotten or misplaced in the lobby. It was foolish, for people to leave such valuables carelessly behind.

At last, Wallace took out the final item from his black bag. It was a large item, I gathered, as he slipped it from the satchel with two hands. I gasped as I saw the item Wallace held - three feet tall and two feet wide!

Matilda's mirror! I stood up, horrified, and lunged at Wallace!

"That's mine!" I shouted, as Wallace struggled to shove me off. Two gentlemen stood up and pried me away from him, then threw me back into my chair. "You don't understand!"

"Clearly, your friend doesn't know the rules of the game, Patch!" Wallace screeched, holding the mirror close. I sat up in my chair, looking at Patch, who sat completely confused.

"He stole it! That's *my* mirror, Patch!" I shouted, in desperation. Patch looked at the mirror and nodded.

"So it is! Looks like you've been robbed, Andrew!" he smirked, and Wallace chortled mischievously, baring his large front teeth.

"You don't understand. I *need* that mirror!" I pleaded. Patch sat looking neither concerned, nor worried. He observed the room slowly, shifting his eyes back and forth between Wallace, Tansy and myself. I could almost see a plan arranging itself in Patch's head. It was a wicked idea, to be sure, but a welcomed one! He spoke to the table.

"Then we shall win it, fair and square!" he smiled, confident in his abilities. The men, along with Tansy, clapped encouragingly. I, however, couldn't bring myself to celebrate until Matilda's mirror was back in my hands.

"If this mirror means so much to you, *why did you leave it behind?*" Wallace grinned, menacingly. His smug manner made my blood curdle, as I felt those familiar pangs of guilt rise up. Matilda had been alone and completely helpless, vulnerable, and in great peril. Yet, there I was, selfishly leaving her as I indulged in a late night poker game. I turned to Patch, who was already peering into the hand he'd been dealt.

"And if we don't win?" I spoke quietly to Patch. He, in turn, rolled his eyes and whispered into my ear.

"Then, we cut the bastard's throat and rightfully take what's ours, like any *normal* person," he laughed. I willed

233

my tense body to ease into my chair. *Patch knew what he was doing. I could trust him,* I told myself. "Relax, Andrew," Patch continued, "I'm a better card player than I am a drunkard," he assured me, with a quick glance at Tansy. I breathed a strained sigh of relief. The game, I knew, was going to be *unbearable*. I sat there, on the sidelines, silently praying to every god, saint, and spiritual being imaginable, as Patch deliberated between his cards. Each minute played was more excruciating than the previous one! It seemed that the game was endless! I nearly wilted in my chair, as my shirt grew wet with perspiration.

Patch played skillfully and represented me well. Halfway through the game, however, he'd only managed to win the pair of shoes, the dagger, and a yellow handkerchief which he tied loosely around his neck. Tansy's lips curved into a smile when Patch handed her the shoes. Her hands caressed them and she beamed with elation. *Of course*, I thought. I should have known that Patch would work his magic on a win for *Tansy*.

At last! The mirror was placed in the center of the poker table, gleaming under the light of the small chandelier above it. I grabbed onto the sides of my chair, every nerve as taut as a piano string. Patch crossed his arms smugly as the dealer dealt him card after card. He raked them over once, and then looked directly at Wallace, who was still in the game. From the look on my friend's face, I knew the victory was ours!

Patch wouldn't lose, I told myself.

With conviction, Patch displayed four aces on the table! Together, the spectators and I all cheered and Patch threw me an arrogant wink. Entirely indebted to Patch, I could have cast myself at his feet from gratitude. We won! The room buzzed, as the pianist played a victorious tune!

"You're an arrogant bastard, aren't you, Patch?" Wallace shouted from across the table. Everyone in the room stopped their hurrahs. The pianist repressed the next measure, the last note still ringing in our ears. We all watched on as Wallace displayed his cards, slowly. He laughed, almost maniacally, as his poker hand revealed a *straight flush*!

"No!" I heard myself shout, and Wallace's laugh grew louder and more sinister.

I saw my world collapse before me. Wallace, with his toothy grin, danced mockingly around his chair. The mirror meant *nothing* to him, but that didn't matter. He'd won the game, and defeated Larouche's best! How could I have, so foolishly, allowed someone to take Matilda from me?

"You're a cheat!" Patch said, pointing directly at Wallace.

He howled with laughter, chugging the gin from his bottle. He stumbled around the table and continued his blaring laughter until my eardrums nearly exploded from the sound.

The earth could have fallen out from under me and I wouldn't have noticed. I sat, too stunned to breathe, barely catching Patch and Tansy's sympathetic glances. The room fell silent. They didn't know what I had lost. Most importantly, they didn't know *who* I had lost. Before I could beg on my hands and knees for my prized possession, I heard Wallace shout from across the room, as he lifted the mirror high above his head.

"That's game, boys! Seems that Patch is not only unlucky in love, *but with cards too!*" he howled. A sea of laughter flooded the room, as glasses clinked together.

Wallace lowered the mirror and stood examining himself in the glass. Smugly, he was mocking its importance to me.

"I look quite pretty, don't I?" he asked the room. When everyone cheered, he happily placed the mirror in his satchel and stood up, victorious. "Let that be a lesson to you, boys!" he shouted, spreading his hands out in the air, as men clapped and stomped their feet along to the piano's tune. Desperately, I made my way to the ghastly man. I knew I would have to plead with him - beg him - to give me back what was rightfully mine. But, it was too *late*.

A dagger whizzed through the air, landing directly in the center of Wallace's neck, pinning him against one of the pillars. It was the same dagger Patch had won earlier.

Wallace, a second after his triumph, was dead, dark red blood gushing down his shirt like a mountain spring. His abrupt death stunned the room. No one made a sound, as Wallace choked and gasped his last breath.

In desperation, I turned and saw where the blade had come from. My heart was in my throat, as Patch lowered his hand and walked up to Wallace, slowly removing his blade from the dead man's neck. Taking the mirror, he walked over to me and placed it in my arms.

"Who needs luck?" he spoke, as he wiped his knife off on his pants. He picked up an almost empty bottle, and tossed the remaining liquid to the back of his throat.

No one seemed bothered by the heinous killing they had all just witnessed. After only a brief moment, everyone in the room resumed their games and idle chatter, while I stood stunned by my friend's brutal attack.

A large man - the man I once remembered Patch call *Anguish* - picked up Wallace's limp frame. He tossed him over his shoulder and removed his body from the Social Hour. It was the last we saw of Wallace, his satchel still on the floor. *What had I done*?

Murder, it appeared, was common in Larouche. It seemed almost to be *accepted*, a thought which left me trembling. With little hope, I searched the faces of the men in the room - anxious to find a person as stunned as I.

I found no one - no one, except the person at the far end of the room, still holding a pair of shoes. Tansy's face bore a similar fearful expression. Her cheeks burned red with anger and utter disbelief. Slowly, she placed the shoes on the table, turned, and left the gathering. Without a word, she was gone, having left the room and *Patch* in it. I saw him, deeply distraught, watch her go, grinding his cigar out on the same card table they had all sat around earlier.

"Now I've done it," he muttered. Then, picking up his coat and heading toward the stairs, he looked back at me. "Coming friend?"

Hesitantly, I nodded, not quite wanting to contradict him. *This man*, I contemplated, *had killed another man before my eyes!* He had ended another's life so casually, it terrified me. This man I called 'friend' seemed to be transforming into a person so vile, so wicked, I could hardly believe it! Tragically, I was witnessing him unravel from someone I admired to someone I feared. It was as if a spell had been cast over Patch, and I scarcely recognized him.

We found ourselves back on the street, heading back to our rooms. The sidewalks, full of revelers that were celebrating and having fun, only served as a cruel disguise for the wickedness within. *How had I not seen it before?*

Quickly, I dismissed the idea. The Hotel Larouche was nothing but a dreamland. I had sought refuge and stumbled upon the greatest wonder on earth. It was a place of great happiness and harmony!

Looking at my friend, however, I saw that there was *nothing* harmonious about him. Patch pulled out a cigarette and lit the end of it, his hands shaking. The man before me seemed so different now. His expression was blank and his eyes seemed to glaze over with a watery look. *Tears?* Was Patch on the verge of *tears*?

In all the months that I had come to know him, I had never seen fear in any portion of his being. He had always radiated nothing but confidence, which was suddenly cast aside and replaced by something that resembled only a hollowed shell. My friend was gone - transformed into some irrational, unknown demon. I pitied him.

"Andrew," Patch said, and he stopped walking. "This is *not* me. This is *not* who I am. I am slowly becoming someone I *hate*," he whispered. As he spoke, his teeth chattered. I couldn't be sure if the action was a result of the cold air or the fear that had overtaken him. Instinctively, I pulled my own jacket to my chest and watched his eyes shift nervously.

"Can't you stop it?" I asked, hopefully. He grimaced and shook his head, the tears still brimming in his bloodshot eyes.

"I'm *in it*."

He looked around where we stood, my eyes following his gaze. The city we were a part of was a beautiful place. Things were wrapped and parceled so perfectly here. It was difficult to believe that some real good could not be found within this small nation of lost souls.

My belief was being challenged, however, as I looked upon my friend. Did he fall victim to the city, or had Patch *always* been this way? I couldn't tell. Wrongly, I dismissed his actions. Clearly, he had forgotten what life was like in the bleak hometowns we hailed from! Myself, being so freshly detached, knew that Larouche offered freedoms I couldn't find anywhere else. I saw Patch look down at the mirror in my hands and smirk.

"Was it worth it, at least?" he asked, and I nodded. It *was*.

Deep down, I knew Matilda would not agree. A life had been taken for her *nonexistent* form, but I *couldn't let her go*. Not yet. Not when we had just begun this new adventure together!

My friend walked ahead in the cold, damp streets. Filled with sudden grief, I looked upon him. He was shivering and lost in a world too vast for him to comprehend or control. Patch walked on, feeling the full weight of the crime he had just committed. How could someone simply erase the memory of taking a man's life... watching him take his last breath as he entered into another world? The unfathomable act would weigh on his shoulders for the rest of his life.

In his drunken state, coupled with his everlasting unrequited love for Tansy, he saw nothing but sheer blackness. No one could help him, but himself.

I pondered what possible harm might have come to Matilda. What if Wallace *had* gotten away with the mirror? Would *I* have acted as brutally as Patch did? To what lengths would *I* go to get what I wanted?

Difficult, it was, to separate the right from the wrong. I felt myself falling into a world far beyond my depth.

Chapter Twelve
Pity the Fool

My friend roamed the hallways, unaware of himself and the world around him. Since the night of that fateful poker game, Patch seemed unfeeling and distant.

In a constant state of drunken stupor, he trampled aimlessly through the lobby looking filthy and out of sorts. We spent evenings together, but hardly conversed, as our conversations usually took a stale turn at any mention of Tansy or the Social Hour. When Patch *wasn't* roaming the lobby, he usually played the harpsichord he inherited from the Widow, often falling asleep at the keys. Whether he was drinking or gambling, we all saw him as only a fragment of the lively character he once was.

On the rare occasions that we dined, I could see that his heart and mind were elsewhere. There were no thoughts given to anything or anyone but his Tansy, and the grief he caused her. In her desolation, Tansy danced rarely, and frequently sought the comfort of her room, where she couldn't be disturbed.

Upon the evening of my first full year at Larouche, I invited Patch to dinner. Over time, I had begun to notice Patch return to his old ways. It was a slow recovery of the man he was when I first met him, but I was glad for it. Too long, had I seen him mope about the hotel. It was one of my deepest wishes to see my friend come back to *himself*, the "prodigal son" celebrated.

To my great surprise, he revealed to me a fragment of Tansy's history, a mystery that intrigued me greatly! It was as if he had been desperate to tell someone -*anyone*- who would listen. Six drinks in, however, and I could tell he felt instant regret.

She was a dancer, cast off into the streets by her eldest brother when she was sixteen. Her parents had both sadly passed on in her early years from the Second Cholera Pandemic. After her brother banished her, she found work as a servant girl, secretly dancing during the late nights to a small audience.

"How she loved to dance!" Patch recalled, his eyes glimmering. "But the lady of the house questioned her nightly excursions, and the poor girl was cast out again," Patch spoke. His eyes welled at the thought of Tansy walking up and down the streets, cold and alone, in a terrible windstorm. He found her a few days later, huddled behind his residence, shivering and on the verge of starvation.

"So, I decided to take her into my home," Patch said, looking past me, lost in a cherished memory. "I've *never* been the same."

Patch concluded his story, and I knew every word spoken was true. I still, however, couldn't understand why Tansy frequently dismissed the man who saved her. She spoke to Patch with an inner anger, often pushing him away, and I wondered if there was more to the story than my friend relayed. What had he done to the girl to provoke such hatred toward him?

I had learned very little about Patch throughout my stay at Larouche, and the eternal air of mystery that surrounded him *still* remained. Was *Patch* even his real name, or was it an alias concealing his true identity?

"Patch is lost, Andrew," Matilda declared, after I revealed all that Patch had said back in the dining hall. She answered honestly, her voice thick with fatigue. "He leads a bleak, miserable life with no direction to a fulfilling future and still, you follow him. I don't understand it!"

"Patch is my friend, Matilda. The only one I've got. I can't let him wallow in his misery!" I said this, realizing that I was trying to convince *myself* more than Matilda.

"So, you allow yourself to wallow in it too, as the ever faithful drinking companion! What about your drawings, Andrew? And your family? You, here in this hotel, will do nothing for anyone," she spoke firmly. I stood, stunned and hurt by her words.

"How can you say that to me? You of all people? Have I not shown you the world?" I said, my voice growing louder.

"You've shown me a great and many things, Andrew, but not the world. This, the Hotel Larouche, is a dangerous place. Can't you see it?" she exclaimed, and I backed away from her, disbelieving.

"Do you realize what you are saying? Do you remember life back in Howell? I've got freedom here, Matilda!"

"Freedom? Endless gambling and a sharpened blade are not freedoms, Andrew. You'll end up as *removed* from life as Patch is!" Matilda yelled.

"Patch was not himself that night. He said so himself!" I breathed out heavily, desperately trying to contain a looming outburst. "I have *choices* here! I can do as I *please*. 'Tis a wonderful place that I shall never leave!" I argued, fixing my tie and shoving handfuls of money into my back pockets.

"Oh, Andrew. You are more trapped than you know," she sighed. Matilda shook her head and began fading into the mirror. I felt myself nearly burst with anger. I felt that if anyone would understand the freedoms of the hotel, it would be Matilda, but she accepted nothing of my present life.

"You are jealous! *You* want all this and wish to bar *me* from it! You wish to keep me from my new friends and send me guilt-ridden back to Howell with my tail between my legs! I'm *alive* Matilda, and you can't expect me to leave the life I've always dreamed of!" I spat out, without a thought.

Quickly, I covered my mouth, almost stumbling into one of the walls. What had I done? Trembling, I rushed to the mirror, but it was too late. She was gone, and hot tears of anguish filled my eyes.

"Matilda, please, *please* forgive me! I didn't know what I was saying! Please!"

I knew she wouldn't speak to me that night, if she spoke to me again at all. I knew it, and I felt a new feeling of bitterness toward her well inside me. Pounding the wall with my fist, I shouted again.

"I demand you to speak to me!"

Silence. There was no one, no pretty face, shining in the mirror. I left the room raging as I slammed the door behind me. Visibly shaking, I made my way down to the lobby where I knew I would be appreciated. I wanted to feel important, as if I had made the correct decision.

My focus, momentarily misdirected, went to my plans for the night. Lately, it had become what I lived for. Patch asked me to accompany him to the Social Hour that evening, and I instantly agreed. It was the first time he'd been out in weeks and I knew the fresh air would do him good. Briskly, we cut through the crowded streets.

Over the year, I had come to memorize multiple faces. General Sugerbaum, retired military, whom I'd become acquainted with during a game of whist, walked down the street with a tightly corseted strumpet on each arm.

248

He nodded a friendly hello and then whispered something into one of the girls' ears, causing an eruption of bubbling laughter. Constant joy seemed to surround us.

Pricilla Graves, a petite woman who often wore men's clothing, rode her bicycle toward us. She threw a wink in my direction. "Where are you from, Andrew?" she called out.

"Nowhere!" I hollered back. She rode past us, yelling over her shoulder.

"You must take me there sometime!" she shouted. I smiled, and I could see Patch smirking beside me. Yes, Larouche was a *wonderful* place

We kept weaving our way through the crowds on the narrow sidewalks until we reached the familiar entry way of the Social Hour. A burst of cigar smoke flew straight at us as we opened the door and headed down the flight of stairs. We entered the room, which was a little livelier than I'd been used to. The tables were packed with men and bottles of whiskey were scattered around the floor. *Rage*, one of Patch's closest friends, spoke in a booming voice from his spot at a table.

"Patch, ol' boy! Where've you been? The poker games haven't been nearly as exciting without you," he howled. Another burly man beside him chuckled and looked at the men sitting around the table.

"Certainly not as exciting as when he rams a knife through someone's neck!" he hollered.

It was the *wrong* thing to say at such a time and I felt my body tense as I awaited Patch's ill-tempered response. Instead, to my astonishment, Patch reached for a bottle of some disgusting dark liquor and finished it off while everyone stared, anxiously awaiting his next move. He wiped his face with his bare arm and smashed the bottle into a thousand pieces on the floor.

"Give me another," he spoke dryly.

Cheers and laughs, mostly brought on by *relief*, raced through the room. Both of us were welcomed at every table, heroes among the men. *Oh, how I missed this!* I thought. Patch took off his coat and threw away the burgundy ascot tied loosely around his neck. I followed him, removing my own coat and taking a seat.

"Andrew, my watch works splendidly! You've got true talent!" one man said, patting me on the back. I recalled

250

mending the man's watch - a fine brass pocket watch - and I smiled.

"Thank you, sir," I replied.

"Still got that *mirror*, Andrew?" a thin man, smoking a pipe, asked mockingly. I nodded self-consciously, but Patch spoke up with slurred words.

"It's special, you see, but Lord knows why..." Patch sneered. I saw a hint of anger flash in his eyes, but it vanished almost instantly as the music blared on. Patch focused on the deck of cards in front of him. He shuffled, dazzling the table with tricks while other men spoke of Larouche and the events of the day.

Picking up a soggy newspaper, I shook it off and flipped through it. There was a small article about Howell Village and, quickly, I scanned the paragraph to see if there was any mention of my mother or brother. To my relief, the article was about our neighbor, Basil Quadray, and his marriage to Ellen Strong. I grimaced with only one question on my mind. *Who would marry Basil Quadray?*

Before I could dwell on it further, Patch snatched the paper from my hands, and tore it to shreds. He stepped up onto the table, kicking the playing chips aside, and sending them scattering about the room.

"News? What's news?! I care not about what goes on in *my* hometown, do you?" he asked, playing ringmaster to the room. Men guffawed and clinked their glasses together. Patch tugged at his suspenders. "Right now my brother's counting money behind a desk... and do you know what I say to *that*?" he asked the room. Several men responded simultaneously, each urging him on in his charade. Patched continued, "I say, DAMN FOOL!"

He lifted his drink in a celebratory toast and the men cheered again, only louder and with even more enthusiasm. Someone shot his gun directly at the glass in Patch's hand and it shattered, startling me out of my seat. Patch merely laughed, drunkenly teetering where he stood, while everyone joined in his hysteria. If I were smart, I would have gone from the place. But inebriated as he was, Patch was my friend and it felt wrong to abandon him. He turned to me, with a wide grin as he pushed his sleeves up to his elbows.

"Did I ever tell you I *learned* to dance? I did! For her!" he exclaimed. His feet began tapping against the poker table. His steps grew faster and faster, his smile widening as

252

the pianist played a lively tune with great force. He continued, spinning around on the table, and speaking to no one in particular.

"I wanted to touch her, you see? I wanted to *hold* her!" he shouted. Whom he spoke of was obvious; everyone knew who he meant. Quickly, his feet moved as if with minds of their own, as we all watched him display his affection in a series of intricate steps. "I wanted her to be so transfixed that she'd *never* fall out of love with me."

Looking on, I noticed sweat trickle down his temples. He looked almost maniacal dancing alone, but he danced well and *that* was admirable. Men pounded their feet in time and clapped vigorously in a torrent of wild excitement bordering on insanity, becoming faster - and *still* faster. Sweat now poured down his face, splashing from his hair and drenching his shirt. I clenched the chair, suddenly feeling the room spin around me, whirling out of my control.

Patch toppled over drunkenly onto two men, who caught him and threw the love-struck fool into a chair. His eyes drifted shut, as multiple conversations filled the room.

Patch was asleep, and I was left looking about the Social Hour for a familiar face. I found none, but happened to notice a particular man stand up from his seat, and make his way out of the room. It was that same strange man, clad in a black top-hat and white silk scarf I'd seen a few times before. During my stay at the hotel, this same gentleman had never stayed long enough for me to introduce myself, always leaving places in a desperate hurry. He remained one of the few residents of the establishment that I had yet to meet.

I hadn't noticed him amid the chaos in the place. How long had he been there? Had he come alone? Before I realized it, I was running out of the Social Hour, searching for the man with the top-hat. Patch, I convinced myself, was in fine company and I would return to him in no time.

Rushing up the steps, I pushed my way through the door and onto the street, but he was *gone*. I looked up and down the wide sidewalks and found no trace of him *anywhere*.

Damn, I thought. *I missed him again.*

The man in the black top-hat had vanished, and the curious cloud of mystery that surrounded him had gone, too.

Chapter Thirteen
Godfrey

Bam! Bam! Bam!

"Andrew! I've got some deliveries for you!" a nasal sounding voice chirped from behind my door.

Greatly irritated, I opened the door and leaned against the frame. Phillip Bravery, head concierge and unicyclist, was making his usual midday rounds. He placed a large bundle of small packages into my arms.

"Good day to you, sir!" he chimed, gleefully. I rolled my eyes at his cheerful disposition.

"Morning," I replied, dryly. With a small chuckle and quick salute, he hopped back onto his unicycle and sped away.

Suddenly feeling a dull stinging near my left temple, I closed the door and noticed a man, slumped over and sleeping on a chair in the corner of my room.

Patch, I remembered, rolling my eyes. I had nearly dragged his limp frame out of the Social Hour, before he unfortunately fell unconscious in the moving machine. Phillip Bravery's loud knock on the door caused him to stir from his sleep, and he gripped his head with a light groan.

"What sort of bastard knocks so early?" he asked, quite bothered. I set the packages down on the table, and began to sort through them.

"Phillip Bravery, that's who - and it's not *that* early. It's nearly two in the afternoon," I answered. Patch pulled the blanket I had thrown over him up to his chin, and groaned.

"Like I said. *Early*!" Patch retorted, with a yawn. I sighed, looking back at the packages.

Nearly two dozen hotel residents had sent their broken watches to room 553 for repair. Lately, I had been receiving more of them than I could handle! I sulked, leaving the parcels on the table as I walked over to the mirror.

Matilda's face *still* hadn't appeared in the glass. I knew it wouldn't, as she was terribly angry with me from the previous night. Regrettably, I remembered our conversation in vivid detail. Word for word, I mentally recited every stupid thing I said with a cringe.

Slowly, I walked over to the edge of the bed and took a seat. Patch looked exhausted and out of sorts. His face stared blankly at the vertical striped wallpaper in the room; gone from reality. After a moment, he spoke up.

"Remember when you thought Widow Sherrigan was *keen* on you?" Patch smirked, and my mouth gaped in disbelief.

"I did *not*," I rebuked, and Patch laughed.

"You did! Your face turned white and your neck flushed scarlet," he paused, lost in thought. I decided to let him believe his assumptions, no matter how far-fetched they were. Then his eyes grew black, turning back into two dark, seemingly endless tunnels. "I envy your youth! Your world is still *white*, Andrew. There are no stains of cruelty or disappointment upon it. It's still that rose colored painting of the whimsical unknown. I was just like you... once."

His observations, though not entirely meant to be offensive, made me clench my jaw. Did he think me wide-eyed and a stranger to the world of sorrow? Brushing his assumptions aside, I scoffed. "You'd be surprised!"I retorted.

I could see that my childish rebuttal had no effect on him. Perhaps, he likely expected no history of the world's troubles from someone of my age. The room was still and quiet, both of us reeling from the night before. Softly, Patch whispered from across the room.

"Is it wrong to love?" Patch asked, disheartened. His question hung in the air between us. I looked over my shoulder, at Matilda's mirror, with mixed feelings. Loving someone meant that you were vulnerable - raw and exposed in your innermost being - something that I was in constant fear of happening. Before I could answer, Patch continued,

"Sometimes, it feels like it is. People often make me feel as if falling in love is the worst sin a person could commit! My family. My peers. But it's *her* that I want. It's *her* opinion I prize most... yet she looks at me as if she finds me the most detestable person of all," he sighed, heavily. Tracing his fingers along the fabric of the sofa, his mind seemed to be absorbed in painful recollections. "I never wanted it to be this way, Andrew. You must believe it!"

"You can change things, Patch! You can make things different!" I spoke positively, as I inwardly braced myself for his sure rebuttal. He walked up to me and placed his hand on my shoulder, however, smiling sadly. I could see that Sleep was not his friend, as his eyes had sunk deep into his gaunt face.

"*Andrew*. My *only* true friend... and *link* to what's good in this world," he sulked, as he headed toward the door. He stopped in front of Matilda's mirror, looking at his appearance as it practically rotted before his eyes.

"Good god, I look like death, don't I?" he said, in disbelief. I nodded in agreement, and Patch laughed. He left the room, shutting the door behind him. I collapsed onto the bed, before I heard Matilda speak.

"He certainly *does* look like death! Nothing a good shave can't fix though," Matilda perked up. I sat back up, anxious to see her face in the mirror. "Don't worry! He'll be fine," Matilda continued, "Men like him aren't easily...*dissuaded*."

Nervously, we both shared an uneasy laugh. There was so much I wanted to say to Matilda, but looking at her just then nearly caused me to forget everything. We both looked at each other, for a moment that seemed to go on forever, each wondering who would speak first. *It should be me,* I acknowledged. I shook my head slightly, rediscovering my voice.

"Matilda, about last night-" I began, but she held up her hand to stop me.

"Let's not speak of it, Andrew. I refuse to believe that you actually meant what you said last night. *You* may have given up on 'you', but *I* haven't," she smiled, and I returned it with one of my own. After a moment or two, I looked away from Matilda with embarrassment. I knew I didn't deserve her kindness, but I was grateful to have it.

"Are you my guardian angel, then?" I smirked, and she leaned her head to one side.

"They couldn't pay me enough for that!" she spoke dryly, and I laughed in response. Holding my hands up in a weak defense, she giggled sweetly and with more happiness than I'd heard from her in weeks! It felt amazing to converse with Matilda again! We were friends, communicating as if it had *always* been this way.

Hastily, I took out my tools to repair the watches piled high upon my desk. The work, I groaned, seemed endless! All the while, I listened to Matilda's faint humming, as I mended each watch and one small clock. Her melodies were among the most peaceful sounds I had heard in a while.

"Did you always want to repair watches?" she asked, as I busily fixed a pocket watch for Mr. Reed, an exiled statesman from Virginia. I shrugged my shoulders.

"I didn't really have a choice. It was my father's trade," I replied, as I fixed the broken chain attached to the watch.

"*Everyone* has a choice," she stated. I chuckled, shaking my head at her naiveté.

"I don't," I confessed. Matilda's eager expression almost begged me to explain. "Have you met my mother?" I asked, and she sighed, knowingly.

"What would you have liked to do?" she asked, coming closer into the mirror with curiosity.

The question, though perfectly normal, left my mind blank. I was *stumped*. In all my years, I had never given a second thought to what *I* would like to accomplish in life. As I faced the question now, I scoured the far corners of my mind - searching for something to say. Bashfully, I shrugged my shoulders.

"Honestly, I'd think I'd love to draw... and teach, if I could manage both! You probably won't believe this, but I think education is *very* valuable. I'd like to give that to

261

children, and to young men like me, who don't think they'll ever amount to anything," I admitted. It felt strange to speak of such dreams, as I had never before mentioned them to *anyone.* Suddenly, shame consumed me. Fancy, a young man like me trying to teach *anyone anything*! I knew nothing, relying solely on my ears and eyes to capture knowledge. My drawings only depicted an *idea* of what life was. The real world was too vast and too complicated for a simple boy like me! Matilda, on the other hand, beamed with excitement.

"Andrew, that is unbelievable!" she spoke, with elation. She placed her hands up to her cheeks, clearly amazed.

"Do you *really* think so?" I asked, apprehensively.

"Unquestionably! Your drawings are wonderful and so detailed. I feel as if I could live in one of them!"

She spun around in her mirror, entirely thrilled. Then, she stopped, and grew more serious. "As for knowledge, Andrew, that is something that doesn't *only* come from open books, but an open *mind* and *heart*. You would have a lot to offer our youth," she radiated.

I smiled at her certainty in my possible success. My confession was a dream, and nothing more yet, listening to Matilda, it seemed that this dream *was* possible.

"Thank you, Matilda. That is kind of you to say!" I responded, sitting up in my chair confidently.

It was ironic that scarcely over a year ago, Mr. Brew had set me back years with his opinion of my character. Now, his *daughter* had managed to lift my spirits with talk of a future bright with possibility. It embarrassed me to know that over the past few months, I had seemed to forget just what Matilda meant to me. She was the singular person who actually *believed* in me.

"What did *you* want to do, Matilda?" I asked, timidly. She shrugged in response.

"Oh, I dunno... something completely nonsensical that would've my devastated my parents, perhaps. A great thespian, I suppose... or a circus clown!" she grinned. We both laughed, but I had a feeling her statement held a lot of truth. Matilda could have done *anything* she wanted. She could have conquered the universe, if she so desired.

Returning to the work on my desk, I picked up the fourth pocket watch, still taking occasional glances at

Matilda. Smiling, I noticed she resumed her humming, taking a few glances in *my* direction, as well.

Pulling myself from the sight of her radiant glow, I opened the next pocket watch in my hands. Inside the bronze object, I discovered a small slip of paper with a nearly illegible scribble written across it. My breath caught, as I read the one-word note:

'Godfrey?'

The watch nearly tumbled out of my hands and onto the floor. Quickly, I retrieved the packaging and examined the name closely. *Black Ben, Room 558.*

Black Ben. He lived right down the hallway from me, or so the package indicated. Most importantly, this person knew my true identity - an identity I'd been so careful to conceal. I shuddered slightly, and re-read my surname over and over again. *How can this be*? I panicked. Setting the watch down, I searched for possible explanations. Black Ben, whoever he was, must have had suspicions about me and my recent inclusion into the Larouche community. Did I really stand out more than I thought?

"Is everything alright? You look pale!" Matilda spoke up. I nodded, and placed my hand up to the mirror. She responded by bringing her hand up to meet mine.

"I think I've been *discovered*."

Taking the slip of paper into my hand, I held it up to the mirror. She gasped, covering her mouth with her hand, as I continued. "I found this slip of parchment in *that* watch there," I said, pointing at the object lying on my desk. "It belongs to a man called Black Ben. Ever heard of him?" I asked. She shook her head, quite fearful.

Desperately, I willed myself to pay no mind to the gentleman's cryptic note. I picked up another watch and tried to continue, as if nothing had happened... *but it had*. I looked at the note again.

Shaking in my chair, I urged myself to relax, but the possibility of someone lurking nearby - knowing my true identity - left me petrified!

Who was *Black Ben*? Was I never to be left in peace and free from the demons of my former life? Larouche had been the perfect destination for my escape, yet I found myself on the brink of having to leave it. Black Ben, I knew, would surely inform my family, and the villagers in Howell, of my whereabouts.

With certainty, I knew returning home *wasn't* an option. In Howell Village, I was a dead man! No one would accept my false resurrection with profound joy. They would berate me for fooling them, and banish their own Lazarus in exile. I wouldn't be welcomed back home or, if I *was*, it would be sheer misery! *What would my mother do if she saw me again?* I gulped; my imagination conjured up nothing but terrible conclusions.

Looking back toward Matilda's mirror, I knew my family would never allow me to keep her. The idea would be *impossible* to them! My mother would likely laugh herself into hysteria at my foolishness and shatter the mirror into a thousand pieces herself!

There were no dreams to be had in our household. No magic. No thoughts of happiness. You worshipped God, worked hard, and died. *That* was the life my family laid out for themselves. For all of us. They would never understand my connection with the mirror. They would never understand Larouche or the people in it. Most importantly, they would never understand *me*. This was, for me, reason enough to know that I would *never* go back. This man who knew me as 'Godfrey', I vowed, would never utter a word of it to anyone. Some way, *somehow*... I'd make sure of it.

I looked at my *own* watch and saw that it was approaching midnight. The day was only just beginning for the patrons so, anxiously, I gathered up the parcels. The mended watches were placed in a large bag that I slung over my shoulder, ready to be delivered. The remaining assortment sitting on my desk would have to wait, as I couldn't tarry a moment longer. I *had* to find Black Ben.

"I'll be back soon," I reassured Matilda, as I picked up the mirror and slid it under my bed. I'd been careful to hide Matilda lately, at the times that I went out alone. Though Wallace was dead and gone, I feared that the mirror would be stolen again, should it be left unattended. There were *far* too many thieves residing in the hotel! Softly, I heard her speak.

"Don't be too long. It's dark down here!" she whispered. *I won't be away long*, I thought. Not when it was Matilda's wish.

I headed out the door, purposely saving room 558 for the last delivery. I wasn't sure why I wanted to wait to meet Black Ben. Truth be told, it was *fear* that gripped me.

***

"Andrew!" Mr. Paavola, a resident on the sixth floor, greeted me cheerfully. He stood at his door, wearing a red lounging robe and eating a puffed pastry. I handed him his watch. "Marvelous boy! Such quick timing, too!" he beamed, through a muffled mouthful of whipped cream. He wiped his face with his sleeve.

"Thank you, Mr. Paavola," I replied, slightly disgusted.

"Then again, I suppose time isn't easy to forget when you're surrounded by it!" he laughed heartily, at his own stale joke. Then, he grew serious.

"Time is my worst enemy - see what it does to me!" he shrieked, bringing his eyes close to me, gesturing toward the sagging bags beneath them. I nodded, terribly uncomfortable with the man's close proximity. "I'm disgustingly old, Andrew. When did this happen?" he frowned, overcome with despair. Mr. Paavola lazily shoved the rest of the pastry into his mouth.

"Time!" he said, heaving a great sigh - the pastry still in his mouth. Then, he sulked back into his room, and shut the door behind him. *People certainly are strange here*, I thought, before heading to the next delivery.

The moving machine, I was reminded, had been named an "elevator" and had become less daunting over the year. After returning a few more watches to their rightful owners, I made my way back to the fifth floor. Mrs. Halloway, the owner of a lovely silver watch with a butterfly carved into it, and her husband, resided in room 527.

I knocked and she opened the door, scantily clad in a loose slip. Averting my eyes, I handed her the watch and she tugged at my tie. I looked down to see her eyes, lashes fluttering, and a suggestive smile spreading across her face. Nervously, I tried to continue with my duties.

"Is Mr. Halloway h-here? I've got his watch to deliver, as well," I swallowed. Stammering, I shook like a nervous school boy at his first dance.

"You won't find him here. He's down in the lobby, making a fool of himself," she replied sarcastically. Then, she inspected me with excitement, as she leaned against the door frame.

"So, are you coming in, then?" she winked, and I stepped back from the door, shaking my head.

"N-no, ma'am!" I nearly choked out. With a singular click of her tongue, I could tell I had offended the woman.

"Suit yourself," she responded, with contempt.

The door slammed in my face. Completely grateful, I breathed a sigh of relief!

Women were incredibly forthcoming at Larouche, and I wondered if any of them ever stayed true to *one* person. If they *did*, were they ever properly courted, or was it commonplace for a woman to make herself open and *available* to any man that caught her fancy? I, personally, had never been good with women, and the females at Larouche confused me even more!

Two watches were left - one that belonged to Mr. Halloway and the other to Black Ben. Mentally trying to brace my spirits, I headed down to room 558, wondering if I should have delivered Halloway's watch first. The short distance between me and room 558 was inescapable, however. It would be foolish not to deliver the watch, now. *I'm so close*, I breathed. Warily, I approached the door.

I must have knocked a few times before a tall, thin elderly man with scattered bits of gray hair opened the door an inch. His eyes looked through the small space, sizing me up.

"May I help you?" he asked curtly, obviously bothered by the intrusion. Trying to catch a glimpse of the room behind him, I nodded.

"Does Black Ben live here?" I asked.

Before the man could respond, however, a noise that sounded like dishes being broken exploded behind him! The man, in a panic, began to shut the door.

"He's not here today, boy. Come back some other time," he urged, but my attention was too absorbed by the commotion I heard behind him. Another piercing scream wailed in our ears, before the man pushed the door closed.

Almost instantly, something rammed into it, with a heavy thud! I looked down at my feet and felt the floor pulsating beneath them, as a deafening shriek blared from behind the door! I was inches away from the monster I had heard about in hushed whispers. Only a wooden door separated us. Quite alarmed, I backed away from room 558, with a heaving chest.

What sort of being made such noises? I shuddered. Black Ben lived in room 558, and whatever creature lived with him and made those horrifying sounds was in that very suite right now. Suddenly, I recalled the conversation I had with Patch, long ago. I remembered him giving the terrible monster a name - one that I would always remember. *Anais*. Since that day, the screams and unearthly noises from the room at the end of the hallway were few and far between. I'd grown *used* to them, hardly having been in my room most days, anyway.

But the name *Anais*, was never far removed from conversations in the lobby. It was whispered, among patrons as nothing more than a passing rumor. Approaching Room 558, however, and hearing the very real screams coming from within, dispelled any notions that *Anais* was merely a legend or myth. I had been separated by a mere door - scant inches away from the monster inside.

Realizing I still had Mr. Halloway's watch in my hand, I decided it would be best to remain far from whatever lurked behind the door of room 558. Decidedly, I made my way down to the lobby in the elevator.

As I arrived at my destination, I approached Phillip Bravery, who sat at his desk, writing. "Where can I find Mr. Halloway?" I inquired. Phillip Bravery, consumed with his work, merely pointed to a darkened lounge area behind me. A group of men sat by a large fireplace, conversing.

Mrs. Halloway's husband had three entirely *different* women sitting around him! One perched herself on his lap and swirled his hair with her fingers. Another fiddled with his tie and laughed gaily, while the other rested her head upon his knee. The false-hearted husband looked dapper in his fine pinstripe suit and slicked hair. He was elegant in appearance and the sort of man who embodied confidence. Cautiously, I approached him, only to find him too preoccupied with the women to notice.

"Mr. Halloway?" I interrupted, and the women snapped their heads toward me in near unison. He looked up and grinned, lazily.

"Hello, young man. What can I do for you?" he asked, caressing one of the girl's arms. Distracted by one of the women fiddling with the laces on my shoes, I held out the last of the small parcels.

"I fixed your pocket watch, sir," I spoke, trying to avoid the girls grasping at my arms and legs. His smile widened, as one of the women took the watch from my hand, and handed it to him.

"Fantastic!" he beamed. He looked at the last package in my hand. "I see you've got one parcel left. Is that Mrs. Halloway's?" he asked, and I shook my head, trying to shake my left leg from the woman's grasp.

"It's for Black Ben, sir," I continued. The girls all 'oohed' in response. Mr. Halloway smiled, devilishly.

"Then you may want to give it to him. He sits over there."

The man pointed behind me, over to the far corner of the room. I turned and saw an amber armchair, lit only by its nearness to the fireplace that blazed brightly. A top hat rested on a small table beside the chair. The man who occupied it, wore a thick black coat and a white silk scarf draped about his neck. His face was concealed in shadows.

Black Ben. It was the same tall man I had seen walking mysteriously in and out of various places at Larouche. He sat, gazing at the fire, and I felt my legs buckle with fear. This man knew who I was! In vain, I knew I had to approach him and discover how that was possible, but my legs felt heavier than lead.

At last, I willed my feet to be brave and move forward, but they were stuck! I felt myself stumble, and then fall, onto the floor. My face slammed into the carpet with a muffled thud! The laces of my shoes, I realized all too late, had been tied together by Mr. Halloway's whores.

A roar of laughter boomed behind me. The women giggled with delight, and the gentleman all laughed heartily at the sight of my limp frame sprawled across the carpet. Quickly, I undid the laces and retied them, not daring to face the gawking crowd. *Ignore them,* I thought.

I stood up, humiliated, but undeterred. The patrons were howling hyenas and, over time, I'd become used to it.

Slowly, I turned back to Black Ben. To my relief, he hadn't taken any notice of my embarrassing tumble. I approached him with courage. My feet dragged along the thick carpet, as I felt the heat from the fireplace warm my cheeks. Nothing moved the man, his gaze so transfixed by the flames before him. It felt almost rude interrupting him then, but duty took hold of me. *I must see this through.*

"Sir, I have your watch," I spoke bravely, trying to appear more courageous than I was. He didn't turn to me, as he simply pointed at the table beside him. I took the motion as a sign to place the watch beside his hat, so I did.

Black Ben still didn't speak, and I realized that - if I wanted answers - I would have to approach the subject myself. In a whisper, I leaned close to his chair.

"Sir, I received your message," I said. Black Ben sat still, his hands folded in his lap. His features, though still difficult to read in the flickering firelight, appeared fixed and unrelenting. "What business do you have with the name 'Godfrey'?" I asked, through shallow breaths. After a moment, he responded, his voice deep and dark in timber.

"Come to my suite tomorrow, boy. I would like to speak with you," he responded. He turned toward me for the first time. I only caught a glimpse of his thick beard and neatly combed hair, his eyes still too hidden in the shadows for me to see them. With a nod, I prepared to bid him adieu. Just then, however, Patch bounded toward us. He slapped me heartily on the back and I winced in response.

"Andrew, you've come at the perfect time!" he exclaimed, as he removed me from the quieter section of the lobby to a crowded area, bursting with cheers. I turned back to where Black Ben sat, alone, suddenly feeling badly for not having said goodbye.

Patch, however, pulled me to the center of the lobby that was unusually packed with spectators. A thunderous voice, the emcee for the night's ceremonies, shouted Tansy's name at the top of his lungs. A bright light lit up a gigantic dangling object in the middle of the room. *A birdcage!* We all looked up, quietly amazed with what we saw before us.

In the large cage, suspended from cords above our heads, was Tansy, wistfully posed. The cage slowly descended to the floor of the lobby, where we all circled around it. She ran her slender fingers around the cage until she came to a tiny latch. With a slight tap, the latch opened and she emerged from the cage, dancing slowly at first, then deliberately increasing her pace - swirling more fantastically than I had ever seen. The sheer fabric of the gown she wore sparkled as if a thousand stars had been woven into it. Tansy glimmered! I glanced at Patch, who stared at her with complete astonishment. I'd never seen him look that way.

He turned to me, placing an arm around my shoulder.

"I haven't seen her in days! Doesn't she look remarkable?" he buzzed with excitement. I nodded, and together we watched her command the audience. Completely enchanted, Patch continued, "She dances with the ring on her finger still. As long as she wears it, she loves me," he exhaled, and I saw his lower lip tremble.

It was then that I noticed an emerald ring on Tansy's left hand. I found it curious that she would wear *anything* that belonged to Patch, especially something as intimate as a ring. I watched him, overwhelmed with pity for my friend. Was he so deluded that he believed the ring was a symbol of *her* love for *him*? There had been times when I, too, saw the mounting physical attraction between them. I couldn't, unfortunately, bring myself to believe it was anything more than that for Tansy. Though I believed she cared for him, she seemed reluctant to completely immerse herself in Patch's world. It appeared that she didn't want to follow his life of wild and complete abandon, as was evident in the languid peaceful flow of her movements in the dance she currently performed.

I was beginning to see, in Patch's life, and in my own, that some affections were not returned and never would be. Patch, through mystified eyes mingled with hope and admiration, clung to a love for Tansy she did *not* want to return. She wanted no part of this hotel - except to dance in it. I wondered if he saw the cage the same way Tansy saw it. Did he see what it meant to her? Did he realize that he could never contain a free bird like Tansy? Did he see that the hotel itself kept her spirit as trapped as she was that night in the cage?

To say that the ring was a symbol of her undying love for Patch seemed unreal. Patch, who was so lost in it, was blinded by a misguided amour and I thought it best to keep my assumptions to myself. Cowardly, perhaps, but I didn't have the heart to tell him what I *really* thought. He loved her and if that love kept him alive, it was not my place to remove him from it... *or, so I once believed.*

There was a time in my life when my thoughts were held tightly inside, as if bound together in a neatly tied *knot*. Any beliefs, feelings, or opinions that I felt - good or bad - were my own, so carefully guarded that no one would ever hear them. Over time, however, it seemed that my days at Larouche had loosened that knot a bit. Sometimes words sprang from my mouth without thought. This new phenomenon was both terrifying and exciting! My inhibitions were being broken down like a concrete wall under the force of a sledgehammer, and I had to admit that it was quite liberating! A strange sort of freedom possessed me. I heard myself saying things I never would have said to any *stranger* - let alone a friend.

"This whole infatuation, Patch... it's a bit *pathetic*. Don't you think?" I asked, but I received no response.

Lost in his distractions, I frequently wondered if Patch ever truly listened when I spoke. I knew now, that he *had* heard my harsh words loud and clear. I saw the hurt in his eyes. He didn't say anything in response, and I felt instant regret. Pride welled up within me, and was too great to overcome. I would *not* apologize. We stood together in silence. *Who was I becoming?*

The dance ended with Tansy back in the birdcage. I guess that was the way it would always be. Tansy would always feel trapped, so long as she remained at the hotel. *What kept her at the hotel?* I wondered. *Why did she feel compelled to stay?*

An astounding explosion of applause filled the room, as she stepped out of the cage and bowed gracefully, purposefully avoiding Patch's gaze. He cheered along with the others, desperate for a moment where Tansy's own gaze would fall upon *him*.

From the crowd, stumbled a man headed directly for Tansy. The short and husky brute swayed with drunkenness, as he waltzed up to the dancer and grabbed her by the arm. Then, he fervently kissed her!

Patch stopped clapping, his knuckles turning white as his hands balled into clenched fists. Enraged, he quickly pushed passed the bystanders. From the look on his face, I knew he meant to tear the poor bastard apart - limb from limb. Before I could stop him, however, he rushed toward the man and, with all his might, pulled him off of Tansy.

"You're a miserable cuss, aren't you?" Patch questioned. He stared at the man with pure contempt. Then, he took him by his vest and threw him into a nearby pool table. The crowd looked on; enjoying the show Patch was giving. The charade, I knew, wasn't *nearly* over.

None of us blinked. If we *had*, we would have missed Patch as he released a single punch so forceful that the man toppled over the table. That punch was only the first of a series of blows too painful to witness. Years of Patch's frustration were embedded into each blow, as one by one he struck the man so viciously, that many of us felt compelled to look away. After what felt like an eternity, Patch left his weak opponent bleeding and jilted beyond repair. We watched Patch circle his rival's stiff frame, as the man lay limp as a dying beetle.

Patch, covered with spatters of blood, pushed up his sleeves and turned to the crimson faced man. "Get some lye on your face, you ugly bastard," he mocked, turning away from the mess he had created.

Tansy watched him, her face returning to its original stone-like appearance. Patch approached her, but she pushed past him and made her way to the elevator. He watched her go and, in turn, we all watched *him*, pitying the fool for trying to love in such a place. Love, we had learned, only led to *sorrow* - and the Hotel Larouche *didn't* involve sorrow.

I'd seen anger overtake my friend before, but this was different. It was nothing short of diabolical in the way that he beat the man. It appeared as if he enjoyed it, *relished* it even! I didn't want to believe my friend was capable of such a thing... but he *was*.

Patch looked down at the man he had pulverized. A flicker of regret flashed across his face, but it was too late.

Just then, another man burst through the crowd from behind Patch, his grip on a wooden chair held high above his head. Anger overtook me, as I saw the man's course of action clearly! I knew what he was about to do but I couldn't stop him in time!

In seconds, the chair came slamming down atop Patch's left shoulder, sending him toppling to the floor!

Overwhelming anger propelled me forward to the center of the action and my fist made contact with the strongest jaw it would ever meet. I'd never brawled before, never even remotely desired to engage in any sort of fisticuffs, but I was overwhelmingly compelled to protect my friend. The man who had just broken a chair over Patch - the man I had just hit across the face - looked at me, stunned, and hurled himself atop my much smaller frame. I fell to the floor, the wind violently knocked from me. Then, one by one, many men piled on me, looking to get into the action. Just that quickly, the brawl had spiraled out of control.

I pushed and shoved, even admittedly *biting* my way through the pile of men all prepared to fight to the death, simply for the thrill of it.

Somewhere beside me, I heard Patch laugh and scream. "It's ANARCHY!"

A glass bottle crashed against a man's head, and a set of brass knuckles tossed teeth from another's! At some point, beneath the pile of crazed anarchists, a heavy boot came down on my ribs. Another wide fist made contact with my face, leaving me with what I knew would be a black eye by morning... if indeed, I *lived* 'til morning! At that moment... I was not much more than a conscious dead man, feeling all the pain, but incapable of doing anything about it!

Like a mad man caught in even more insanity, I clawed my way out from under the unbearable weight of over a dozen men, my fingernails ripping as I dug them into the carpet. My ankle had been seized by a brutal man who was actually gnawing on it until I miraculously shook him loose... I was terrified! The people I had been surrounded by for almost a year were no longer humans! They were savages - barbarians who possessed *everything*, but felt *nothing*!

At last, I was free from the pile, and in a state of trembling consciousness. Slowly, I backed away from the mass of brawlers, with revulsion. Patch stumbled from the pile too, with a bloody nose and a ripped shirt. Unbelievably, and much to my displeasure, however, I found him *smiling*!

"Andrew!" he yelled, as a man attacked him from behind. Patch turned and issued the man three forceful punches that sent him flying back into the pile. He then turned back to me, as if nothing had happened. "Andrew, where are you going? Come back! I know what you're thinking!" Patch smiled, with defeat. "You're thinking I'm a fool. A *pathetic* animal clinging to something that will *never* be," he shouted, above the groans and yells. He placed his hands on my shoulders, and gave them a small, but firm shake.

"Sorry to let you down, friend."

For a moment, I saw true remorse in Patch.

He was yanked from his spot by yet another man who tossed him back into the pile. Patch continued fighting along with the other drunken men in the lobby. Despite always doing as he pleased, reacting radically and without justification, Patch had always appeared *free* to me. In our time together, however, I saw what terrible things that freedom had done to my friend.

When I *first* arrived at Larouche, freedom was all that I wanted. Back home, I dreamt of a place where I could be free of responsibility and duty, and my inhibitions would be gone. I looked down at my bloodied hands, shaking fervently, and slowly backed away from the cruel horseplay. It was nothing but *chaotic devastation.*

What was I doing?

I turned away from the lobby and made my way to the elevator. *Responsibility* had curled her long arms about me, reminding me I wasn't ready to let go of that part of myself entirely. I hardly recognized the person I was becoming, and it *frightened* me.

There was only one person I needed at such a time - the only person at the hotel that I had *abandoned* these past few months. *Matilda.*

I was no different from Patch. In the exciting swell of the hotel and its sin, masquerading as pleasure, I sought the comfort of the only woman I loved. It was wrong of me to believe that I had no weaknesses of my own. There was only *one* person who could remind me of who I was, and that was Matilda.

As I entered my room, I instantly retrieved the mirror from under my bed and hung it back on the wall. There she was, immediately appearing in the glass, as she always did. Her face fell at the sight of my mutilated appearance, and I felt my teeth chatter as I spoke to her. The room began to spin about me.

"Matilda, I've been so blind! You may think you need *me*, but it's really *I* who need you - most of all."

She didn't speak or, if she did, I was too wrought with fatigue and pain to hear her. In a haze, I crashed onto my bed, shivering madly and pulling my knees toward my chest as I rocked myself to sleep. Every bone within me rattled - the sudden, undeniable side effects of a life without limits... without *restraints*. Sleep, such as it was, finally claimed me, but it was one of the worst night's "rests" I had ever had.

It would have been a *blessing* to have never awakened... had I only known *then* what was to come.

Chapter Fourteen
Black Ben

"Andrew? Are you *dead*?"

Matilda's voice whispered, as I cracked open my right eye the next morning. My entire body felt stiff, and I feared making any sudden movements.

"Alive, unfortunately," I muttered. My jaw cracked slightly from even speaking those two words.

"Shame. I should have liked someone over here... on *my* side of the mirror," she teased. I smiled in response, wincing slightly at the pain I felt on the left side of my face.

"Sometimes, I think that would be magic," I admitted, and she grew serious.

"Never, *ever* say that Andrew. You're a fool if you think I wouldn't trade spots with you in a second!" she reprimanded. With embarrassment, I lowered my head. She continued, running her eyes over my disheveled appearance, "I was going to ask about the bruise on your face... or the blood on your hands, but I'm not. I think you got what you deserved," she scoffed, and my mouth fell open. "Only wish I'd done it myself!" she smirked, and I rolled my eyes.

"Tell me how you *really* feel!" I blushed, while she laughed at me. I couldn't be too offended, however, as I became terribly distracted by the way she sparkled in the glass. I wished, more than anything, that I could capture her wholesome expression in a portrait. *If only I had my charcoals!* Clearing my throat, I sat up and looked at Matilda. She stood, playing with the lace on her dress.

"The charcoals you gave me were the *best* gift I have ever received," I admitted, my face warming at the confession. I hadn't meant to say anything, but after the night I had in the lobby, nothing seemed to frighten me. Matilda smiled, and I could tell she was fondly considering the memory.

"You sketched with such passion when you were in school. I only hoped you would *never* stop drawing. I thought if I could give you something, some sort of encouragement..." she trailed off.

"You gave me more than that, Matilda. Every time I used those charcoals, I thought of the girl who believed in me," I spoke, truthfully. Perched on the edge of the bed, I sat biting my lip. Matilda shook her head, dismissing my heartfelt admission.

"I always wished you would talk to me, Andrew. You were intriguing and mysterious... and *handsome*, of course," she spoke, looking away from me. Incredibly, I had just witnessed Matilda become *uncomfortable* before my eyes. Instantly, I knew we had reached some sort of milestone in our friendship. Matilda had been rarely embarrassed, and I almost couldn't believe the words she had chosen to say. *Me? Mysterious? Intriguing?* And... had she said, *handsome?*

"For a girl, whose life was an open book, I dreamt of the day that we could be friends," she confessed. She looked around the room nervously and then, reluctantly locked her eyes on mine. "Well, truthfully, I should have liked to have been *more* than friends."

My lips quivered in disbelief. All the pain from the night before was gone, as my entire body numbed from Matilda's words. *Please, tell me those words are really hers*, I silently prayed. If they *were*, I knew I could never let her go. Selfishly, I would protect her soul and the mirror all my life and she would live beside me forever.

"*More* than friends?" I asked again, for much needed reassurance. She nodded and, through cascading tears, spoke softly.

"So much more. Of course, *love* does that to you. It makes you terrified and strong at the same time. The night the doctors told me to stay in bed, I knew I would never leave it. There was nothing for me to live for, because the boy I loved was in love with someone else, or *so I thought,*" she cried. I shook my head and pressed my nose against the mirror, aching to feel flesh upon flesh. I wanted to have her with me... just once. I spoke as my stomach nearly performed somersaults.

"You've got it all wrong, Matilda! I was yours from the start! *Only yours*. If I'd known then how you felt..."

"You were mine?" she asked, wide-eyed.

"Oh Matilda, I've lost you, haven't I? I've lost you, without even knowing I had you to begin with!"

"You loved me?" she questioned, her spirits lifting.

"No, Matilda. You don't understand - I *love* you...I loved you then, I love you now - and I always will," I professed. It felt unreal to be saying such things. Finally, after so many years, I could confess all that I felt. She looked at me, and her eyes smiled.

"It's not too late to say 'I love you, too', is it?" she giggled, and I laughed along with her, feeling an overwhelming wonderful sensation flood over me.

Slowly, I leaned my face closer to the mirror and allowed my lips to press into the glass. Undoubtedly, I knew it was foolish to share a kiss with a *mirror*, but it belonged to Matilda and that was enough.

Suddenly, her lips fell against mine, in a burst of soft warmth, and I felt an unexplainable tingle, foreign to the cold feeling of the glass. My hands brushed against locks of soft hair that fell along my face. Somehow, I had managed to fall into the mirror!

Looking around, I saw something very different from the small hotel room I had just been standing in. Her world was *black*. Cold as an ice bath, I felt my fingers grow numb as panic set in.

This was what absolute darkness looked like. A claustrophobic fear enveloped me, and I reached for Matilda, but she was no longer there! Then, as I took steps further into the strange cloud of nothingness, single beams of light soared through the darkness. They floated above my head in a space so vast, the night sky seemed *minuscule* by comparison.

Suddenly, the lights zoomed around me and formed images so powerful, I forgot where I was! Out of the lights, images of children appeared, happily engaged in a game of chase. A brilliant Merry Go Round whirled at a dizzying pace just a few yards from me, majestically filling the space with light. Moments later, I noticed not one, but *two* Arabian horses prance past, following closely by a mermaid with a long flowing tail.

I often daydreamed, but a world such as this was *unfathomable!*

My body radiated with warmth as I saw the light beams form themselves into a grove of trees around me. The lights danced like fireflies in the night sky, illuminating a glowing figure moving toward me.

It was her.

Matilda's hair was resplendent in the shimmering light, and her porcelain skin appeared translucent. We were each seemingly mesmerized by the other, not wanting to disrupt the dream. I didn't want to forget this moment. I didn't want her to fade back into the darkness, as she had done countless times before. *This is our moment*, I thought.

Her gown shone brightly, flowing elegantly about her. I saw our time at the Bloomington Ball happening again, before my eyes, and I knew I had been given a second chance! Matilda would, at last, get her dance with someone who was madly in love with her, and I would hold her in my arms for the first time.

Approaching her cautiously, I held out my hand and she took it in silence, smiling at me with new meaning. No words were exchanged, as I took her hand in mine. We swayed softly, to music only *we* could hear.

"You're a lot taller than I remember," she said, with gentle sarcasm.

"And more muscular too, you mustn't forget that," I winked, and she rolled her eyes.

"Right," she replied, then she placed her hand on my heart. I knew that she could feel it rapidly beating to its own rhythm. "Why didn't we do this before?" she asked, and I lifted an eyebrow.

"Because I'd be in line, waiting, for the rest of my life! Everyone wanted to dance with you, and why wouldn't they? You're beautiful, smart... and life... just *begins* with you," I sputtered, blindly. Matilda bowed her head with embarrassment, and I lifted her chin so her bright eyes could look at mine.

"I read in a book, once, that stars explode when they die," I began, then stopped. I knew she was confused by my abrupt change of subject, so I continued. "Seems like the way to go, doesn't it? When a star explodes, they've left particles of themselves *everywhere*. That means they haven't really gone at all!" I spoke, with great enthusiasm. Matilda, however, tensed in my arms.

"Why are you telling me this?" she asked, and I shrugged.

"I think we should have had a wonderful *celebration*, perhaps a parade when you passed away!" I smiled, and then I froze. Her eyes widened with offense, and I realized that the conversation was *not* going how I planned.

"Gee, thanks!" she sarcastically retorted. I shook my head, as I pulled her in close.

"What I'm saying, is that you should have left this world in an explosion of your own. Just like a star! We should have celebrated all that you did for everyone - all the happiness you created."

Matilda let go of my hands, and looked down. She brought her delicate fingers to her face, concealing it from me. "I didn't do *anything* for *anyone*, Andrew. I left this world, having given it nothing!"

"You gave *me* something. Life didn't seem so terrible knowing I might get the chance to see you!" I felt my neck flush with excitement. To my astonishment, Matilda flung her arms around my neck, as she pressed her lips against mine in the single, most wonderful kiss.

Life was a funny thing. When the door of my past closed, a mirror of possibilities was placed before me. It was the love that Matilda and I now shared that would keep me searching those opportunities for *hope*. Whether what I had just experienced was real or merely an illusion, I didn't dare question it.

When I opened my eyes, I was standing back in my hotel room, facing the mirror. Matilda was gone. I placed my hand up to the warm glass, not sure what to believe.

Glancing at my watch, I realized it was nearly three in the afternoon.

Smiling to myself, I recalled with clarity all that I had just lived through. I yearned to see Matilda's perfect face - yearned to step *back* into the mirror. My wishes were unfortunately interrupted, however, by a knock on my door. I could only assume it was Bravery, with more watches to mend. I opened the door, still in a daze from my time with Matilda, and saw Patch standing there... smelling of smoke. His right eye was nearly closed from a purple bruise that covered it.

"Patch!" I exclaimed, as I gave him a cheerful slap on the back. His eyes were bloodshot and his mustache was left untidy, and caked with dried blood. I was quite relieved to see my friend. He was alive and, for that, I was grateful.

"Why are you so annoyingly... *chipper*?" he asked me, clearly irritated. I chuckled, as I held the door open for him. He entered the room, and flung himself onto the chair.

"Can't a fellow be happy?" I asked. He cocked his head to the side.

"*Happy*? What's that? Is it expensive? Can I buy it?" he asked, dryly. I picked up a bottle of wine from my desk and took a swig, hearing my stomach growl from hunger.

"Some men do!" I jested, smiling at my own tasteless joke. Patch sat up and picked up an embroidered pillow, tossing it up and down. I was glad that Patch had come to my door. It gave me the opportunity to apologize for my harsh words the previous night. Hesitantly, I cleared my throat. "Patch, what I said last night, before the brawl-"

"Forget it, Andrew. I *am* pathetic. Pathetic Patch! You were right," he scoffed. With frustration, he tugged at his hair, clearly upset with how the evening had played out. Something else appeared to be on Patch's mind, however. "I've heard rumors that Tansy may be leaving the hotel," he continued, his look both hard and sullen. "If that's true, this may be the worst day of my life!" he said, throwing the pillow across the room. Then, he covered his head with his hands, and groaned.

"A bit melodramatic, don't you think? You've had plenty more days worse than this!" I joked, trying to lighten the situation. He smirked, and grabbed the bottle of wine from my hand. "Be patient," I advised, "If she loves you as you truly believe, she *will* come around. Give her time... and perhaps, *space*."

Patch groaned again, clearly repulsed by the idea. I knew he was finding my advice unfavorable, but what more could I say?

"Space?" he asked, feigning ignorance.

"Ah, so you've heard of it!" I responded, and he smirked. Then, Patch noticed my desk in the corner of the room, the parcel of watches still waiting to be mended. Realizing the mountain of work that lay before me, he rose from his seat.

"I've interrupted you, I see! I'm sorry, Andrew. I only meant to stop by to let you know that I'm still alive... though, only just *barely*. Some stupid jackass gave me this sweet gift last night," he said, pointing to his black eye with annoyance.

"I've got some aches as well!" I said, rubbing the top of my head. Patch sighed, ruefully looking at the watches with disdain.

"You will never be out of work to do, Andrew. Best give up now."

"Why is that?" I asked. Patch tossed his own pocket watch onto the bed.

"Time stops when it's being ill-used. My *own* watch stopped just yesterday!" he smirked, as he opened the door, about to leave.

His departure was delayed, however, by a parade of three men striding down the hall, in the direction of the elevator. The two taller men each held onto a Great Dane, attached to long leashes. I recalled seeing them on my first day at Larouche. The third man turned toward us as he walked past our room. It was the same *priest* I'd seen before, only this time, he wore an eye patch. I noticed that it concealed the better part of a large scar going directly over his left eye. The priest nodded his head at us, in a solemn greeting, and continued walking,

"They must have just seen Anais," Patch concluded, as he stepped into the hallway. He turned back to face me, my gaze still following the peculiar trio with curiosity.

"Work or not!" he continued, "You must come to the dining hall tomorrow! There's a celebratory feast for Monsieur Larouche. You won't want to miss it!" he smiled, before heading off down the hallway, running his hands along the walls as he left.

Monsieur Larouche. Ringmaster to the sinful circus of the hotel he created. My mind buzzed with intrigue. During my stay at the hotel, I had never once laid eyes on him. Here I was - a guest in his fortress, and I hadn't even thanked him for his gracious hospitality. Some said he was a traveling man, who seldom stayed at the hotel. Others proclaimed him to be a hermit, stuck in his suite for months at a time. I didn't know what to believe, but my thoughts surged with anticipation. I'd never thought about the day when I would meet the man who had unknowingly given me a chance at freedom.

Shutting the door behind me, I stepped into the hallway, looking down toward room 558. I couldn't think about Larouche just then, as I had pressing matters to attend to - questions that needed to be answered. Looking down the grim, solitary hallway, I felt my throat tighten with dread. Black Ben had asked me to visit him. He had theories about my true identity. *What did he know?*

Cautiously, I moved slowly toward the door of his suite, knowing that it was not only Black Ben who resided here, but *Anais* as well. I knocked thrice before the austere servant, whom I'd met before, opened the door. His sunken eyes shrank even further into his skull as he looked up at me.

"Back *again*?" he brooded, and I nodded.

"Black Ben expects me," I informed the ill-tempered man. He held the door open, rudely staring at me with annoyance as I entered. Slowly, he made his way to another room in the suite, muttering under his breath the whole time.

With a sigh of relief, I began to take in my surroundings. The room was nearly dark, lit only by the waning sun peeking in through two small windows. The lace curtains and wallpaper, I noticed, were both faded and torn. The sparse furniture in the room was also damaged, as bits and pieces of broken wood littered the floor. Taking a seat in an armchair, seemingly made from bull's hide and bone, I grew tense. *This must be Black Ben's chair*, I concluded.

In my days at Larouche, I had been frightened, bewildered, shocked, and every emotion in between. Sitting in Black Ben's chair now, I felt oddly safe. The room was silent and still. It wasn't long before the old man came from behind one of the doors, carefully locking it behind him.

"The master will be with you shortly," he uttered, leaving the room through another door on the left. I scanned the dismal looking room, with sadness. What once was a beautiful hotel suite was now *destroyed.* What sort of existence could a person have in such a place? The room seemed to hold nothing but despair. If not for the rays of sunshine that poked their way through the dusty windows, I might have left the place.

Interrupting my thoughts, a man entered the room and closed the door behind him. I knew, instantly, that it was Black Ben - though I struggled to make out his features in the room's dim light. Immediately, I stood up to greet him, but he motioned for me to sit. He took a seat in another armchair, several feet away.

"You asked to see me, sir?" I spoke, hesitantly. The gentleman's gaze was focused on the carpet, his hands gently rubbing the face of a gleaming pocket watch in his hand.

"I did," he nodded, and I abruptly stood up.

Mountains of anxiety overwhelmed me and I found myself nervously pacing the room, thinking of what to say next. I looked at him, noting a self assured expression on his face, as he watched me nearly melt away from fear. The seconds felt like *years* under his open scrutiny.

"You are away from home. Why?" he asked in a voice both deep and smooth... like a river.

"I couldn't stay there any longer," I admitted. I looked toward the front door of the man's suite. *Nothing good can come of this, Andrew. Run!* My thoughts were commanding me to leave this room, and run through the beckoning doors without a single backward glance.

A part of me, however, knew that it was too late. I had been caught in an invisible net by Black Ben, who would ultimately relay the news to my mother, and everyone back in Howell Village. It would be impossible to run from *everyone.* The long list of people I wanted to free myself from was growing, and I didn't possess enough strength to outrun them all.

"You shouldn't be here, boy," Black Ben spoke, earnestly.

Bitterly, I scoffed at him, to hide my offense, "Why should it matter to you?" I asked, feeling the tips of my ears burn. I was losing the little bit of control that I had when I first entered the room. Bravely, I stopped pacing and turned to Black Ben. "I'm allowed my secrets, *aren't I*? Same as any man living at the Hotel Larouche!" I heard myself speak in a commanding voice. My hands shook with anger. "Are you trying to frighten me?" I continued. "Do you want me to go back to that miserable place?" I kicked over a side table and felt my anger spiraling out of control. "I'm a free man! Just as free as anyone else!"

My hands raked through my hair, as my legs led me around the room in an aimless pattern. Like a child, I was having an uncontrollable outburst, and finding myself incapable of stopping it. In losing my temper, I couldn't find the dutiful, good natured boy I once was. *Andrew, where are you?*

Black Ben simply watched as my hysterics continued. I felt foolish having him stare at me, as if I was some scientific study, but I couldn't restrain myself.

"I have friends here. I live a full life here! Don't you see? You *can't* take that from me!" I pointed at Black Ben, who remained unfazed. *He wants to take me away from the Hotel Larouche!* I thought. *This man wants me to leave... but why?*

Losing my balance, I slumped to the floor wanting a drink - *anything* to dull the stinging headache I had. Where was that familiar cigar that calmed my nerves? Where were the bawdy women of the hotel who helped me drown my sorrows with their flattery? Reeling from my unexpected outrage, I looked at Black Ben.

"You won't take me back, *will you*?" I almost begged.

"Larouche is no place for you, *Andrew*."

The tone of his voice was reminiscent of a voice in my past. I stood up, still lost in my own fears, and turned to a picture hanging crookedly on the wall. Attempting to regain my composure and restrain my anger, I walked to the image.

"What qualifies you to say all these things to me?" I questioned, with resentment. Approaching the simple wooden frame, I stood in front of the photograph and stopped. *The image was of my mother, Anvil, and a young boy, all dressed in their finest clothing.*

That young boy was me!

Quickly, I turned around and saw Black Ben standing in the light of the window, with his face framed in the sunlight. For the first time, dark, piercing eyes stared back at me. They resembled eyes I had seen in a picture back home, long years ago. It was a picture that had hung in my mother's room. Craning my neck and straining my eyes, I stared at the man in disbelief. It took only a moment for me to realize the identity of the man who stood before me.

Clear as day, I recognized Black Ben as my *father*, Alben Godfrey.

Chapter Fifteen
Tansy Tells

"Is this some sort of trick?" I exclaimed. My mind refused to allow me to believe that the man before me was my *father*. Slowly, I backed into one of the walls. "You're dead! You died before I knew you. You're dead. You *must* be!" I shouted. My fingers grasped at the torn wallpaper, tearing it to shreds. Black Ben stood still, as I took in his features. Hard as I tried, I couldn't deny that this man was *me*, simply more advanced in his years. His eyes... his hair... both no different from my own.

"Are you disappointed, son?" he asked, and I looked at him in awe. *Son.* The word sounded so right when he said it.

It was impossible for me to be disappointed, as I wanted to shout from the heavens that miracles were real, and that my own father was alive and well! I wanted everyone I had ever known to acquaint themselves with Black Ben, as I introduced the man as my *father*.

Instead, I ran to him, like a child, and threw my arms around him. He, taken aback by my sudden boldness, received me and held me close. It felt good to know I *wasn't* alone. After I released him from my grasp, I pulled him toward the armchair and took a seat on the floor beside him.

"Come, you must tell me how my father has come back from the dead! What peculiar sorcery is this?" I asked, as he took his position in the chair. He smiled, and ran his hand through my hair.

"I'm afraid it's a long-winded story to tell!" he warned, and I shook my head, urging him on.

"You must tell me, your *son*, or I might believe the walls of Larouche have finally closed in on me and I'm going completely mad!" I laughed. My father chuckled, and relaxed in his chair.

"I think that's already happened, boy," he spoke, with a hint of sarcasm. I shifted uncomfortably. After some time, he relented, "Very well... pull up a chair."

Eagerly, I rushed to retrieve the chair I had been sitting on and moved it closer to my father. He looked out the window, then back at me and I saw him close his eyes, while he rubbed his wedding band with his thumb.

"You should know that when your mother and I married, we agreed to have only one child. One child was all we could afford, and we were firm in this decision. When Anvil was born, we were so incredibly happy. We often dined with the other families and paraded around our precious boy - I remember it well," he stopped, as if lost in the memory, and then continued.

"What a time that was! Howell Village was so different then. But all it took was *one* night of thoughtless passion, one night that would alter our lives forever. Soon, your mother discovered she was expecting another child. Though it was not part of our plan, I was glad for it! I built a beautiful cradle, prepared a fine room, and waited. When the day finally arrived, I thought surely I would lose your mother... she looked so ill, so close to death. The midwife didn't think she'd come out of it alive - but she did... *with twins*."

"Twins?" I asked apprehensively, as I felt my heart pound wildly! "I don't understand!"

"*Twins*, Andrew."

I stood up. Fear gripped me as I began to absorb the pieces of this astounding information. *I had a twin! But who?* Listening carefully, I ignored the tension mounting inside me.

"The night of your birth, your mother, had fallen into a very deep sleep, past exhaustion after the difficult delivery. The midwife, who had stayed by your mother's side, was asleep in the rocking chair. I placed you, Andrew, in the cradle next to your mother's bed before I went to the parlor. The other child, your *sister*, stayed with me. Carefully, I bundled her up and watched her sleep. It felt so wonderful to hold her. Your mother was still in a deep slumber. Though we did not expect another child, I truly believed we could be *happy*. I went to bed with so much hope for the future, but the future had other plans for me.

"Shortly before midnight, I was awakened by a violent rattling! My bed seemed to shake - the walls vibrated! The curtains swayed back and forth! It was as if a turbulent storm was raging over our house! If I had fallen into a nightmare - I couldn't be sure. Fearing for our lives, I picked up your sister, only to immediately set her back down again. Her skin boiled beneath my fingertips! She writhed and screamed, as I've never heard a child scream before. I *still* remember that sound."

"Did the shaking ever stop?" I asked, now on the edge of my seat.

"If it did, I didn't notice. I found myself lost in my poor child's features, twisted and almost inhuman as they were."

He paused, his forehead wrinkling with despair. My father stood up and walked to the window, before he continued.

"I swaddled the girl in many blankets, and carried her to the closest hospital, to find that the only available doctor had gone home for the night. That's when I looked down at the child in my arms and saw her future destroyed, as she would inevitably be shunned by the harsh criticisms of the villagers. I knew I could no longer remain in Howell if I wanted to protect her, and my family.

Certain that Father Joseph could determine what was wrong with her, I fled to the church and pounded on the heavy doors. He took one look at the child in my arms - one look into the infant's eyes - and backed away from us.

"'This child is marked! Her soul is *his* now!' I recall him yelling. The way he spoke terrified me. I refused to

312

believe him! I pushed past the old priest, pulling aside her coverings, and looked into the girl's face for myself.

"What I saw, Andrew, were only the whites of her eyes so clearly belonging to those of a *monster*! All I could do was look away in horror. If I had the courage, I would have ended the unfortunate creature's life, but I began to see Anais for what she really was... *my daughter*.

"I'll admit to you now, Andrew, that at that moment, I fled the church not knowing what I would do next. I left her in the hands of the priest, in fear of what she would do to our family. I worried about the harm she would bring to you boys, and the despair she would cast over your mother. It would mean our ruin in Howell Village. Desperately, I ran down the streets searching for a miracle, before I found myself - instead - near the river.

"The skies were not kind that night. They brought torrents of rain and wind so strong - trees were uprooted and large branches violently flew about the air. I must have been mad to have been out in such a storm! And then... I saw my answer.

"The body of a man, not much bigger than I, lay crushed under the weight of a fallen tree. I ran to him,

313

hoping I could help, but when I saw that his skull had been smashed beneath the heavy trunk, I knew he was gone to the storm.

"Frantically, I searched the dead man's pockets. *Who was he?* To my dismay, I found nothing, but the man's belongings tied together in a handkerchief beside him. He was a vagrant - a wanderer - and nothing more. He was a man searching for a new home on the wrong night.

"And that's when it occurred to me that the dead man I stumbled across was my solution. *This* was the way I would save our family's future from complete devastation. It was my plan to trade places with the unidentifiable corpse and leave Howell Village with your sister. In the morning, they would declare Alben Godfrey *dead*.

"With a heavy heart, I pushed the tree aside with all my might and took the dead man back to the church, where Father Joseph received me - still carrying the swaddled infant in his arms. Together, we took the corpse to the back of the church, and I told the old priest of my plan. Immediately, I switched clothing with the dead man, and placed my wedding band upon his ring finger. It was enough, I hoped, to keep any suspicions at bay.

"Before I prepared to leave Howell Village, I headed home one last time. Your mother was still fast asleep when I kissed her goodbye. I could only imagine what life would be like for her when she awoke from her slumber. Then, I stirred the midwife from her sleep and revealed my plan to her. Being the only other person who knew about the second child, I wanted to ensure her silence on the matter. I wanted her to confirm the delivery of only one child... *one boy*. With the woman's faithful promise to keep my secret, your sister and I left Howell Village.

"The child was miraculously asleep in my arms when the carriage stopped at Larouche. I had only meant to stay the night. The next day I would head to a local monastery and pray that God would cast the devil out of our girl. Just like so many others, however, I became trapped in a world that *accepted* my daughter, cursed as she was. She could scream night and day and no one thought anything of it!"

It was all a lot to digest, so I sank back in my chair and let it wash over me. I had a sister who was in league with the devil. My father was alive, and my mother had lost everything the day I was born. A part of me already knew

315

the answer to my next question, but I had to hope I was wrong.

"Father," I began, "What is her given name?"

He looked out the window, and let the sun shine upon his face. Then he turned to me, and spoke.

"I called her *Anais,*" he said, with resignation.

I could have fallen over from the sound of that name! *My sister* was that very creature that had everyone in the hotel talking. She was the monster we all feared! My father didn't look at me when he spoke again.

"Her name means 'grace', as I hoped God would shower his grace upon her... but here I am... *twenty* years later - a fixture of this prison," he sighed. My father looked around him, with despair, and I rushed to comfort him. He only pushed me aside, however, as he made his way over to his chair.

Taking a seat, he continued. "I've tried just about everything, but when all else fails and I am ready to give up, I see our family in her and know that Anais *must* have a chance one day. She could grow up to be as remarkable as you are, son. One day," he said, with a familiar dream in his eyes.

Remarkable? I thought. With all that happened over the past year, I didn't believe anyone could find *me* remarkable!

"*That's* why mother hates me so… I'm a painful memory of the day her husband died," I said, with a hint of bitterness. Father looked at me sternly and sat upright in his chair.

"Your mother loves you, Andrew. I am certain of it!"

"Perhaps, she wishes it were *me* who died. She despises me father, I *know* she does," I spoke, with growing frustration. The anger in me simmered, but he quickly suppressed it with a stern look. His eyes, kind and honest as they were, led me to believe he was telling the truth.

"Have faith, boy, and compassion. Your mother's life hasn't been easy. If only I could have spared you all from such grief," he said, looking down at his hands, folded in his lap.

"My sister? Anais? Where is she now?" I asked, in a whisper. Part of me was worried that she would appear out of nowhere, and frighten me to death! Quickly, I scanned the room as I braced myself.

317

"She sleeps," he hesitated, and the room grew still. My skin prickled with unease. Some minuscule fraction of me *wanted* to see her. I wanted to find my sister within the monster... but fear controlled me. Hesitantly, I asked my father another pressing question.

"Those men - and the priest with the wounded eye - do *they* visit her?" I sat in my chair, upright with great curiosity.

"Yes. Every month since I first brought her to Larouche. They perform something called an *exorcism* on Anais. They try, in vain, to cast out the demon that's latched onto her... but it won't relent. I imagine the only thing they *really* do is wear the creature out from exhaustion! The priest received a horrid gash just last month. Anais threw a crucifix at him!" he said, standing up. He paced back and forth, same as I had done earlier, and then buried his head in his hands.

Shame burned within me, as I saw that my father had given up his own life for the greater cause of saving our family, while I had only been bringing us down. His devoted battle with Anais and her demon had become his sole existence. *Twenty years*! For twenty long years, he had watched over my sister who was possessed by an entity much more powerful than any human. *If only I had known!* "Is there nothing that can be done for her?" I pressed, but my father shook his head.

"If there is a miracle out there, it does not seek Anais as the recipient," he spoke, with defeat. There was still one question I *had* to ask.

"Why Anais, Father? Why did the devil choose her that night, a mere infant?"

Just then, a defeating scream blared from beyond the wall. At the sound of the loud shriek, my father turned to the door of my sister's room, his face white, knowing what was to come. He stood, suddenly gripped with fear, before he could respond.

"Another time, perhaps," he answered. I covered my ears, pierced by the sound, and watched my father take action. In a series of long strides, he reached Anais' door, opened it and entered her room. With a slam, the door shut, and he was gone.

Any courage I possessed vanished as I ran to the door leading out of the apartment. I closed it behind me, suddenly feeling a surge of guilt take hold of me.

Pathetically, I had left my father alone with my demonic sibling. Was she capable of killing him? Would I lose him, just as soon as I had found him again? My mind cared not for answers, however, as my feet led me away from the room. *My father is accustomed to the ways of my sister*, I convinced myself. *And I'm not ready to meet her, yet!*

Quickly, I walked back to my room and stumbled against the door. So much had happened and the day wasn't even over. I had a *father* again, and a *twin sister*! The girl I adored loved me back! Everything was different now! My life had changed overnight - and I found my new enthusiastic self return - if just for a moment

The only thing I could truly think about, however, was how hungry I was! My stomach rumbled with anticipation, as I saw the hallway practically sway before me. With shaking legs, I managed to stand on my own, maneuvering down the hallway with great difficulty. As I took the elevator down, I hoped that I would stumble across some sort of muffin or vegetable before I passed out on the hotel floor.

The dining hall was almost empty, with the exception of a large couple stuffing their faces at a distant table. Fatigued, I almost collapsed into the nearest chair and was grateful when a waiter placed a large pitcher of ice cold water on the table. Without thinking, I grabbed the handle and poured myself a glass, guzzling the cooling liquid as fast as I could. It wasn't brandy, but it certainly quenched my thirst!

After sending the waiter off with a large order for lobster and a side serving of oysters, followed by chocolate mousse, I sat weakly in my chair. Somehow, I had managed to skip meals for *two days*! When the full plates were placed in front of me, I delved into the steaming seafood with glee! Such food was splendid already, but when you were starving for a good meal, everything tasted *even* better. Such food awakened your senses and comforted your soul.

What seemed like minutes later, the lobster and oysters had made their way down to the pit of my stomach. With great delight, I wrapped my mouth around the crème de chocolate and nearly cried with joy! Forget that I had just seen my father alive and well! Forget that I had just been told by the woman of my dreams that she returned my love! Currently, I was devouring the most sensational mousse... and I could *not* be happier.

Gluttony was my only friend, at that moment.

Out of the corner of my eye I spotted a woman wearing a long burgundy cloak, carrying two small suitcases, make her way past the dining room and toward the front door of the hotel. The couple that was eating stopped to look at her with appalled expressions. *The woman is leaving the hotel*! I thought.

Without a moment lost, I stood up and followed her. In all my time spent at the hotel, I realized I had never seen anyone choose to leave it! Now, a woman was headed for the door with conviction, and I found I had to see her departure for myself. I looked on as the woman, whose face was concealed by the cloak, made her way through the lobby. Her hands, still firmly grasping the luggage she carried, revealed a small glittering object that caught my attention.

A ring.

Stunned, I followed the woman out, moving past clowns and acrobats all twirling about in the lobby. The woman headed quickly toward a black carriage and, just as quickly, I followed her. She stepped inside and, without a second thought, I did likewise. Panting, I closed the door behind me so that we were the only ones in the carriage.

As I suspected, I sat directly across from Tansy, whose large eyes almost burned holes into my flesh, "Why have you followed me?" she demanded. I responded to her with a question of my own.

"Why are you leaving?" I inquired, with a raised eyebrow, and her eyes narrowed.

"You should get out this carriage, Andrew. It will be leaving soon!" she warned. I shook my head, not wanting to leave Tansy without putting up a fight, for Patch's sake.

"You're not leaving - not like this, Tansy!" I pleaded. She smirked, and her face warmed a bit.

"I should think you'd be glad for me. Larouche isn't exactly the *holiest* of places!" she scoffed. Just then, the driver poked his head through an open window. He looked at Tansy, his eyes nearly bulging from their sockets.

"Why... Miss Tansy? What are you doing?" he asked, looking back and forth from the dancer to me with suspecting eyes.

"Drive please," she spoke, with defiance.

"You *can't* undo this, girl. You know what they'll do!" he whispered, terror filling his eyes. She ignored him and callously lit a cigarette. The driver shook his head in disbelief and left the window, muttering obscenities as he went. He thumped his way to the top of the carriage, sending me into a complete panic, as I heard his whip crack loudly. The carriage began to move!

"Driver! Wait!" I hollered, and instantly, the carriage stopped.

"What are you doing?" Tansy, exclaimed.

"Forgive me for being selfish ma'am, but I care *more* for the feelings of my friend. You've met him before, haven't you? Most call him Patch," I continued, openly baiting her to protest. Her eyes grew cold, as she turned toward the window, visibly distraught.

"If only you understood," she whispered, under her breath.

"I might if you only told me," I said softly, as I reached for her hand. She stared at me for a moment, deciding whether or not she could confide in me. When I nodded my head as a sign of encouragement, she sighed, and relaxed in her seat.

"He was a *good* man, Andrew. He was the best person I knew," she said, softening a bit.

Patch? I was bewildered. Though it didn't surprise me to hear that Patch was good natured, referring to him as a "good man" seemed somewhat *far-fetched*. I broke her silence.

"What was his occupation?" I asked, and she smiled fondly, as if recalling a more pleasant time.

"He was a *doctor*. He put smiles on children with sicknesses that could lead to *death*. He cured people even when the odds were stacked against them. Everyone had such admiration for him, Andrew. He even nursed *me* back from Scarlet Fever."

"He had seen me dance before, and then, saw me shamed and cast off by my brother. When I fell ill, he took me into his home without any thought. It was on my deathbed that we fell under each other's spell. Every day he'd spend long hours reading to me, and making me laugh with his ridiculous humor! Every day, he told me that my dancing brought a joy to his heart, and that he would nurse me back to health so that I could dance again. For a girl from the slums of the street, that was all I ever wanted to hear. A

325

wonderfully intelligent man was in love with *my* dancing... my *soul*. He was in love with me... *and I loved him back*. The summer we spent together, I knew my love for him would be everlasting.

"But slowly, I saw his reputation as a man *and* a doctor dwindle. He made house calls less and less. Whispers spread throughout the streets as we walked passed. The town's most beloved doctor had joined hands proudly with the village trollop, ratty and poor as she was. Though he never appeared to think much of the gossip, you must know what *I* felt. I watched the man I loved become the filth of the streets... *like me.*"

"Then, one evening, he proposed an offer of marriage... but it did not bring me the joy I expected. I only saw his future destroyed as he placed that ring on my finger. I boarded the next carriage out of town and arrived at the Hotel Larouche, where my dancing was *not* a sin," she paused, briefly. Quickly, she wiped away an escaping tear.

"You must know how it crushed me, Andrew, when I found Dr. Patrick Rhodes, standing in the lobby of the hotel two days later. That man, the man I grew to despise, would henceforth be known to all who encountered him as Patch.

He had given up his occupation and good name for me, and I could have *murdered* him for it. My life has been wrought with guilt and pain ever since. I do my best to dissuade him but, still, he persists!"

"But, you *do* love him?" I asked, though I realized I didn't need to hear the answer. It was written on her face, written in the way her fingers stroked the ring he had given her.

"As long as this ring stays on my finger, my heart speaks only *his* language. It's our unspoken secret. I find removing the ring, for me, is so much harder than a person would think."

I recalled Patch's excitement over the ring when she danced. He must have *never* wanted to remove his eyes from her hand, in fear the ring would one day vanish. Even still, when Tansy chose to leave Larouche, her finger remained adorned by the fine jewel. Foolish, was I, to think Patch chased an empty dream. His heart was filled with the hope that he and Tansy would live their lives together.

"I do love him, Andrew. Patch is the most fantastic man alive! There is not a person who comes in contact with him who does not instantly fall under his spell... his charm...

his wit..." she spoke, her voice trailing off. Tansy produced a smile and then, a laugh, so great... I wished she would always be that happy.

"Sometimes," she continued, in this new found revelation, "It's hard to believe he's real! It's even more difficult to believe he loves me enough to give up his life's work, and live *here*. I fear that Larouche is turning him into the worst sort of man! He is supposed to *preserve* life, not take it away, as you so plainly saw the other night. That *villain* is not the man I fell in love with!"

Tansy was right. Patch *had* come a long way from being that good and wholesome doctor she spoke of. Knowing him now, I could hardly fathom him serving others in such a way. Larouche had corrupted him, I saw, as it had so many others...

"What will you do?" I asked, and she straightened her posture, the coldness consuming her once again.

"The best thing I can do for him is to disappear, so he *cannot* follow me. I would appreciate it if you wouldn't disclose our conversation to anyone," she said, as she looked out the window. I grabbed her hand, begging her to reconsider.

"Tansy, it will kill him! You cannot leave! Take it from someone who had his love stolen away from him by death. Divided affection is something I do not wish for anyone," I stated, but she withdrew her hand from mine.

"If I leave, he can start living again! He can return to his practice and leave this place. He will be better for it and, though my heart nearly rips apart at the thought of it, I know what I am doing."

Perhaps, he would be all that Tansy hoped for him. The only times I saw his eyes light up, however, were when *she* was there. If that light went out, *what would become of him*?

"The sensible person in me is inclined to agree with you, but no one ever said love was sensible. There is love that awaits you with open arms and, when it's gone, you'll realize what you missed," I warned, but she shook her head and spoke more to herself that to me.

"I won't," she whispered. I sensed an inner conflict, so I continued with my reasoning, hoping Tansy would understand.

"There are some of us who face a love that is seemingly improbable. There are some of us, Tansy, who will never experience the passion that I've seen between you and Patch. If you don't believe it, then I suggest you come with me," I said, rising from my seat, uncomfortably cramped in the small carriage.

"Go with you? Where?" she asked, clearly puzzled. Stepping out of the carriage, I extended my hand. As I predicted, Tansy looked at me with intrigue. I worried, however, that what I would show her would not be enough. There was only *one* way to tell.

"You can trust me," I told her, with a nod of positive affirmation.

"Why should I? You are no one to me," she spoke, her brows furrowing as she stared at me. I saw all that she hoped for, all that she wanted to disconnect from, crumble before her eyes as she looked up at the hotel, reluctant to step inside. A small fraction of myself, in turn, wondered if *I* was doing the right thing.

"I'd like to think I'm your *friend* and, right now, I'm the mirror to your mistakes. Tansy, I once stood as afraid and as defiant as you. I know how you feel, but I also know the consequences. Follow me and, if you do not see my meaning, then allow me to pay for your carriage ride out of here."

It was the *least* thing I could do, after all.

My hand remained outstretched. Tansy stared at it for a moment, caught between decisions, before taking hold of it. Stepping down from the carriage, she pulled the door shut behind her, and I pulled her back inside the hotel.

I was taking her to room 553, where I would show Tansy something I hoped would change her mind.

***

"Your room's a lot smaller that mine," Tansy said, and I nodded in agreement. We had made our way to my room on the fifth floor, where a familiar mirror hung.

Tansy removed her cloak to reveal a black dress with a high collar. Suspiciously, she looked around the room, and spotted the watches. Taking a seat beside them, she took great care, as she examined each one. After she was finished inspecting all the watches, she turned to me and crossed her arms.

"So, what is it you wanted to show me? Better be good since you dragged me all the way back!" she smirked, and I tried to manage a smile in return. Awkwardly, I stood in the room, unsure of how I could unveil Matilda without frightening Tansy.

"Hello!"

A light and airy voice chimed behind me. I turned to the mirror and saw Matilda smiling and waving at Tansy. With a scream, Tansy teetered on the chair, shielding herself with a pillow.

"Tansy, meet Matilda Brew," I smiled. Matilda gushed with excitement at the sight of Tansy, who was still clutching her chest in shock.

"Oh, Miss Tansy, I've wanted to tell you what a wonderful dancer you are! You know, I used to dance a few jigs here and there. Tell her, Andrew! Tell her!"

Tansy looked to me and then back to Matilda.

Apprehensively, she stood up and walked toward the mirror, placing her hand on the glass. After a moment, she looked at me for reassurance, and I smiled back at her. In utter disbelief, Tansy lifted the object a bit and looked under it, checking to see if there was something, or someone, behind it. When she discovered there was no trick to the magic of the mirror, she rested it back down against the wall.

"Remarkable! Andrew, how did this happen?" she exclaimed, in awe. I shrugged, mildly embarrassed.

"It was sort of a happy accident... let's call it '*mirror-aculous*'," I joked. I'd been thinking about that one for a while! Matilda and Tansy, however, returned my ill-timed jest with deadpan expressions, before Matilda spoke up.

"When I passed away, they forgot to cover all the mirrors. A *commotion* distracted them," Matilda said, throwing me a glance. To my dismay, I reddened from the memory. Matilda continued, with a small sigh. "So, I guess you could say that I'm sort of stuck now," she explained, as Tansy continued to examine the mirror. Then, she stepped away, still lost in silent wonderment.

"I have always heard of that silly superstition, but I never really thought it was possible!" she marveled. Suddenly, she covered her mouth and looked at me with large eyes. "Is she your betrothed?" she asked, and I shook my head, looking directly into the mirror.

"If I had only known, then, what it would be like to lose her... I would have done all that I could to tell her exactly what she meant to me. Perhaps, she would still be with us. Love heals all, just as Patch cured your ailments with *his* love," I spoke, and saw Matilda smile sadly.

"You are so lucky to have him, Miss Tansy. You are lucky to be alive *and* in love. 'Tis a beautiful thing," Matilda said, as her voice wavered. Her eyes began to moisten, and she started to fade from the mirror. "Excuse me, Miss Tansy. I don't mean to behave this way. It was truly wonderful to make your acquaintance."

Before I could call out to her, Matilda's image faded from the mirror. She was gone, and it pained me to see her go.

Tansy witnessed all that I wanted to show her. Through the pain and tears, I knew Matilda had reached out to Tansy's cold heart... but I was not sure it was enough. Tansy stood up and headed out the door, without a glance back into the room. I followed closely behind, in silence. As she stepped out into the hallway, Tansy pulled the door shut the door with great concern.

"What?" I asked, but Tansy didn't respond. She looked at the thick carpet beneath her feet, then back at me.

"What will you do now?" she asked, and I saw her own eyes begin to water. "Will you live the rest of your life attached to a woman who is confined to a mirror?" she said, hiding her emotions. "What will become of *you*?"

"As long as I am with her, what does it matter?" I responded, quiet irritated. She shook her head, and placed her hand on my cheek.

"She knows that is *not* the way, Andrew. If she loves you, she will let you go. Until then, you cannot move on with your life," she said, her face taking on a sullen expression. "Trust me. I've seen it happen before," she said, thoughtfully rubbing the ring on her finger. Shaking my head, I dismissed her statement.

"My life started with Matilda," I explained, defensively. Tansy merely looked around the hallway, gazing over the wallpaper, with true sadness.

"This is *not* a life, friend. This is *delusion*."

Like a saw, her words carved through me. They were *not* what I wanted to hear, especially when the only "delusion" I saw was that happiness could be found back in the village. The towns we were all from only served as reminders of what we could not fix. Surely, Tansy knew this. As I watched her go, I heard her words over again in my head. *This is delusion. This is delusion. This is delusion.*

In my repetition, the simple phrase became more and more real to me. Her words chipped away at my defiance, because some part of me knew they held the truth.

Somehow, I found my way back to the poker tables that night. Once again, I fell back into the heat of it all. I wasn't even sure how I managed to get there. Like I'd taken a drug, I found my way back into the trap, stumbling back to my room at four in the morning. I hardly ever had dreams anymore. Even a nightmare would have been a blessing, as it would have reminded me that I was still alive, and conscious.

I seldom dreamt, but *this* night... I did.

***

The house smelled of pies. A woman with a lovely face cooked and sang a merry song. A wonderful large golden retriever curled itself around my feet. Somehow, I felt content. The simplicity was enough. Suddenly, a hand reached for mine. I looked up and saw my mother, much younger than I had ever seen her. She smiled at me with the sweet fondness that I had always dreamt of.

In the corner of the room, I saw my Father and Anvil discussing the paper with enthusiasm, sharing a hearty laugh. A knock on my door sounded, causing me to jump from my seat. I opened it, knowing it could only be the girl of my dreams. There she stood. Matilda, smiling her lovely smile. We dined and sang merrily around the piano. It was the only dream I had ever wanted.

Larouche, the most sinfully, wonderful place where dreams were a reality was not what I wanted at all. There I sat, back in Howell, enjoying my surroundings.

In my tranquility, however, I didn't see a small, shriveled, dirty hand with bloodstained nails, reaching out from beside my seat. Slowly, it crept toward my own hand, which rested on the chair's arm. The hand, I knew, belonged to Anais. Her arm began to wrap itself around my torso. Dozens of small cuts, I noticed, covered the limb that encircled me. With great anxiety, I gasped. I was about to look into my sister's eyes - eyes that reflected all my sins back at me.

*** *

In the darkened room, I awoke in a sweat - desperate to leave the nightmare. I sat up, looking around me with a fresh perspective. This room was becoming increasingly difficult to look at - to reside in. Quickly, I closed my eyes again, sealing them shut. Overwhelming guilt consumed me. I didn't want to acknowledge my surroundings. I didn't want to feel the inevitable guilt that came along with choosing a life at Larouche as a means of escaping responsibility.

A warm fire. A soft bed. Food at my disposal. Women at my door.

All the while, my mother and brother were at home... *eating Stone Soup.*

Chapter Sixteen
A Gala For The Citizens

Oh, how they danced! In a heated combination of excitement and lust, I saw men and women cavort with wild abandon. They swayed to the music in the large decorated dance hall, spinning and twirling without any cares or worries. Patch's eyes lit up at the lewd vulgarity on display before us.

"Isn't it brilliant?" he grinned.

In a strange sort of way, he was right. It *was* brilliant! The dancing at the ball that night was unlike anything I had witnessed back in Howell. Back home, we danced at arm's-length at all times. Everyone was stiff as a wooden soldier on the rare occasions that there were to dance. The villagers would certainly crack in half performing the bends and turns that the hotel patrons currently achieved with ease!

Before I could respond, however, I was pulled from my stance beside Patch by a large female whose firm grip on my jacket sleeve told me I had no choice but to follow her to the dance floor. Her emerald colored dress, with its low cut bodice, left little to the imagination as she pressed me to her chest. I stood there, limp as a dead fish, not actually wanting to dance as she rocked us back and forth. Patch, I saw from the corner of my eye, was laughing hysterically before he finally came to my rescue.

"Pardon me, miss, but this boy *isn't* drunk enough yet!" he howled. The woman, to my surprise, didn't fuss. She quickly moved on in search of another dance partner.

"Thank you," I said, as soon as I collected myself, but Patch had already departed, weaving his way through the crowd. His hurried departure, I knew, was most likely in pursuit of Tansy.

It would seem impossible to host a party for a group already accustomed to constant nightly charades! This night seemed intensified, however. Watching them all now, in dresses with long trains, and suits woven from satin and silk, I knew that the citizens of Larouche had readied themselves for the most jubilant evening of all their soirées.

As I watched the lavish extravaganza before me, I felt a familiar twisting knot grab my insides. This was certainly *not* like the parties back home. *Here*, women wore jeweled corsets and guzzled wine from the barrels themselves! Men danced on tables, and juggled beer bottles! Slowly, I saw the party unfold from a reasonably civilized affair to downright unrestrained mayhem. The wanton gala became no more than wild carousing! It was the way most soirées at the hotel went, and tonight was *no* exception.

A short, red haired man balanced one of the barrels on his head, wavering unsteadily. It didn't take long for him to lose his balance and topple over, sending the remaining liquor spilling out onto the floor. A few revelers began rolling around in it, while others lapped the foamy liquid up off the porcelain tiles, like wild dogs.

Hair was freed and let loose from their elegant coifs! Ties were undone! Stockings removed! Jackets were opened and shirts were untucked, as many patrons waltzed across the dance floor. Other spectators roared with uncontrollable laughter, as another man boldly urinated into one of the potted plants in the corner of the room.

One man recklessly jumped up onto the chandelier and swung from it, singing at the top of his lungs. The ceiling began to crack as he rocked to and fro. I stood back, preparing myself to run from the swiveling pendulum of lights that was undoubtedly about to break loose and shatter into a million pieces.

Thankfully, the man leapt from the candelabrum - but landed squarely onto a seven tiered cake, crushing it beneath him. Quite astounded, I watched as he lay on the floor atop piles of smashed cake, laughing and creating snow angels out of the frosting beneath him.

Desperately, I looked around for someone with a shred of sanity, but found no one. What I found, however, was something much *more* captivating.

The room was buzzing with chatter and in its center sat a man, with slicked hair and a roguish smile. He was seated on an adorned throne, and being swarmed by numerous women from the party. The handsome man welcomed their affections, bowing his head as one of the harlots proudly placed a silver crown onto it. His suit, I noticed, was made of deep red velvet. It was an eye catching garb that had black thorned roses sewn into its collar.

It was the devil himself... appropriately dressed. *Larouche*, I thought. *It has to be!*

A king on his throne, he exuded absolute power, and great satisfaction at the scene of the debauchery that surrounded him. *How could he not be satisfied?* I thought. *He created it!*

Another familiar man stood beside Larouche, looking all too serious for such an event. It was Harvey Nicholas, the rigid man with a pencil still tucked behind his ear. Occasionally, Larouche would whisper something to him, and Harvey would jot it all down on a small pad of paper. I wondered what the man's relation to Larouche was. What was his hobby?

I didn't ponder this for long, as I was too preoccupied with Larouche, arrogant and cavalier as he was. He was much younger than I thought he would be, and much more self-assured. Mentally, I sized the "king" up as a man in his forties, who had lived a privileged life. Wealth and excitement seemed to be his creed, and I saw every gentleman in the room stare at him with envy.

As I looked at the man seated on his throne, I found that I could neither admire nor envy him. Though I was grateful for the hideout he had provided, I saw that he had created nothing but an escape for people running from any sort of responsibility in their lives. With embarrassment, I nearly crumbled at my hypocritical thinking, for here *I* was -

in the same sinful boat - running from a life and memories I did not want to face.

The Hotel Larouche, the most sinfully, wonderful place in the world, no longer seemed like fun.

"Drink up, Andrew. The best is yet to come!" a familiar voice declared. Patch, who had returned with two glasses of whiskey, handed me a drink and smiled. "Tansy should be here soon!"

Nodding, I drank the odious drink, cursing myself as it seared down my throat. I was tired of the numbing concoctions Larouche offered, but drowning one's self in alcohol at an event seemed to be almost mandatory at the hotel. It's what *everyone* did.

"Look at Larouche, sitting there among his whores. 'Tis the devil himself!" Patch scoffed, with a smile.

He gazed at the man sitting on his throne. Was he admiring Larouche, or did he see past the illusion and find the mayor's attendance a stamp on whatever was left of his sanity? My curiosity was full to the brim, and I found that I couldn't help but ask my friend a few questions about the man everyone so admired. I was eager to know how

Larouche acquired his millions, and came into power over the small and the erratic nation of sinners.

Patch took a seat on the table, carelessly tipping over baskets of bread and bowls of cranberry sauce, as he scrambled through the food.

"There are plenty of stories that go around, Andrew. No one knows for sure," Patch said, sorting through a bowl of confections. "The most popular myth is that sometime, long ago, Larouche stumbled into *great* wealth. He was left with a large sum of money from his father and, as the story goes, was given two options by his old bedridden mother. He could invest in a hospital where the sick could receive free care *or* build a church. Well, unfortunately for the old woman, he took a *different* route. He killed her instead. He put sweet poison in her sherry - and gambled the fortune away.

"One day, with two coins in his pocket, he made his very last bet at the local tavern where he'd become a permanent resident. He struck a deal with a peculiar fellow traveling from out of town. The man was a betting man, having earned his *own* sum of money during the late night poker games. The man, Larouche learned, was also the owner of a beautiful hotel a few towns away.

"The bargaining chip was great, indeed. Should Larouche *win* the game, he would be the owner of the man's hotel. If the *traveler* should win, Larouche would give the man his *soul*. The owner of the hotel loved a good bargain and he counted himself as a lucky fellow, so they placed their bets on the table. *A soul for a hotel*," Patch sighed. He looked at Larouche, who was busily engaged in conversation with Harvey Nicholas. "If only the traveler had won!" Patch said, in awe of Larouche's presence. He continued, after finishing off his whiskey.

"You can't *really* bet a soul when you don't have one to give in the first place!" he chuckled, with an odd sort of reverence toward Larouche.

My eyes returned to the makeshift monarch and my stomach tensed.

Power. Larouche had seized it with no remorse! He had murdered his own mother and gambled for a living. He had opened the gates for other sinners to live as they pleased. It was a strange kingdom he'd made for himself... and yet, it was his own. What did I have that belonged to me? Was there anyone in the world that would follow *my* lead to such lengths? The longer I stared at the man, who had gotten away with everything, the more envious I became. I wanted there to be a world where *I* could have that power and admiration. I wanted Patch and the others to appreciate *me* and see *me* with that kind of respect.

The rules, however, were *not* that simple. You either joined the lifestyle and surrendered your soul, just as Larouche did, or made your way home to the other miserable fools who never amounted to anything. Certainly, I'd have my goodness, but that's all that I would have. I knew with a profound certainty that I wasn't ready to go back and mend watches in the old shop with Anvil. I wasn't ready to let go.

A trumpet blared, bringing me back to the moment. Patch had turned his attention to the center of the room, where the seas of the crowd had parted. Everyone stood watching the entry way. For a moment, the chaos subsided and we all waited anxiously for a sound - a movement.

"This is it," Patch smiled, handing me his empty glass.

"Ladies and gentleman!" the master of ceremonies boomed, "As is tradition, the beautiful Tansy will dance for the patrons of Mr. Larouche's marvelous hotel!"

The residents all cheered and clapped their hands, looking with utter devotion at their patron. Many of them actually cried with overflowing gratitude and joy. It was strange to see them lifted to such a state of euphoria over the sight of their dauntless leader. They praised him as if he'd come from beyond the stars, delirious in their fervor, looking at him with extreme admiration.

Larouche, in turn, merely raised his hand, as if to silence them all. He was a man of few words. His confident magnetism was compelling, creating an irresistible allure. It was hard *not* to put all your trust in him. When the group finally settled, the music began. Patch's fingers fidgeted, anxiously.

The music began as violins and cellos played their melody so vibrantly, it lifted our spirits instantly. I *wished* that Matilda had wanted to join me, but she had been so quiet lately - so pensive.

The music continued much longer than it should have. The orchestra played the few introductory measures

348

again and again, the repetition creating rising anticipation among the anxious citizens. *Where was she*? I thought. The crowd, including Larouche, looked about the room in hopes that they would find Tansy arriving from a secret entrance, *but she never came.*

"Where's Tansy?" Patch spoke with alarm, as his face grew serious. Protectively, I placed one hand on his shoulder. A terrible feeling sunk in, as I began to realize that Tansy had *run away.* Somehow, I knew that her absence was entirely my fault; it was my responsibility to guard my friend from the hurt that inevitably awaited him. *I* was supposed to keep her from fleeing the place, but I found that I could not accomplish it. With my own advice, I had mistakenly set her free. In showing her the mirror, I had provided her the necessary example for leaving.

Somehow, I couldn't feel sorry for it though. Was it the right thing to do? I wasn't sure. Unknowingly, I had enabled her escape from the danger we were all enmeshed in. Looking around the room at this crazed gathering, however, I couldn't help but feel that my actions weren't as wrong as I thought.

Bravery rode in on his unicycle and jumped off, making his way to Patch with something in his hands. Nervously, I swallowed the lump in my throat. Bravery's arrival, I knew, did not bring pleasant tidings. With his head hung low, he handed Patch a small light blue envelope. I saw my friend's hands tremble with anticipation and worry as he took it. His name, I saw, was written across the envelope in small, delicate handwriting. He opened it, dreading what he knew he would find inside.

Time seemed to slow down, as Tansy's ring rolled out onto Patch's open palm. The sight of it nearly shattered my *own* heart in two. The beautiful shining stone meant *nothing* now. With the ring's return, she had provided the necessary gesture that would confirm that her love for the desolate doctor was no more. She had given it back to Patch without any explanation or words of farewell. She left the hotel with no final words for the man who had always watched her from afar, with unconditional love. She was gone, and she *wasn't* coming back.

Patch knew it, too. I saw all hope in his eyes vanish. His shoulders slumped forward and, for the first time, I saw Patch look weak with despair. It was a look I thought him incapable of - something I thought nearly *impossible*. He had strutted around with such confidence, such bravado. The man in the suddenly quiet dance hall stood surrounded by many, but really... he was more alone than ever. His world had shattered before our eyes, and we all had ringside seats. I knew this was the singular event in his lifetime from which he would *never* recover, and my heart broke for him.

Looking around the room, he shrugged his shoulders, attempting a weak grin, trying to overcome his humiliation... but it was too late. We all knew what happened with Tansy and we all saw that she wasn't coming back. She was gone without a word, and likely miles from the hotel. As Patch trembled with anxiety in his distress, I felt his hopelessness as if it was my own. I knew what it felt like when cold reality struck and you were left knowing that you would never see your loved one again.

Patch didn't look at anyone. He placed the ring in his jacket pocket and made his way out of the room, far away from the onlookers. Instantly, I began to follow him. My friend needed me, and it was much too dangerous for him to be alone at such a time.

I was thwarted in this attempt, however, by the large group of patrons that flowed back into the center of the room, readying themselves for more dancing. Pushing my way through the crowded area, nearly twenty waiters rushed toward me with plates of food and more drink.

Caught in the sudden commotion, I was abruptly taken by my arm and rushed to a nearby seat by someone with great strength.

Slowly, I turned to find *Larouche* standing behind me, a slight smile playing at the corner of his mouth. I looked up into the man's hazel eyes that bore down on me from his considerable height. Those eyes conveyed much more than any amount of words ever could, and they were daring me to try to figure him out.

I couldn't and, as that smile spread across his face, I knew I would *never* interfere with a man like Larouche. Slowly, he bent down close to my ear, and whispered so that only I could hear him.

"Terrible, isn't it? Your friend was so in love with the girl," he spoke, with a trace of mocking condescension. Fearfully, I nodded, and he patted me on the back. Indirectly, I knew this was his way of showing me my place under his supreme superiority. This was *his* world. These were *his* rules. Gripping my shoulder, he continued.

"Stay smart and choose *me* as your god, Andrew. Love is meaningless, as it will eventually die. Everything we think is good for us must come to an end. If you don't believe me, then I suggest you ask your *friend* in the mirror," he grinned. With that, Larouche turned and left me, moving back into the crowd. I felt the wind knocked from me.

He'd known about Matilda all along! This realization left me unnerved. My one secret was his, just as the rest of my life had become. The singular tie to Andrew from Howell Village was discovered and I felt myself grow sick with disgust. What had I become? Nothing was sacred anymore. I could have walked around naked and shocked no one. As I watched people feed off each other's cruelty, I knew my life would never be my own again.

Larouche's theory of love was jarring, but as I tossed his disconcerting philosophy around in my head, I began to find the truth in it. What did love bring to Patch but misery? What did love do, but stand idly by as death ripped Matilda from me? Larouche showed the world that true love was unnecessary and that happiness could be found in *other* pleasurable activities.

In fact, the longer I stayed, the more I realized that everyone in the dining hall was sick with all-consuming joy. Larouche was laughing with robust enthusiasm, while my fellow diners were stuffing their faces with delicious food and wine. If this kind of happiness was within my grasp, why would I ever leave it?

Men and women kissed and fed each other grapes and stuffed pastries. They chatted with each other about nothing at all, and yet their smiles were wide and their eyes were bright. Desperately, I wished Matilda was beside me, supporting my decisions with a comforting smile. She didn't seem to understand this world, however. In fact, she seemed uncomfortable in the setting I had provided for her and now, basking in it on this night, I could see why. She so belonged in Howell, with its simple goodness. She was pure and refined, and too much of a treasure to be tarnished by decadence such as this.

I was different. Over time, I had felt myself becoming one with the walls of the hotel. I was no better than the rest. I was weak and, suddenly, I didn't care to hide it. Trying to relax in my chair, a woman looked at me and tossed a crème filled pastry in my direction. I caught it, and she smiled.

"Eat up darling! Stuff your face with everything your parents said was bad for you!" she squawked. The man next to her laughed, as he slipped his arm around her and leaned toward me.

"Andrew! Rumor has it that you fix watches. Be a good boy and fix mine," he demanded, tossing his watch at me. The girl beside him piped up.

"Why should he, Henry? You haven't used it in years!" she cackled.

They all laughed manically, as the man popped open a bottle of champagne, shooting the cork toward the ceiling as foam flooded the table. Passing it down the row of diners, they each took swigs from the bottle. One man poured some of the champagne down a woman's dress! She returned the lewd behavior with a thunderous smack across the man's face. To my surprise, the man and woman roared with laughter at their own horseplay.

"Hit me again! Again!" the man encouraged, begging for another slap across the face.

Disgusted, I felt the need to turn my head away. What I turned toward, however, was a portly man sitting a few seats down, dipping his head into a bowl of gravy. He slurped the thick liquid up like a pig eating from his trough. He oinked loudly and everyone around him howled with laughter. *Another* man, who wore a black and gold cape, sat in the corner of the room, holding a woman on his lap. The pair kissed fervently, simultaneously shoving strawberries into each other's mouth. Quickly, I adjusted my chair and refocused on my meal.

Would I ever see that with love came responsibility - pride and respect - for what you cared for most? The patrons of the hotel thought only about themselves. The wasted food of the banquet hall on this one night was my family's food for a month. Every drop of water spilled, I knew, would be deprived of them in hell. It was difficult to take part in the mayhem. Though the pleasures of the hotel were endless, the residents' actions were selfish and benefited no one but themselves, as they all rolled around in their odious nature and tonic. There I sat, witnessing it all, and feeling miserable. I was caught in a struggle between what was easy and what was *right*.

A stout woman sitting across from me climbed onto the table and yanked forcefully at my tie. She plastered her lips against mine without warning, smashing her face into me. Appearing as though she wanted to smother me to death, I desperately pried the woman off.

"C-control yourself!" I weakly demanded, as she squealed with delight. The others around her all laughed at my torment, thoroughly enjoying the "enthralling" spectacle. The woman grasped my tie again, undeterred, and I realized her strength was much more powerful than I imagined! I gasped, a sudden harsh feeling of suffocation overwhelming me, as the woman's hands went directly to my neck. *What was happening?!*

Just as I thought that I was about to take my very last breath, a loud commotion drew the woman's attention from me. She released her firm grasp on my neck and stepped away - drawn to something in the room.

As I collected myself, my eyes darted to a group of people frantically running from something under the table. Screams began to sound from the crowd, as the women cowered behind their equally terrified dance partners. Panic quickly spread across the room, as many patrons ran to protect themselves behind various pieces of furniture. They hid behind large vases and statues, and used chairs as shields. Terror arose, as everyone backed away from the disturbance, clinging to one another in fear. The ruckus, I knew, *must* have been caused by some sort of animal, trampling through the celebration!

At last, the creature climbed onto one of the chairs. To my horror, I saw that I had been terribly mistaken! It *wasn't* an animal at all. It was a human being, with animal-like behavior.

It was my sister, Anais.

None of the descriptions I had heard of the poor, unfortunate creature were anything like facing the flesh of the monster itself. Her eyes were hollows of madness and evil, showing all white pupils that conveyed no emotion, but only a glimpse of the terrifying world of the unknown. Her hair was attached in fragments. Thin and stringy, most of it was pulled out of her skull in clumps, leaving large scabbed patches. Her mouth was perhaps the most grotesque of her features. Surrounded by a ring of dried saliva, her cracked lips were white and large. Her teeth were short and blackened. In her crouching stance, her knees and legs were nothing more than a pile of bones held together by skin. Her feet were bare, and the smock that she wore was nearly ripped to shreds. Her body, which was covered in countless bruises and scratches, was enough to raise the hairs on my neck. Fear choked me, as she ripped her nails along the table cloth, yanking it out from beneath the dishes, calamitously.

Like a wild beast, she scampered toward a large pheasant a couple had been eating only moments before. She jumped on the table, crouching over the cooked bird, ripping it to shreds and shoving the pieces ravenously into her mouth. Strange growling noises that sounded like a combination of multiple voices living inside her nearly left me paralyzed in fear!

The gathering all shrank back in fright, but no one left the room. We all watched, horrified, but too mesmerized to look away. Our curiosities were all being satisfied. The air of uncertainty around the poor child now unfolded, as her mystery vanished before us. We saw her for what she was - the body of a girl hosting the deformities of a *demon*. Looking around, I saw a mass of intrigued bystanders gaping at her unsightly appearance. The people around her were transfixed by my sister, much like a feral dog they stumbled upon in an alleyway. But very quickly, I saw their looks of terror become stares of amusement!

Her clawing, wild behavior became a farce as the guests' fear began to fade. Fright was replaced with jeers and taunts, cruelly indicated through pointed fingers and tittering laughter.

The creature saw that it was being watched through eyes as *cruel* as its own. Slowly, she crawled her way to the center of the table, writhing in the middle of it - like some demented centerpiece. It lurched, heaving spit at the surrounding crowd, only encouraging more delight in the scene before them. Through rhythmic clapping, they urged her on as she became their new form of entertainment.

A smiling musician followed the crowd's enthusiasm, and pounded on his drum in time. My sister slowly stood up, and every eye in the room locked on her. Unbelievably, she raised her arms and calmly levitated her up way to the ceiling, crawling around the chandelier. As she moved along to the painted walls, she looked down as if to taunt us.

The sight before me was a sick abomination! She was their game... their sport! As I looked among the faces beside me, each one staring up at her and still clapping, I felt my heart heave. I wanted to cry. The hatred I felt overwhelmed me. *This* was why my father hid her away. *This* creature, and the creatures of the hotel, was the last twenty years of his life!

Staring up at the ceiling, I felt the next few minutes pass in a blur. I didn't know where Larouche - or anyone else - was, for that matter. I saw my sister and *no one else*. Consumed with great guilt, I nonetheless feared her and I backed away from the table, anxious to run as far away from the Hotel Larouche as possible!

It was excruciating to look at her, and I felt a vice-like grip on my lungs. Frantically, I tried to remove myself from the party. With small movements, I took a few careful steps back and slowly made my way from my spot at the table. Perhaps, I thought foolishly, I could sneak out unnoticed and unharmed.

I wanted to run, just as I ran from everything else in my life.

Then, I *stopped*. Something inside me screamed for me to stay. My feet wouldn't allow me to flee so soon. A brother, I knew, could not let his sister - even one with the devil's soul residing in her - become swallowed alive by the people of the hotel. They all stood there, watching Anais as if she were some circus performer. They mocked her and laughed at her! I knew I had to try to stop them. Hopelessly, I looked around at the line of faces, but I found support or compassion in no one's eyes. Stepping from the crowd, I shouted as loudly as I could, with all my might.

"Stop this! Stop this now!" I yelled, finding my *true* voice for the first time. The room quieted for a moment. Everyone gawked at the intrusive boy who dared to ruin their fun. They stopped their chants, but only long enough for me to notice my sister, still floating in the air. Her head twisted toward me in a swift motion! It was the first time I had looked directly into my twin's gruesome face, and I was paralyzed with revulsion.

As I stood, nearly frozen in time, I saw her white eyes almost burn themselves into my own. Her hollowed orbs locked on my face, visibly beckoning me to dare to stop the amusement. She floated back onto the table and crawled toward me. My legs felt as weighted as bricks, glued to the floor beneath my feet. It seemed that I could not move away fast enough, as I saw her creep over with a wicked smile.

This was it! I gasped. The end of my life was quickly approaching, and I was only twenty years old! I was going to be torn apart as quickly as that bird Anais devoured moments before! Slowly, she slithered toward me with a determined look. She was so close; I could almost feel the overwhelming heat she emitted sear my flesh! I turned my head, so as not to see my executioner approach further.

Apprehensively, I stuck my hand out beside me as a weak shield of protection, and felt an odd, wet sensation. To my horror, I turned my head to see that the demon child was *licking my palm and snarling*. She did not bite. She did not scream. She crouched beside me, sadistically marking my hand with her demonic symbols and salivation.

Daring myself to look into her eyes, I searched eagerly for any sort of familiarity. This was my twin. My sister was lost in the darkness of evil and, as I stared at her, I wanted - more than anything - for her to find the goodness I believed she was born with. I wanted her to find the goodness I, myself, had *lost*.

Looking around at the sinister faces of the dinner party guests, however, I knew that compassion would never be found at the Hotel Larouche. The patrons all stared at her, no longer afraid, but *fascinated* that a child could succumb to such evil. They were glad that they did not share her cruel fate, and thought themselves all so fortunate.

One thing I realized as I looked about the room, however, was something I never saw so plainly; this girl was no more hideous than the monsters that occupied the hotel rooms. I stood there, rooted in fear, as I realized that what we all should have been terrified of... was *each other*.

We were the demons - masked in fine clothing and wealth.

Before I could remove myself from my sister's snarls, I saw a large hand pull her from me. Relieved, I looked up to see my father take her in his arms, as she squirmed in an effort to free herself. His strong limbs, to my surprise, contained her well. He had restrained her like this, I presumed, *many* times before.

Without a word, he pushed past bystanders and headed out of the hall with fury in his eyes. As I stood and watched him go, I wondered what it was that angered him most of all. Was it the child and her blatant disregard for him, or was it the crowd of cruel onlookers that ogled his child as a sideshow and nothing more? Though she may have been accepted as a resident of the Hotel Larouche, she was certainly not welcome amongst the patrons. Their jeers resounded in my head! With a heavy heart, I realized that Anais would *always* have to remain hidden.

With tremendous gratitude, I reflected upon the man who had given up his life for our family's protection. He was a dead man in one place... and a *joke* in another. As I saw the crowd dissipate and resume their merrymaking, I knew there was only one thing for me to do.

I decided to follow my father.

Chapter Seventeen
An Unusual Exorcism

The first thing I heard, as I stepped out of the moving machine, was an ear splitting wail that echoed through the hallway! I was on the fifth floor, my head still abuzz from the mixture of alcohol and tumult.

New found compassion replaced the dread in my heart. I didn't know my sister at all. I had no knowledge of her existence, yet there I was... eager to protect her. She was my family and the only relation, apart from Anvil, who shared my parentage - my blood. I wanted her to learn and grow as *I* had, not relegated to living like an animal in this bizarre environment. She was robbed of a life that, I now realized, I had been *privileged* to have. She needed to know what home felt like. I wanted her to dream, as I once did, about changing the world with her very own aspirations and ideals.

When I cracked open the door of room 558, I realized I wanted to give her those dreams more than *anything*.

The salon was empty and only the curtains ruffled back and forth from the mild vibrations in the room. Standing in the suite, I could hear my sister's muffled wails from behind one of the closed doors.

This was what my father had witnessed over the past twenty years of his life. His days were counted by the markings Anais scratched upon his face and arms. Most of his life had been a series of failed demonic expulsions, none of them offering a cure. The future must have looked awfully dark for a man and his sick child, who battled a seemingly endless possession. The room just beyond the door was an unfinished grave waiting to swallow whatever bit of life it could find. I wanted to step inside, but my feet were weighed down by the familiar cowardice within me. I felt powerless to face the demon just beyond the door.

When the door finally opened, my father rushed out of the room, exhausted and dripping with sweat. He closed the door behind him and looked at me with astonishment.

"Andrew, boy, you shouldn't be here!" he scolded. I nodded, a weak attempt to remain obedient. The childish boy in me, however, couldn't be contained.

"I know, but I *had* to see her. She's my sister - my twin! What do you expect me to do? Continue celebrating with the other guests?" I argued. My father pensively approached the familiar picture of our family on his mantle and lightly touched it with sincere fondness.

"You'll find that it's the only thing you *can* do, son. I've waited twenty years for a miracle, yet Anais' heart weakens every day. Her soul is so far removed, that I can no longer see the girl inside her," he sighed, sinking wearily into his chair.

His sleeves were rolled up to his elbows, and his bow tie was undone. "The demon is powerful, Andrew. Every day, it drains more and more of her frail body. Anais has open wounds that we cannot touch," he continued. Setting the picture down on the table beside him, he looked down at his hands that were covered in scars and scratches. I hadn't noticed those markings before. "She *will* die, of this I'm certain. She cannot go on this way!"

Through my father's love and care, Anais was still alive, but just barely. It was impossible for my father to keep her alive much longer. The creature who took possession of Anais *would* eventually consume her, and she'd be lost to the terrible wickedness that my father fought so hard to spite.

Throughout our conversation, I continually glanced at the door that led to Anais' room. Some part of me wanted to see her. A strange, dark curiosity came over me and I turned to my father, hearing myself speak words I didn't think I had the courage to say.

"May I *see* her?" I asked, and my father shook his head firmly.

"That's not wise, Andrew. She is dangerous and you are a stranger to her," he said, staring off into the distance. I looked toward the closed door to Anais' room and saw it rattling ever so slightly. Quickly, I dismissed his cautions. She was no stranger to me.

For years, I clung to my love for Matilda to fill the sense of complete emptiness I often felt. Was it possible that the missing part of me - the part I ran away to find - was none other than my twin sister who lived but a few miles away?

"You're wrong, Father. Anais and I know each other *better* than you think," I spoke, firmly. My father stared at me with astonishment, but I couldn't let him prevent me. I was *determined*.

Reluctantly, he slowly walked toward the door and I followed behind him. As I approached it, I felt a rumbling and looked down. The floorboards just outside Anais' door vibrated, as if shaken by an earthquake. I inhaled sharply and held my breath. What I was about to face was no game or nonsense found in fairy tales. There were entities behind that door that could do *far* worse damage than any monster I could dream up.

"Beware boy, should the devil latch onto *you* instead," my father warned, as he opened the door to Anais' room. A cool blue light peeked from the crack, as the door began to open... slowly creaking, as if *begging* me to enter. Trying to remain as composed as possible, I walked into the room.

Then, a new light, bright like the sun, flooded the bedroom. A warm, golden glow overtook the blue hues and the rattling ceased. A humming sound, as lovely as Matilda's humming, floated in the air behind me. *Anais!* I smiled, and turned around. There she was, sitting on her bed, removed of any scars or marks on her face. Her eyes were brown - same as mine!

Was this some sort of trick? Anais looked back at me with no trace of any demon dwelling inside her body. She was absolutely *beautiful*! Her smile was angelic and I felt my own lips part into a wide grin. It was miraculous! The demon appeared to be gone!

Before I could call out to my father behind the door, Anais spoke, her black curls bouncing from her excitement. "Brother! I've been waiting for you!" she said, sitting up. She clapped her hands together with enthusiasm, as I took a seat at the edge of the bed, observing her features. She was my mother's daughter, but bright and joyous! I chuckled at her thrilled expression.

"Anais, is it *really you*?" I asked. She nodded her head, and I took her hand in mine. "I know we've never met, but I feel like I've known you *all my life*," I spoke earnestly. She beamed and squeezed my hand, then she ruffled my hair with a laugh.

"I've seen *you* before. You live here don't you?" she asked, and I nodded. Perhaps, behind the devil's eyes, she *had* known me all along.

"You're *exactly* as I pictured you, you know? I always wanted a sister!"

"I pictured you this way, too, Andrew. Almost exactly!" she beamed. Quizzically, I lifted my eyebrow.

"*Almost exactly?*" I asked, with a grin. She nodded, and reached for a rag doll beside her, brushing its yarn hair through with her fingers. I continued, not wanting my first conversation with my sister to end so quickly.

"Am I *different* from what you expected?" I pressed on, and she nodded again, her eyes still distracted with her doll. Anxiously, I lifted her face so that her eyes met mine. "How am I different, Anais?" I asked again, with growing agitation. She smiled slightly, and then threw her arms around me, pulling me in for a tight hug. It felt so good to hold her!

Then, she whispered words in my ear that I strained to hear. "*I thought you were a good person.*"

The words she spoke suddenly struck me! Surely, I had misheard the girl's sinister words! Before I could ask her

372

to repeat herself, I felt my sister's skin turn hot beneath my fingertips! It nearly boiled beneath hands, almost smoking from the heat. As I pulled myself away, I looked down to see her dress - stained with dirt and blood! Cuts ran along her arms that gripped my own so tightly. Her hair shriveled before me, into thin pieces of wire-like strands. With a blood curdling scream in my ear, I knew the demon had tricked me!

The room was deep blue once again and I felt sharp nails dig into my forearms. Instinctively, I pulled away to find Anais grinning - her eyes white, and her face scarred just as I'd seen her the first time. It was the demon's face I saw inches from mine and, from the way it stared at me, I knew I had become its prey!

Quickly, I tore myself away from her, stumbling into the wall and landing in a pile of rotted bed sheets. Hot tears sprung from my eyes. The demon had played my heart strings as if they belonged to his own rotted violin. Deep down, however, I knew the creature was somehow right in its observation of me. *I was a good person once... long ago*, I thought, as I shrunk back into the corner of the room.

Anais, still on her bed, growled in my direction as if to challenge me to some twisted standoff. Freed from her restraints, I cowered in fear, prepared to be overtaken.

"Leave him alone, Demon!" another voice yelled. I turned, and noticed the same priest I'd seen before - standing in the corner with a bible in his hand. Still wearing the eye patch over a scar that ran along his face, he looked as tired as my father did. With his hand on his crucifix, he held up the holy relic to Anais as his own form of protection. His makeshift shield of armor, however, only angered my sister and she bared her teeth to him, as saliva dripped off her large gums.

"Alben!" the priest called out.

In seconds, my father bounded into the room, as if he had been waiting for such a call the entire time. They both somehow restrained Anais as they began forcefully binding her arms to the bed post. Each of them struggled, as they held her down, narrowly avoiding her violent kicks as she lashed out. I could see that they had gone through this routine countless times before! As I watched the terror unfold before me, I knew I should have run to their aid, but something prevented me. In fear, I sat there, shivering pathetically, and watching bravery as I'd never before seen it.

Beyond her blackened smile and the whites of her eyes, I reflected on what *really* frightened me about the creature in the room. Anais was my twin and the only one who shared my likeness. I knew that it could have very easily been *me* in her place. Twenty years ago, the demon could have chosen *me* as a host, if he so desired it. I closed my eyes with a realization the crushed me.

The monster didn't possess my soul. He didn't *have* to. I managed to walk into the arms of evil all on my own.

I looked around the room, mentally recalling my first day at Larouche. It seemed so magical then. The lights, the music, the laughter - all of it masking the darkness that I had so foolishly fallen into. So, I sat there in the corner of the room weeping, just like the day Matilda died, wishing it was me instead. *My* soul was just as damaged as the dark spirit in the room.

Resolutely, I watched Anais - tied to a bed and writhing in the twisted sheets. The priest repeated his Latin prayers, while sweat trickled down his forehead. Strands of his brown hair covered his face, as he held onto his bible, never ceasing his chants. His demeanor remained steady... focused and undeterred. I was grateful to the man who had remained by my father's side all these years, never losing hope.

My father, by contrast, looked defeated. His stance appeared as though he'd become lost in terrible storm - drenched with exhaustion. With each episode, I concluded, he lost more and more faith in the possibility of a bright future for his only daughter.

Multiple voices echoed throughout the room, all emanating from my sister's small body. With a spine chilling shudder, I knew the three of us were *not* alone. There were other spirits, other demons, present... and they would not leave anything untouched. The curtains shook as the bed posts rattled, while my sister's limbs contorted well beyond the limits of *any* human endurance.

The prayers kept her calm... for only for a short while. It seemed, however, that nothing could be done to save her. The words the priest read left the monster unaffected, as after each brief interlude of peace, the turbulence escalated to new heights. Anais could not find the love and tenderness she needed, because she'd never experienced it. Her memories of true happiness were nonexistent, as she was cursed at birth.

Now, she was expected to search deep within for a light that was unknown to her. I knew that handling the task alone was next to impossible. If *only* she could experience that kind of love. Certainly, my father had expressed his love throughout the years, but maybe that kind of compassion could only come from someone who knew her as well as they knew their own person. Maybe that person was *me*.

The love she required to defeat the creature had to come from the only other person, who felt as she felt, *lived* as she could have lived, and *loved* as she could have loved. There was a lot of love in my heart, though it had become tainted over time.

I'd seen what such a powerful emotion could do to me when Matilda was living. After her death, love propelled me *even* more and I knew it was the one spark of my old self that I still had. Perhaps, the only person who could save Anais was herself, or at best, her twin!

The door of the room slammed behind us, as the two men in black entered the room with their large black dogs. The dogs didn't bark or fuss. They simply glared at the child as if challenging the demon inside. At once, the priest stopped his chants and turned to the newcomers, speaking commands to them in a low voice.

Apart from Anais' constant moaning, the room was oddly still. I saw my opportunity and approached the bed with an arm extended for protection. With no direct plan, I took steps toward my sister.

"Anais," I spoke quietly, through chattering teeth. "Anais, it's your brother. It's Andrew."

My legs brushed up against the bed, as I knelt down beside her writhing body. Smelling the hot sweat and vomit that stained the sheets, I felt my stomach twist unbearably! All eyes, I knew, were focused on *me*.

My sister's attention snapped toward me, wide-eyed and enraged. Her eyes locked with mine, so intensely, I found it difficult to look away. "Come back to us, Anais." I pleaded.

There was a certain weary look on her face that gave me the courage I needed to continue. She was now tranquil and still, though the look of Satan was still written on her face.

"Sometimes we want to resort to the darkness, but if we search for the light... we will lead better lives. We will find our way. Don't play into the evil that surrounds you. Rise above!" I heard myself say. A long forgotten voice was calming me with these words... or was it something I believed in all along...

A wash of cool air came over me. I couldn't explain the beauty I found in the revelation, but I felt something new - something that I *hadn't* felt before. I wanted, so much, to be that person who chose the straight and narrow path to goodness... and there was that *light, pulling* me back. It was a light I found - oddly enough - in my *sister's* eyes. The demon had all but begged for my soul, but I couldn't relinquish it... *not yet*.

"I've been so foolish, haven't I?" I chuckled, to myself. "Search for the light, Anais! It's all around you. There *is* good to be found outside these walls!"

As if the angered spirit was listening, the flames of the candles in the room began to flicker. Spiraling hot wind now filled the cramped space, nearly scathing my skin! The floorboards seemed as if they would break free from the nails that held them down! Everyone, but Anais, braced themselves against the walls as we prepared ourselves for the worst. To my surprise, I realized that my words had greatly upset the demon! With a sudden burst of courage, I decided to speak directly to the monster itself. There was something I *had* to say.

"Monster!" I yelled above the roaring wind in the room. "Take *my* soul! It's yours! I deserve it, for all that I've done. Lord knows, I've been the worst brother a man could be. Take my soul, but free *hers!*"

My father gripped my shoulder. "Andrew, stop this!" he demanded, and I shook my head at his command.

"I should *never* have run away. I know this now! I fell prey to evil. I was deceived by the false beauty of the Hotel Larouche," I said, with defeat. Turning back to my sister, I looked into her white eyes and spoke to the monster again. "Take me, and let my sister go!"

Through streams of tears, I chanted the words, 'let her go', over and over again. Without thought, my hand reached for hers and, to my surprise, she let it remain in mine! Never was I so sorry for something I'd done. It felt so wrong to be alive and well, while my sister was haunted by spirits.

Anais growled and moaned but her grip on my hand never slackened. The priest resumed his prayers and I continued to encourage my sister to find the light. The bed shook and the curtains swung side to side, but my eyes never left my sister's.

Suddenly, the bed stopped its quaking and the room quieted. The hot air escaped the room almost as quickly as it had arrived. The demon let out a long, deafening scream, and I covered my ears in complete terror.

Then, just when I thought the demon would take hold of us all, my sister fell back onto her pillow, collapsing from exhaustion.

We all stood still, not exactly sure *what* had just happened. I visibly examined my body. Was the demon inside me? I looked at my father, who looked at Anais with wide eyes. Her *own* eyes were closed; she had fallen into a deep sleep.

"Is it gone?" I asked, of no one in particular. The priest, still gripping his bible, walked toward Anais and placed his hand on her forehead. We all watched the color seep back into her face, with unbearable anticipation. No one moved. We all feared that what we just witnessed was no miracle, but another one of the demon's jests. The priest removed his hand and looked at my father with a smile.

"It is *gone*... for now. Only time will tell," he said.

In disbelief, my father ran to the bed and collapsed to his knees beside us. He held his daughter, sobbing into her shoulder. I saw my father's tears pour out his years of care and concern for Anais, as he held her. He had been with her every step of the way. He gave up his life to protect her and now, she was free. I wasn't sure how that was possible, or what I had said that righted years of pain and suffering, but it was *over*.

The overwhelming emotion, coupled with the high temperature of the room, was enough to send me out into the salon, leaving my father and the others alone for a moment. With all that had happened, I felt the need for fresh air and a soft chair. I needed, just for a moment, to remember myself. Though Anais' soul had been returned to her, I felt that -in a strange sort of way- so had *mine*.

I reviewed everything I experienced since I woke up that morning. A haircut... a dinner party... an exorcism - you know, just your *everyday* sort of things.

The door to Anais' room opened behind me, and then closed shut again. The priest and his peculiar henchman made their way to the front of the salon, toward the entry way and stopped. "Wait outside for me. I will only be a moment," the priest directed, quietly. The two large gentlemen nodded and left the room, their dogs still at their sides.

When the entry door shut, the priest turned around to look at me, a small curious smile forming on his face. Calmly, he walked around the room, taking occasional glances at me. Together, we remained in the room, too bewildered to speak about what had just happened, perhaps fearing that our words would somehow jinx our good fortune. I was certain that the man had many questions for me, some that I, myself, couldn't even answer. After a few more agonizing minutes under the priest's close scrutiny, he finally spoke.

"Twenty years, I've visited your sister," he said, continuing his slow pace around the room. "Twenty years, and I could not get through to the demon that was inside of her," he paused, then he stopped his languid stroll and stared at me. "What's your secret?"

After a moment, I shrugged and thought up the best answer I could. "A good heart?" I suggested. The priest, taken aback by my response, raised his eyebrows with amusement.

"Are you suggesting that I do not possess a *good heart*?" he questioned. I shook my head, apologetically.

"I'm just saying that *my* goodness is a... surprise. *Yours* is expected. The devil didn't see my goodness coming!" I confessed. The priest chuckled, extending his hand for a handshake. Graciously, I took it and firmly shook the man's hand. The expression on his face seemed to search my own for some sort of clue that would lead to understanding.

"Andrew Godfrey, your father spoke of you so often! You and your brother, Anvil. I recognized you right away when I first saw you. You're the spitting image of your father, you know," the priest observed, smiling. "Look at you," the man continued, "Sophisticated and so refined... and yet, still so *green*," he grinned. The priest was *certainly* different from the old, hard-nosed clergymen back home. He walked toward my chair and, without my consent, disheveled my hair so that it stood out in every direction.

"Much better," he said, taking a step back and observing his work.

It was father's turn to walk into the room. His head was wet with sweat and his shoulders slumped over, with immense fatigue. He stood against the wall, peering out of one of the large windows, his mind preoccupied. I didn't understand it. *Why did he not rejoice in the reclaimed life of his daughter?*

"I presume that there is no need for *me* anymore," the priest said, cutting through the silence in the salon. The statement drifted in the air, as neither my father nor I spoke up in response. I sensed that the priest felt my father's agitation, same as I. Cautiously, he approached my father, stood beside him, and joined him in looking out the window.

"It's a *miracle* what happened today, Alben," the priest spoke, reverently. *Too* many years, had they battled the creature. Now, it was time for them to leave all of it behind.

"What happened here tonight, Father Caius? What did I *fail* to do?" my father asked, perplexed. The priest placed a hand on his shoulder.

"Do not blame yourself, Alben, for a curious thought came to me when I was in that room," the priest said, as he motioned for my father to sit. After my father sat down, the priest continued, "You mentioned Anais had a twin, but you never knew of the great amount of love he carried. Peculiar isn't it? A boy who lives among the vagrants of Larouche was so ready to sacrifice himself for the sister he didn't even know existed! It was too difficult for the devil to corrupt him, even in a filth ridden place like this hotel. You can search the ends of the world for the right answer, but I believe her association with Andrew gave her what she's always needed. Twins hold a powerful connection and through it, love and the ability *to* love found Anais."

"But I'm *not* a good person, Priest!" I exclaimed, "Look at where I am! Look at all that I've become! No one sent me away. I left of my own will. I ran away like a coward! I am not bound or gagged to stay here, yet I remain in this prison by *choice*. I'm just like *them,*" I said, arguing with the pair who believed me so undeniably good. My admission surely conveyed all my wickedness and shortcomings.

I am no better that the rest of them, I thought, as I remembered that all the patrons were still engaged in the celebration for Larouche downstairs.

"There is no man alive who has never been tempted, but it's your ability to recognize it and banish that power over you that matters. By sacrificing your soul for your sister's... well, that's about as selfless as it gets," the priest said, gripping my shoulders playfully. "Don't be so severe on yourself, Andrew! This place was designed to lure in the innocent and sinful alike. What separates them is their decision to *stay* or *go.*"

The priest looked at me with challenging eyes and a smile. He stepped away from us to warm his hands by a small fire that glowed softly in the fire place. "Though, I'll admit, I've never met someone who tried to *leave* this place."

The priest gazed at the room around him, in the same way that a spectator observed an art piece did. My father, who had retreated into the stern, distant exterior he often wore, spoke to me from his chair.

"Andrew, what are you doing here? There is so much you have to give to the world, yet you choose to waste it away," he said, with great concern for his youngest son.

"If I told you, I fear you'd be disappointed in me," I admitted, not looking at anything but the floor. *The priest was wrong*, I thought. I *had* been seduced by Larouche and all its finery and I didn't think leaving it would possible. Once I walked through the lobby, or conversed with Patch... I would be lost in it again. "I left to save someone and I failed. I was selfish! All I wanted to save was myself. Now, I'm stuck and every day I seem to care less and less about the person I used to be-"

"So what will you do?" my father asked, with frustration. "What's your plan? Do you wish to become part of them and give up your life? Or do you wish to fight back?" he pressed. *Fight back?* My father sounded so passionate. Right now, I only wished I had grown to be more like *him*. The priest interrupted, shaking his head.

"'Tis a fools game, Alben. The boy *couldn't* do it alone," he cut in. Then, the priest picked up his hat, and put on his coat which was hanging on a rack by the front door. My father shook his head in contradiction.

"He wouldn't be alone!" my father urged. The way they spoke to each other made absolutely *no* sense to me whatsoever. In vain, I struggled to keep up with their

388

conversation, but it was too late. The priest looked around at his surroundings once more and nodded to no one in particular. Then, he looked at me, with that same knowing smile, and tipped his hat.

"If you should ever seek refuge, I've a little chapel not too far away. You are *always* welcome," he said.

With that, the priest patted the wall and opened the door for what was most likely his last time in room 558. He closed the door to the suite, leaving my father and I both alone and speechless.

I didn't know what either of them wanted from me. The notion of leaving seemed to be the best idea, but the way they both had looked at me, with a strange sort of sadness, it seemed like they thought it wouldn't be easy. It seemed as if they knew that no amount of convincing could make me leave the hotel. The decision was mine, and mine alone.

"If you would have asked me to leave a few months ago, I may have laughed at you. I may have even argued with you, and called you vile names," I said, timidly at first. As I spoke I could feel my courage rising. "I *don't* want to be that cruel person again. That person I became... well, I don't think I like him after all."

My father, at my response, beamed with pride. I, however, was still trying to figure it all out. The priest's theories were clear, though. There was undeniably a love for Matilda, so strong and powerful, but a new and different love reserved for my sister. I didn't believe I was as good as the priest thought I was, but I *did* believe that most of the choices I made were from my the very bottom of my heart.

"I'm glad to hear it! You should be out there Andrew, creating opportunity for yourself! There is nothing here for you, but ruin," he said, looking truly exhausted. Woefully, his eyes pleaded with me to continue my life with a renewed sense of purpose. The idea, though terrifying, was exciting - but I didn't think I could do it alone.

"What about you? Won't you come back? Anais will be well again soon!" I said, taking a step closer to my father.

"Howell Village would be mortified if *one* person came back from the dead, let alone *three,*" he chuckled. "Perhaps, it's better to wait until Anais is fully recovered. I'd love to come back and continue my work at the ol' watch place again... *someday,*" he said, a smile reaching his dark eyes.

The words were a *dream*. They were what I'd always wanted to hear. *A family again.* Waiting for his return to Howell, I realized, would prove agonizing, but knowing he'd come home one day would be hope enough. My father continued, as he circled about the room.

"You remember that abandoned brick house close by our shop... just down near Quarry Street? Is it still there?" he asked. Eagerly, my father stood, gripping his hands together as I recalled the old place.

"I believe it is, yes. At least it was a year ago!" I replied, and he continued, walking about the room in long strides. Then, as if struck with an idea, he stopped walking. "What a fine hospital that would make, don't you think? The people of Howell would *certainly* benefit from it!" he smiled, with enthusiasm. I, on the other hand, was *entirely* confused. *A hospital?* He continued, "I've always thought that building *should* be put to good use. Perhaps, you could find someone, a person of medicine, to assist you," he winked, and I knew instantly who he meant.

The construction of a hospital was an almost unimaginable project for such a simple person as myself. Where would I even begin? Brick by brick, I would make a promise that the hospital would be the very place the sick and helpless could turn to. My father was right. Howell needed a hospital, a place where the sick could visit to be cured and comforted. It would be hard work. My days would be filled with sickness and worry. Demanding hours would pass by and I would seldom have any time for my own leisure...

At the Hotel Larouche, there was no *need* to work. A resident had a hobby - if they so chose -and received food, lodging and merriment in return. I could be comforted by the fact that the next day I could work leisurely on a few watches. I set my own schedule and was accountable to no one. Then, I could head to the lobby, and surround myself by the same mischief that Patch often did...

I was stuck in the middle of an unnecessary struggle. There was only *one* thing I truly needed to do. "May I bring a friend?" I asked. My father smiled, as relief washed over him.

The next day I would be leaving the old hotel. I'd be heading back to Howell Village for the first time in over a year. I'd be going *home*.

Chapter Eighteen
Parting Is Such Sweet Sorrow

Arrangements were made and plans were settled! I'd head out in the evening, and my father and sister would return to Howell Village when the time was right. It could be months until we were reunited, but I knew they were *alive*... and that was enough! I had a new life before me and it thrilled me beyond anything the hotel could provide.

My father's son, proud and feeling ten feet tall, I walked out of the suite with restored ambition. With excitement, I made my way to find Patch. Before I could return to Matilda, there was much to tell my friend. After the previous night, I only hoped the news I had for him would be received well.

With enthusiasm, I opened the door of his room and found him seated on the floor in the far corner, lost in devastation. His undershirt was stained with wine, a drunken stupor washing over his slack-jawed face. He took no notice of my presence, or if he did, he didn't show it. He stared vacantly through the window, appearing to study the sunrise, but not really seeing anything. Inching closer, I saw that he noticed me, but continued his blank observation of the sun.

"She is *gone*, Andrew," he quietly declared. "There is no *color* anymore. I walk through shades of black and gray," he muttered, looking about his unkempt room - articles of clothing and empty beer bottles littering the floor. He smirked bitterly at the filth around him. "*This* is my life now."

His room was larger than mine, and much more... *disorganized*. Playing cards and half smoked cigarettes carpeted the floor. The place *was* rather disastrous, and I wondered if the housekeeping staff had *ever* visited. I crossed my arms, trying to make light of the situation.

"Forgive me, for not wading in the pool of self-pity you've filled for yourself, but love was *also* taken from me. I know your grief, but I also know that you cannot go on this way! You must move forward - out of this place," I pleaded with him. "If you stay here, any goodness that you have will leave you, and you will become just like *them*."

Patch laughed and took a swig out of one of the nearby bottles that still held a bit of liquor in it. "There is no goodness in me, Andrew. *Tansy* saw that."

"That's not true," I started, but Patch's outrage ripped through the room's stillness.

"THEN WHY ISN'T SHE HERE?!" he shouted.

In his fury, he picked up every bottle and savagely hurled each one against the wall. The ear splitting sounds of each one breaking were hideous, and flying shards of glass flew through the room. It was only a miracle that neither one of us were harmed. It somehow seemed fitting that by breaking those bottles he was releasing the hurt and rage he had bottled in his heart.

Once his outburst had run its course, he slumped to the wooden floor and quickly wiped any trace of a tear away. He crawled to the closest corner, shaking uncontrollably, as he wrapped his arms around himself. At last, he quieted, completely exhausted. Cautiously, I spoke.

"Tansy saw you seep into the wicked wallpaper of this hotel and become one with all its cruelty, but she *never* questioned your initial spirit. It was that part of you that she fell in love with. Don't you see? Don't become one of them, Patch. Walk away from this place!"

Carefully, I brushed aside some jagged pieces of glass and sat down on the floor beside him, as he spoke. "I wouldn't even know where to find that light anymore. *She* was my light and now that darkness you speak of is all I see."

"It doesn't have to be that way," I argued.

Slowly, I began stringing together words that I hoped would alter my friend's dismal perspective.

"I have just spoken with a man, a *relative*, who has hopes of restoring a hospital that would give free care for the poor. He would like me to run it, but I haven't the first notion about what medicines we would need or what tools we would use! I would need a *doctor's* help," I outwardly hinted. I could see that Patch was listening, but was not following my proposed plan of action.

"And?" he asked, with the smallest hint of curiosity.

"*You're* a doctor, and there's no way around it. I need your help. I want you to come with me back to my hometown - back to Howell Village. I'm taking the carriage that leaves at four this evening," I stated, matter-of-factly. Patch leaned his head against the wall, smirking slightly with amusement.

"You wish *me* to enter society again? I'm not even sure I remember how to behave like a human being!" he laughed, incredulously. "I'd be better off here, at Larouche, with the other heartless creatures."

He stood up and walked to the door, holding it open for me to leave. I tried to mask the hurt I felt, but it came nonetheless. *Patch was wrong,* I thought with conviction. A part of me knew that my friend spoke a half-truth. He was right on the brink of total destruction, but *not* past reclaiming his old life. As I made my way out the door, I turned to face my resistant friend, and saw complete defiance in him. He had made up his mind, and nothing I could say would change that. No one could convince Patch of anything, *except* Patch.

"The way you sought Tansy out, I'd never believe you were heartless," I said, making one more attempt to persuade my friend. The sound of her name turned his face to stone. Patch leaned wearily against the doorframe, his eyes shutting for a long moment. Then he opened them, abruptly, fighting the sleep that was finally overtaking him.

"I'll stay here, Andrew. It's all I know," he said, resolutely. "Go on, and save yourself. I wish to remain at Larouche... *alone.*"

His words were almost enough to boil my blood with contempt. I was his friend, yet he chose to stay among those who only laughed at him! The offer I made was his one chance at reclaiming his life as a doctor, but it was not enough. It was difficult to believe that Patch, so consumed with his own loss, could not see the opportunity set before him. Regrettably, I knew I should have left without another word. I should have gone from his room and left the self-destructive doctor behind... but I *couldn't*.

"What will you do, exactly? Waste away while your mind turns to mush for the maggots?" I questioned, with frustration. Patch merely smirked. I could tell that he heard my plea, but chose to ignore it. Nevertheless, I continued, "Remember something, *friend*. It's difficult to care about others, because they can be lost in an instant. When you *don't* care, though, you lose the very part of yourself that makes you human. Patch, you don't belong *here*!"

"You don't know me. Not *really*. If you did, you'd see that I'm exactly where I belong," he said, motioning to the walls around him. With conviction, I believed he was wrong. He was *me*, but a few years advanced. He had arrived at the hotel years before I had, with more time to be beaten down by his existence here. We had all made stupid choices for the people we cared about and the dreams we believed in, but Patch was deeper into the pool of disillusion than I was. That didn't mean, however, that his life *couldn't* be saved.

"I think I *do* know you, Patch," I spoke, bravely.

Remembering something from a novel I attempted to read a few years back, I threw in one last pleading statement before I made my departure. It was something, I felt, that suited our current situation well. "Man is rarely given a second chance. If fortune smiles upon him and thrusts another opportunity his way, he'd be the biggest fool not to take it. I've never taken you for a fool, Patch. A bit of an *ass*, perhaps, but not a *fool*."

My hope was that this remark would initiate a challenge to my friend, who normally delighted in a good protest. My eyes pleaded with him, but he merely smiled sadly in return, his hand still on the door.

"You're too good for this place, Gunshot. *Goodbye,*" he said, shutting the door firmly. With that, I bid farewell to my friend, the only true friend I had ever had. Disheartened,

I replayed his parting words in my head, hearing his voice as the one remaining anchor to this hotel.

Gunshot. It was the name he had given to me during my first night at the hotel. Nearly a year at the hotel felt as if it had really been two *decades*. I felt that I had aged a lifetime in such a span. I was in a never ending dream that turned into a nightmare, so gradually that I failed to see it happening. Patch had taken me in like a brother, and we'd experienced many extraordinary times together. When the door closed, I felt a small tug on my heart. It was likely the last time I would ever see Patch. Silently, I thanked him for being the guide on my unexpected journey, and wished him well. There truly was *no one* like him.

It was nearly morning, and I still hadn't slept. I couldn't, however, as I had so much to tell Matilda. There were so many discoveries I'd made that I knew she'd be glad to hear! She had never liked the Hotel Larouche, and I loved her for that. Now we would be leaving the place, and I couldn't wait to tell her all about the new plans I had for us.

In complete exhaustion, I headed back to my room, where I nearly collapsed. It was six in the morning, but I had to see my dearest Matilda before I prepared for the next chapter of our life. It felt so good to say it like that!

"Matilda?" I said, knocking gently on the frame. Her face appeared rather quickly in the mirror, radiating with that ethereal glow.

"Here I am!" she grinned, and I returned her smile with one of my own. Over the days since we'd come to share our love, I'd noticed her waver between happy delight and hidden distress. I knew she worried about our uncertain future, but I also knew that I had the perfect solution for our happiness. Everything would be remedied once we left the hotel.

"There you are indeed!" I beamed. "Did you miss me?" I asked. She furrowed her eyebrows and laughed.

"Of course not. It's not like I've been thinking about you or anything!" she replied, sarcastically. Naturally, she was lying.

"Matilda, there is so much to tell you. I hardly know where to begin. Maybe because every time I look at you I remember that you - you magnificent being - are the cause of it *all*. You are the one who gave me freedom, so how can I possibly thank you?" I sighed, in profound admiration. She shook her head and smiled.

"Andrew! Come now, don't be silly. Tell me everything. How was the party?" she asked, as she spun around in her mirror to show her enthusiasm. Inspired, I took the time to relay everything to her, starting with the party. I spared no detail of the events in my father's rooms. I told her of my twin sister and how she came to be cured, and then ended with my new ambition to head back to Howell. She applauded and jumped up and down excitedly, and I laughed at her sweet cheerfulness.

"Andrew, your father is *alive* and you have a *sister* and a new life ahead of you! This may be the most exciting day of my life... and I'm not even alive!" she giggled, but I flinched at the reminder of her condition. "Are you excited?" she asked. Nodding, I stood up and loosened my tie.

"A bit nervous. Everything is so different, isn't it?" I asked, "I'm afraid I've greatly changed from the 'Andrew' you remember."

"You are the same boy from Howell Village, Andrew. Only, perhaps, a little *wiser* now," she said, grinning in response.

She was the love of my life, and her laughter would always warm my heart. How I missed her so! Even after everything I had done, she remained the ever constant source of light that propelled me forward. I wanted to better myself. I wanted her to look at me with the same proud eyes she looked at me with now. As I gazed at her reflection, I realized what true love meant and how *lucky* I was to have it. Matilda interrupted my love-sick stream of thought, with an observation.

"Your friend is very distraught, isn't he?" Matilda asked.

Remembering Patch's sullen face, I nodded. My heart grew heavy to think of my friend, so lost in his ways. I didn't want to think of Patch. I didn't want to think about the choice he made, and my failure to persuade him to leave with me. With a wrenching pang of sadness for my friend, I felt the desire to move away from this topic of conversation.

"He misses Tansy, just as I missed you," I said, with a heavy sigh. I leaned my head toward the mirror, yearning to feel her close to me. Her thoughts, however, lead elsewhere.

"Maybe, just maybe, Tansy was *right* to leave," Matilda, said pensively. Though I couldn't help but agree with her, I wondered why *Matilda* had come to that conclusion. I saw her stare past me, almost as if she was living in another world. "'If you *love* him, you will let him *go*'... I remember her saying something like that once," Matilda quoted, and I nodded, apprehensively. Her mind worked as it formed its conclusions.

"Matilda?" I spoke to her, trying to read her thoughts, but she only aimed a half smile in my direction.

"Funny story, actually, the walls aren't as thick as you'd think."

For once, I found it difficult to follow what she was saying. *The walls were not as thick?* I didn't understand. Before I could ask further, she continued talking, "You know something interesting? The day I died, this peculiar thought popped into my head. I thought that I would be happy if I had loved a friend - a good man - with a dream for something *more* gleaming in his eyes. I wanted to find someone I greatly *admired*. Did you know that admiration is sometimes greater than love? It's true!" she said, her smile widening. "Andrew, I admired you. I admired your inner strength, and your desire for better things. It was just a thought then, but now it all seems so clear..." she drifted. Nothing was clear to *me*. She spoke nonsensical words that I desperately tried to piece together.

"What seems clear, Matilda? I don't think I understand."

"I'd like to think that *this* is what I was always meant to do," she said, looking around the room, then back at me. *What exactly are we meant to do*? I wondered.

"You were always meant to reside in a mirror beside me?" I asked, teasingly. She shook her head, and looked at me with piercing eyes.

"*Release you.*"

As if I'd been plunged into freezing waters, the words stung me with sudden clarity. They shocked me, forcing me into senseless desperation, as they were not at all what I expected. What did she mean? Why should Matilda want to release me from her spell when I so ardently enjoyed being tangled in it?

"I don't understand," I said, weakly. She lowered her face and I noticed a soft glow beginning to surround her.

"Oh, Andrew. You've done things for me that *no* other person has ever done. You showed me how exciting life could be! We danced and I felt what I've always wanted to feel... hand in hand and heart to heart. I'd like to think that those things may not have happened had I not died and demanded that you find a way to free me from my captivity. You found the *strength* within you. You are a wonderful human being with an illuminated soul, and it's rewarding to know I had a small hand in that."

It was unbelievable to hear such praise from Matilda, but there was no need for them. "You have done more for me than you know," I replied, from the very bottom of my heart.

"Good. I'm glad. I can move on knowing that," she sighed.

Move on? Right! We had to leave!

We were leaving in a few hours and headed back to our small town. Everything would change. I hurried over to the closet and searched around for any belongings I would need to pack. Realizing I had nothing to my name, I laughed.

A year ago, I was a boy with stolen money and a mirror in his hand. Now, I found that I no longer had *any* money left in my pocket, and only a mirror to my name.

"I'm not going with you," Matilda spoke softly from her place in the mirror. I stared at her in complete disbelief, aghast that she would want to stay at Larouche.

"Of course you are going! It's no problem... I've got a hook on the door in my room that's got your name on it!" I teased and she smiled gently, but her look was more serious than I expected.

"You don't seem to understand, Andrew. *I'm moving on... and I can't go with you.*"

The realization hit me. I heard her words, but my heart wouldn't accept them. She wanted to leave this world for good, and I wasn't prepared for that. Surely, she knew she couldn't leave yet. Not when there was still so much of the world for us to discover!

"Wh-what do you mean? How can you leave? You're stuck in the mirror! You're mine. Always!" I nearly cried. Though I realized my words sounded selfish, I knew they must be spoken. It would be *impossible* to go on without her.

Matilda looked around her, oddly nervous, and moved hesitatingly within the mirror.

"I can just feel it!" she said, unable to explain much more.

She was lying, I thought. She wanted to leave me and, in my distraction during the past few months, I had neglected to make her feel wanted and loved. If I had spoken of the love in my heart for her every day, she would not want to leave. Tears filled my eyes, but I would not allow them to spill over. *I would not cry for her... because she was not leaving me.*

"You can't leave Matilda. You're coming with *me*. We have so much to see together. I want to take you with me!" I pleaded.

"You would keep a *mirror* by your side for the *rest of your life*? What about when you get married and start a family?" she asked. It was an absurd, miserable thought - too impossible to even consider.

"I have no plans to marry! I'm yours, remember?" I reminded her. Could nothing be said to alleviate her worries? There was only one love for me, and I desperately needed her to know that. My conviction was strong and I wouldn't relent!

"You'd be a fool *not* to try to find love again. There's a wonderful girl out there, lonesome and as shy as you once were, who *should* be loved by you," she said, looking away slightly. "Your life *must* continue. I will only get in the way," she said, her voice trembling. Angered by the words she spoke, I pounded my fist against the wall.

"How could you say that?" I yelled, overcome with sudden despair I felt. Slowly, I saw her visage begin to fade away from me.

"Leave me here and live your life, Andrew Godfrey, for the both of us!"

Her face, in all its radiance, drew back into her world and she was gone. My beautiful guardian angel was *gone*. I placed my hands firmly against the glass. "Do not leave me, Matilda!" I called out, begging and pleading to no one at all. I pounded on the wall with my fists again. The sounds of my sobs grew louder as I wept. She was gone. All that remained was an empty mirror.

Taking it off its hook, I wrapped my arms around the frame, shaking in misery. Suddenly, the mirror felt cold beneath my fingers. Matilda's warmth no longer emanated from it. The most wonderful gift I'd ever received had been taken from me. With sorrow, I clung to the majestic treasure, *never* wanting to part with it. It was almost worse than the first time I had lost her. "Please, Matilda, don't go! Come back. *I love you.*"

There I sat, weeping on the floor, only moments before having judged Patch for the very same thing. Again, I pounded my fists against the wall, heaving guttural sobs. For Matilda to be given to me, and then taken away was cruelty at its finest. All I could do was shake with anger as I cursed everything about my life... just as I had finally started to appreciate it.

There was no one to be angry at, I thought. Who could I blame this time? Fallen, had I, so far from the branches of my carefully crafted willow, I wondered who I could pin my blind descent on. My mother? My father? Matilda? As I looked in the mirror, willing her to come back, I found my answer. I saw that the only person at fault was *myself.*

I removed the mirror from the wall, clutching it close to me, as my body fell to the floor.

Crumbled dirt beneath my feet.

In a mirror did we meet.

You were gone, I lost you then.

The sun will never shine again.

Chapter Nineteen
False Beginnings

"Good morning, *sunshine*!"

A loud, unusually chipper voice roused me from the deep sleep I had fallen into. My cheek was pressed against the cool wood floor, and my arms still cradled the mirror.

Heavy boots stomped up to my slumped body, and I knew that *someone* had entered my room. I cracked open my right eye to see Patch, standing above me, cleaned up and carrying two bags in his hands. He took one look at me and smirked. "Is it me, or did we exchange places?" he jested. I was in *no* mood for his jokes.

"I'm not going," I managed to say, through a hoarse throat. Patch dropped his bags to the floor and scoffed.

"Forgive me, Andrew, for not *wading* in a pool of self pity," he teased, mockingly. To this, I rolled my eyes. Wounding whatever was left of my ego, he continued, "You did NOT, however, pull my weeping ass from the comfort of my room just so we could have this lovely chit chat. Now,

let's go!" he nearly demanded. "The carriage leaves in less than an hour."

Opening the front door, he beckoned for me to follow him. In my groggy state, I sat up, and wrinkled my brows at his sudden change of mind. "I thought you weren't going?" I asked, dryly. Patch merely shrugged.

"Yeah, well, I don't really have anything better to do," he said, looking down at the buttons of his jacket. "And you don't know shit about medicine, so I don't want you looking like a fool in front of your mother or nothin'," Patch lied, clearing his throat. I smirked and rested my head against the wall. Right now, I only wanted to drown my sorrows away in the hotel. I didn't want to leave without her, though she seemed capable and ready to leave *me*.

"Why must *they* go, Patch?" I sulked, as I continued to dwell on Matilda's unexpected farewell. To my dismay, I felt more tears leak across my face, unwontedly. I didn't want to leave for another place that would distract me from Matilda. I wanted to think about her *always*. Patch crouched down beside me, his expression seemingly hardened but oddly sympathetic.

"They 'go' because we're worthless sons of bitches and they can do a whole lot better. Only *they* think that, without them around, *we* can do a lot better and we will all be better for it. It's this very strange female logic that is best left untouched. If we try to make sense of it, we'll *never* leave this place!" Patch said, sarcastically as he stood up.

Still in a heap on the floor, I clung to Matilda's mirror... not entirely ready to let go. My friend looked down at me and sighed, as he leaned against the wall. "They 'go', Andrew, because they've got to find their way back to us for themselves. Maybe not today or the next day... but *someday*. Hell, at least that's what I keep telling myself. Now get up, you ugly piece of shit, and stop crying!" he said, lightly kicking my knee.

"When did you get so smart?" I asked, with annoyance. Patch crossed his arms and smirked arrogantly.

"I'm a doctor, boy, and a damn good one, too," he said, with confidence. It was strange seeing Patch this way. Doctor Patrick Rhodes had made his appearance at *last*. He pulled me up and shook me out of my despair. "Come on now. Stop being a stubborn fool," he said, as he pulled my arm and brought me to my feet. Angrily, I shook my arm free of his grasp.

"You have no authority over me!" I bellowed, "I can do what I like!" I shouted in defiance. Then, like a flash of light, he backhanded me across the face, so harshly, that it felt as if my cheek had split in two.

"Did anyone ever tell you that you whine a lot?" he laughed.

"Ow!" I yelled, shoving him into the wall. He laughed again, while I massaged my right cheek. "What's *wrong* with you?" I shouted, as he checked his watch.

"A whole lot I'm afraid, but we don't have time for storytelling. Let's go, or the next hit will be with my knuckle dusters!" he warned. I had *no doubt* he was telling the truth. In a haze, I collected myself, still reeling from the slap I had just received. There was just no telling what Patch would do next! I sulked and agreed, with the enthusiasm of a child getting ready to head off to school in the wee hours of the morning.

"Got your bags?" he asked and I shook my head, then he stared at me curiously. "No bags for the school girl?"

"Remind me again why we're friends?" I asked, with annoyance. Patch shrugged and bent down to retrieve his own suitcases before he headed out of the room.

"Because all of *your* friends are imaginary!" Patch grinned, as he held open the door with his foot. Instantly, I thought of Matilda, who had left no proof of her existence except the savored conversations and memories in my mind. With overwhelming sadness, I hung her mirror on the wall.

"Right," I replied. Before I made my way out of the room, I stopped and looked around. A sudden feeling of uncertainty overcame me. The walls of the hotel offered safety, but who knew what was out *there*? Real life awaited us, and I instantly found myself doubting my decision.

"Is this a bad idea?" I asked Patch, and he nodded as he held the door open.

"All ideas usually are. Just depends on how well you can convince yourself that they're *not*," he said, as he looked behind me, into the room. Patch furrowed his eyebrows.

"What about *that*?" he asked, looking at the mirror hanging on the wall. "Aren't you going to take it with you?"

Silently, I shook my head. Matilda was gone, so what purpose did I have in keeping it? It only served as a reminder of what I could never have. Matilda was in heaven with the angels. She would not think of me anymore. With a heavy heart, I took one last look at it, picked up my bag, and walked from the room for the last time...

My mind seemed to be playing tricks on me, as I could have *sworn* that Matilda stood in the mirror, just as she always had! Her image, in seconds, quickly vanished and I counted the occurrence as merely an illusion - something I desperately wanted but would never have again. Still, it felt as if she was there, observing me from her spot on the wall. I guess I had grown accustomed to seeing her there, every day for the past year. I knew I would never really be ready to say goodbye. My mind briefly toyed with the idea of her returning one day. It would be miraculous to see her again...

Pull yourself together, Andrew. She'll not be coming back.

"Days of dragging that thing around and now, you're not even going to take it with you!" Patch said, shaking his head in confusion, and then he closed the door. We walked down the hallway for the last time and rode the moving machine down once more. *Nifty invention*, I thought. *Hope it catches on!*

"You should tell me about that mirror, sometime," Patch smirked, and I nodded. I highly doubted he would ever believe the story I had to tell, but maybe *one day* I would share my secret.

Nothing had changed. The party in the lobby still went on. It flowed from the dining room and upward, to every floor. Though a small part of me would miss the world of fantasy and glamour, the greater part of me was relieved to be free of it. But then again, it was also the place where I had found *myself*.

Patch walked through the crowded frivolity with a hand shielding his eyes, trying to resist the temptation of joining the throng. I knew it was much more difficult for Patch to leave the hotel, as he had lived there much longer. I laughed, and he smiled back. We were *leaving*, and that was an adventure in itself!

Patrons called out to us left and right, each begging us to join in their fun, but we ignored them. That life, I knew, was behind us now. I didn't think we would ever find our way back to that sinfully wonderful place. Still, my experience at the Hotel Larouche was incomparable. During my time there, I had discovered what was *truly* important to me.

A boy with a mirror and stolen money, now left the hotel as a man with no mirror and not a cent to his name. But he left a *good* man, and that was all he really needed to be.

Matilda. Matilda. Matilda. Matilda.

Would I never stop thinking of her? She had started everything. In life, she led the crowd and danced to her own rhythm. In death, she changed me, seeing something in me that no one else did. She loved me, and because of it, my life could now move on. It *had* to. She would want it no other way.

Perhaps, Matilda had been an excuse to leave behind what I thought would be my doom, but in her death she saved me. In *life*, she had saved me, back in the village. I'm not sure where the will to live would have come from without her smiles. Matilda twirled in a garden of life. She made flowers bloom in cold winters; the sun was her closest friend. I loved her and I always would.

***

My father awaited us at the steps of the carriage. Patch threw his bags up by the driver's seat and made his way inside. Then, he leaned his head out the window and smiled. "Goodbye, sir!" Patch said, extending his hand to my father, who shook it firmly.

"Watch my son," he ordered, and Patch, in immediate confusion, turned to me with wide eyes and lifted brows. I nodded and he turned back to Black Ben, suddenly spotting the resemblance.

"Small world, ain't it?" Patch smirked, as this new realization dawned on him, "So does that mean your sister is..." his voice trailed off, as I nodded once again. "You've got one twisted family, Andrew!"

My father laughed, and then took my hand in his, gripping it tightly. "I have one *last* proposition for you," my father began, and I listened intently. "When the time comes, I would like you to teach Anais how to read and write, and draw too, if there's time for it. Word is that you are quite the artist," he winked.

The proposition was music to my ears. I wasn't sure where the high praise about my craft had come from, but I was flattered nonetheless. It thrilled me to think that I could

421

help my sister out with anything she might need. She and I could grow close through a love of learning. There didn't seem a better way to get to know the sister I had only just met.

"You have no idea what that would mean to me," I grinned. Father shook my hand again and opened the door of the carriage. Abruptly, I stepped in and poked my head out the window. My father tipped his hat to the both of us.

"With practice, maybe you can teach your own class one day," my father said, swelling with pride. "Goodbye, boys!"

I waved and Patch tipped his own hat, taking a swig from a bottle of gin he managed to swipe on his way out. "Fare thee well!" he said, after a big swallow of the gruesome jolly-juice. My father snatched the bottle from his hand and held it away from Patch's reaching arms. Mildly amused, my father cheerfully reproached him.

"Maintain your mischief, Patch. Just keep it in a *different* bottle," he winked. With that, he left and returned to the Hotel Larouche. Hopefully, it would not be long before I saw him again. In time, I knew, we would all be together at last.

Just then, Bravery rode up to the carriage on his unicycle. My first acquaintance at the hotel, I'd forgotten to thank the ever busy concierge for putting up with my questions and random requests over the past year.

"Bravery! Come to say goodbye, did you?" I asked cheerfully. There was nothing lighthearted in his look, however. His expression was serious and genuinely fearful as he looked at me with wide eyes, his teeth actually chattering. He held out a small red envelope, as his shaking finger pointed toward the very top of the hotel.

"Message... *from above*," he whispered. Following his pointing finger, I spotted a window with thick velvet curtains concealing the very room of the man whom everyone revered. Of course! The room undoubtedly belonged to Larouche, who, from that spot, had a clear view of the streets below.

I took the envelope from Bravery's quivering hand and opened it. A thick wax seal with the letter 'L' had melted against envelope, making it difficult to open. At last, I managed to tear the seal and removed a small card with an even smaller message written on it.

Don't come back.

M. Larouche

I re-read the words and breathed a sigh of relief. He didn't have to worry about me coming back. I had no intention of doing so. I knew, however, that Larouche was displeased with me and a small part of me wondered what he would do if I ever returned.

He'd kill me, I thought. It was that simple. No one would question him for it either, because he was Larouche and one never wanted to entangle one's self with that sort of power. I had chosen to leave his palace, thus denouncing him as my king. I should have known that my plan of action wouldn't sit well with him. Quickly, I turned to Bravery.

"He has my word."

With that, Bravery left - without a single goodbye. I found I couldn't pass judgment on him. Despite his name, Bravery was as much a coward as I had been. Victim to Larouche, he was one of the mayor's many lackeys and I didn't want to cause him any further trouble. Watching him enter the hotel, I heaved a sigh. *Farewell, Bravery.* Then, I looked up at the room with the dark curtains. *Farewell, Larouche.*

I sat back in the carriage, oddly unsettled. A peculiar feeling overwhelmed me. *What was I missing?* I had no luggage, but somehow, I knew I had left something behind. I sat up and checked my pockets, not really knowing what I was looking for. Then, it struck me!

Quickly I jumped out of the carriage. There was one thing I had to do before I could leave the hotel. "What now?" Patch sighed.

"Give me one second!" I pleaded. Before he could stop me, I took off in a hurried dash down the street. Panting, I pushed passed a large group of women, carrying dozens of shopping bags. One of the women nearly whacked me with a large hat box she held! I glanced back at Patch, who was leaning out of the carriage - frantically swinging his pocket watch, pointing to it dramatically. The carriage would be leaving, but there was still someone I *had* to see.

Finally, I approached Madame Luelle's dress shop and stopped in front of its large window. Valentina was there, in her usual spot, still and focused as always. During my stay, I had made it a point to stop by her window often to wave hello. Occasionally, she looked back and smiled, ever so slightly. Now, I waved, desperately trying to get her attention. She looked at me and held out her hand so that her palm faced the glass of the window. On it, written in black, were the words "*Hello Andrew!*" I smiled and waved again. She had discovered my name!

Hurriedly, I entered Luelle's shop and found her busy at the rear of the shop with a customer. I whispered to Valentina, careful that I was out of earshot from the vile owner. "I'm leaving today. Would you like to come, too?" I asked. She looked at me, both puzzled and uncertain. "Quickly! The carriage leaves now!" I urged.

Valentina drew her shoulders up, jutted out her chin, and with a look of spite and disgust in Luelle's direction, hopped down off of her pedestal.

"I'd *love* to."

She took my hand and we were out the door in seconds, hearing Luelle's screams behind us.

"Come back here girl! Come back! Come back now!" she screeched. In our haste, we ran to the carriage. I held the door open for Valentina and jumped in after her, laughing as I closed it behind us. We both slumped in our seats, grateful to be heading out - unscathed. Tapping the roof, I called out to the driver.

"Howell Village, please!" I yelled.

"Your funeral," I heard our driver mutter dryly. We all sat there, listening to the sounds of his boots trample over our heads as he took his place at the top of the carriage. Patch looked over at Valentina and then back at me with a smug smile.

"I see you went shopping!" Patch grinned, then he glanced out the window as the carriage began to move. "Don't look now, but I think we've got some spectators," he said with amusement. He opened the window, and outside I saw nearly a *hundred* patrons, head to toe in their finery, watching our departure. No one so much as waved or said goodbye. They simply watched the moving carriage with narrowed eyes that practically warned us *never* to return.

In the middle of it all, I spotted a familiar face. There was *Harvey Nicholas*, the man I had seen frequently during my stay at the hotel. Hastily, he had always jotted down notes on his small pad of paper. I left the hotel learning nothing more about the odd man than what I saw. All I knew for certain, was that he was entirely too focused for the world he inhabited.

We looked out the windows for our last sight of Hotel Larouche, watching it become smaller and smaller as we rode away. Even from a distance, it seemed impenetrable. It was a fortress of beauty that could never be equaled in splendor. I found myself considering what it meant to each of us, as we rode away. Patch looked as if he was in true mourning. Valentina seemed to be glaring at the hotel with contempt. As for me, I was simply happy to leave that place in one piece. The air *already* felt clearer.

"Howell Village then... to see your... *wife?*" Valentina asked, biting her lip. I smiled and shook my head.

"Mother," I corrected. Patch rolled his eyes and covered his face with his hat, as he settled into a nap, while Valentina and I began a long multifaceted conversation covering many topics. She was different from most of the girls I had met. There was, of course, no one in my mind who could replace Matilda, but I saw Valentina making a wonderful companion for someone someday. She was humorous and maybe a bit odd, but it only added to her charm.

"I always thought it would be smart to name a dog Here," she remarked, and my eyebrows formed a rigid line.

"*Why?*" I inquired. It wasn't the first bizarre thing she'd said, more like the fifth or sixth, but each one took me by surprise.

"That way you wouldn't have to say, 'Come here, boy'. You could simply stop at 'Come, Here'. It would save lots of time, and Luelle always said that time *shouldn't* be wasted!" she said, smiling smugly - quite pleased with herself. I wanted to laugh. I wanted, so badly, to laugh, but I could tell she was proud of her idea, as if she'd been thinking about it for some time. I didn't have the heart to tell her that naming a dog *Here* would save *no one* time if it was repeatedly followed by laughter. One could argue that it would *waste* time. She sat quite contentedly, however, so I kept my mouth shut and nodded as if her idea was terrific. One thing was certain. Valentina was becoming one of the most interesting people I had the pleasure of meeting. How could she not be? After all the time she'd spent sitting in the window, she must have had dozens of thoughts like *these*.

After a while, the carriage began to slow down. Peeking my head out the window, I saw it. A year away and it still looked *exactly* the same! Before me was Howell Village standing there, looking no more odious than it had before - but far more beautiful seen now in a new light. It was *home* and it always would be.

In my eagerness, I didn't wait for the carriage to stop. I raced toward my house, careful to remain undetected by any of the villagers. The way I looked, with my hair relatively combed and wearing new fitted clothing, I doubted I would be recognizable to anyone anyway. I was determined, however, to make sure my mother was aware of my presence first, before the town was notified of my return. Dodging between trees and hedges, the cool wind prickled my skin as I jumped over rickety wooden fences to get to my house.

It felt *wonderful* to be back.

It was worlds apart from the Hotel Larouche. People had jobs and children to feed. There was a measured sense of responsibility here and rules to follow. My opinion had greatly changed over the year, as the small town I returned to quickly became the most beautiful place I had ever seen!

Reaching my house, the last one the block, I pushed open the small wooden gate and looked at the garden.

Though it was poorly maintained, the flowers were wild and in bloom. Taking one step up the crooked porch stairs, I stopped as the floorboards creaked. If I went in, they'd want to know what I'd been doing this past year. They would want to know where I had *lived*. If I went in, they would possibly decide to cast me out! Though I had changed so greatly, they remained the same people I left a year ago. In fear, I knew I would find myself stuck in the *same* situation. My mother, whom I had learned had suffered much more than I imagined, would scold me only to conceal her pain.

It took courage to take another step forward. I'd run away from all this, so did I really want to go back? Did I want this life again? I knew my friends back at the carriage would wait for a word that I was alright. Their lives were about to change, too. They had followed me, awaiting a signal that it *was* possible to return to civilization and live to tell the tale. I wouldn't let them down.

Most importantly, I wanted to be home more than I realized. I wanted someone to scold me and box my ears when I did something wrong. I wanted my family, plain and simple as they were, to be with me no matter how hard they tried to push me away.

The door was still hung unevenly, sending bits of twigs and leaves rustling beneath it and into our home. My brother never *did* fix it, but I suppose if he had, I'd hardly recognize the place. It felt as if it had been ages since I left!

Before I could open the door, I heard a deep somewhat familiar voice, preventing me from making another sound. "Don't you understand, woman? Property was damaged! Goods were stolen - and all at the hands of *your* son."

"My son is *dead*! Have you no compassion?"

"Just days ago, your son was spotted among the deviants at the Hotel Larouche. He is *alive* and I will see to it that I am rightfully paid for my loss."

I caught my breath, as I could scarcely believe what I was hearing. *It couldn't be.*

Cautiously, I peeked through a crack in the door and saw three men, in a heated dispute with my mother. Anvil stood behind her, looking thinner and more helpless than I had ever seen him. The man who spoke was none other than Baxton Brew himself! He looked haggard and extremely out of sorts. He nearly spat as he spoke.

432

"Your son was a strange boy. Anyone could see that!" Baxton yelled. For a moment, I witnessed a look of hurt on my mother's face. It was unusual to see any form of tenderness in her eyes, and I desperately wanted to run and comfort her.

"You speak out of pain from the loss of your daughter, Baxton, but do not forget that I, too, have lost a child. Do not pursue this. *I beg you,*" she pleaded with him, and the two men beside Baxton awaited his next move.

"As long as there is no body, I cannot confirm anything - but no one burns down someone's house and gets away with it! You understand that?" Baxton said, pointing a finger at my mother's face. "Now, if he should *resurrect* and show his face around here, I *will* undo him. I promise you, your boy's life will *not* be his own," he warned, lowering his finger. Baxton turned from the room and he and his men made their way to the front door.

In a panic, I jumped off the porch and over the side fence that surrounded our house. Then, I took off in a hurried sprint, running as fast as I could! I fled our house, knowing that I would only endanger the lives of Anvil and my mother if I stayed there a moment longer.

All actions had consequences. These were mine. It was foolish to believe that I could return to Howell so easily. It was foolish for me to believe I would find Baxton in fine sorts and not harboring any sort of ill will toward me. He had always despised our family, most especially me. I was foolish to have believed he had ever wanted me involved in his daughter's life, *strange* and *bizarre* as he proclaimed me to be.

I ran from the house knowing I would never be able to return. *Not this way*. A future in Howell seemed impossible, so where would I go? Suddenly, the list of people who wanted me dead, both in Howell and back at the hotel, was growing! I made my way back to the waiting carriage, where Patch and Valentina stood, hopeful. Regrettably, I saw that I had dragged my *friends* into it, too. My knees buckled and I fell to the dirt road, weary from the turn of events, completely incapable of finding a solution.

"Andrew! Are you alright?" Patch shouted as he ran over to me. Hearing his voice only in a distant fog, I nodded. I was aware of my surroundings and fully conscious, but my mind was frantically lost in other places.

"We can't go back! They'll kill me!" I blurted out. I saw Patch and Valentina stare at each other with confusion. "They think I started a fire a year ago. It was the same fire that allowed for my escape - but I swear I did not start that fire! They want me *dead*! What don't you understand?" I yelled. Patch paced back and forth and Valentina anxiously bit away at her fingernails. After a moment, Patch spoke up.

"Well, Andrew. What are we to do? We can't go back. Larouche will tear us limb from limb! You saw the way they eyed us as we left," he said, looking at me through anxious eyes. I wondered how *I* had suddenly become the leader of our small group.

Truth was, Patch was right. I *had* seen the looks from the surrounding patrons. I saw the snarls from the onlookers daring us to return. In leaving, I'd managed to jeopardize everyone I cared about. What were we to do? Where were we to go? The answers all rested squarely upon my very own shoulders. Frantically, I replayed the eventful past few days over and over again. I remembered everything my sister had done that day. I thought about everything my father had said to me, every word the priest had spoken...

Looking at Patch and Valentina's worried faces, I stood up, dusting myself off with renewed confidence. It was then that I realized *exactly* where we needed to go.

"I know a place."

Chapter Twenty
A Bit of Sky

Above the door of what appeared to be a small, humble chapel some distance from Howell Village, a wooden plank proclaimed just one word:

"SANCTUARY"

Finding this peculiar, I looked at Patch, who was already making his way out of the carriage. He stood, pulling out another cigarette, seemingly unfazed by the building, located in the middle of vast nothingness. Valentina, under the shelter of a red parasol, stood looking away from our driver, who was relieving himself a few yards away. The surrounding terrain was cold and we all simply stood there, lost and without a single plan.

Valentina took a seat on a lonely bench and Patch, his cigarette now lit, made his way to the old building. Apprehensively, I followed him.

The doors were open. A small sign, nailed to one of the towering doors, read:

"For all who wish to remember what they used to be."

It was a church - one that had the ancient appearance of a melted candle. Had the place been under siege once? Had it been burned in a treacherous fire? Everything seemed to be followed by questions these days.

Taking a seat near the back, I looked down the wooden pews in the empty chapel. It felt strange sitting in a place so quiet... so still. In the extraordinarily rare calmness we had stumbled upon, I allowed my aching shoulders to settle, as my frenzied nerves relaxed in the old church. I hadn't realized the physical toll the Hotel Larouche had taken on me. As I sat, trying to gather my thoughts, I realized my breathing was abnormally rapid and my right knee was bouncing uncontrollably.

Settle, I told myself. *You're in good hands now.*

I knew, however, that it would take days - if not months - before I could find the kind of tranquility found in this church within myself.

A part of me, too insignificant to dwell on, wondered how the old hotel was doing. I thought fleetingly about the glamorous parties and late night gallivanting. Quickly, I reminded myself that it was all a mirage.

Then, there were those painful thoughts that I knew I'd never leave behind. *Was she there? Did she find her way back? Was she waiting for me?* It would take a very long time to convince myself that Matilda was gone and that I would have to move on. It seemed an impossible thing to do.

Through all the tear stained memories, she had been the one person, the sole motivation that led me to the hotel in the first place. Her life - her *death* - would be forever captured in the chambers of my mind, a vessel loaded with misfortune. I simply could not relinquish thoughts of her. They would remain there, like sticky sap on a wilted tree.

Footsteps sounded in the church and I looked up to find Patch beside me, staring straight ahead at the image of Christ nailed to the cross. He looked at it, his eyes tired. His fatigue paled in comparison, however, to the restless, pensive expression he frequently wore at Larouche. Certainly, his health would improve being away from the hotel, but I had yet to discover how his sanity would fare. After a moment lost in his disarrayed thoughts, he collapsed into the pew next to me, and exhaled.

"This place gives me a case of the guilts. How can you stand it?" he asked, and I held my hand up to my ear.

"Listen," I told him. He looked around, expectantly.

"What?" he asked, straining to hear. I smiled in response.

"Silence. You ever heard a sound so magnificent?" I spoke, in awe. He shrugged, clearly unimpressed.

"I prefer the sounds of cards being shuffled and an endless tap, myself!" he chortled. Rolling my eyes, I saw his mouth spread into a familiar grin, as he leaned back in his seat.

Meanwhile, I looked up at the solid beams of wood that created the church's ceilings. Man made this, I observed. Hard working men had labored to create a place where all could find solace in prayer. I'd never seen it in that particular light before, but now that I had, the appreciation had me staring up in complete astonishment. Then, I turned to Patch, whose leg bounced uncomfortably, as he shifted in his seat.

"I'm glad you've decided to join me, Patch. I don't know what I would have done facing Howell Village without you. To be honest, I'm *not* sorry I dragged you into this mess. Life doesn't look so bleak with a friend like you beside me," I spoke, sincerely. He elbowed me in the side, trying not to appear too flattered by the compliment.

"Don't say shit like that to me," he smirked, trying to appear unfazed. "You've got pretty low expectations for your friends, Andrew," he added, sarcastically.

Smiling, I resumed looking at the beams. Then, foolishly, I turned to Patch, hoping to ask him about a certain thought I knew he still dwelled on. We would soon be a long way from the previous lives we led, and I only hoped he felt he could confide in me.

"Patch?" I began, but before I could ask about the person closest to his heart, he shook his head as if he'd seen my question coming all along.

"Don't ask me, Andrew, or I'll have to knock you senseless again... in front of Him," he said, pointing to the crucifix. I laughed at his honest brutality. He hadn't lost *that* since leaving Larouche. His response, however, was enough to tell me that he would live as I lived... Tansy would always be with him, but he would move on, concealing his greatest loss.

The question I almost asked was enough to send him to his feet. He looked down at me and patted my shoulders, a hint of a sad smile forming at the corners of his mouth.

"Come on, Godfrey. Let's get out of here before we burn," he said, only half joking. In response, I laughed at the worried look on his face.

We made our way out through the doors when Patch looked back to the altar and stopped, a distant look lingering on his face.

It was certain that, during the time I'd known him, Patch had battled with himself on numerous occasions. Time away from the hotel would put life into perspective for him, I felt, and would return him to his compassionate self. He could resume his practice again, and help the sick as he had before. I feared, however, for that mischievous burst of light that would inevitably dim over time. I worried about that cannon-like spark that fueled Patch, and created the ball of fire within him. What would he be if that burnt out? What would he do then? Very few, if any, escaped from Larouche and I worried that without the *hotel*, without his *Tansy*, I would no longer recognize my friend.

"Godfrey? Is that *you*?" a voice asked.

442

Patch and I turned to see a gaunt figure in black moving toward us from the shadows of the arches. It was the priest I'd seen before at the hotel, whose name my father told me was *Father Caius.* He was hardly recognizable, as he stood beside a single row of lit candles. He squinted, trying to make my face out in the flickering light, and then lifted his hands up as if to rejoice.

"It *is* you! And you've brought a friend. How wonderful!" he grinned, with enthusiasm. He came closer, and I felt Patch take a slight step back.

"I've come to seek your help," I told Father Caius immediately. There was no point delaying the inevitable. The priest nodded, as if he had expected a moment like this.

"Follow me," he spoke directly. As I prepared to follow him, I turned to Patch. My friend waved me off, his motion telling me he'd be fine on his own, as he lit another cigarette.

Into the dark crevices and corridors of the church, I followed Father Caius. Mentally, I tried to formulate my plea to the old priest. Would he be able to spare a night of warmth and a hot meal for the runaways? I'd hardly known the man a day and yet, he appeared to be my only salvation. Who else could I turn to?

We approached a dark room, near the back of the church and Father Caius lit a few candles to provide much appreciated light. Various garments hung about the room, and a few books were scattered about. He motioned to a chair beside a modest table and I took a seat. I interlaced my fingers and sat up straight, prepared to approach the priest with my plea.

"Andrew Godfrey," the priest began, "I knew you'd stop by eventually. I just didn't know it would be so soon!" Father Caius said playfully. He poured water from a pitcher into two cups and took a seat at the small wooden table.

"I can't go home, Priest. There are men back in Howell Village that want to kill me! You know everything that the Godfrey family has gone through. I wouldn't want to bring them more trouble," I admitted guiltily. There was more trouble in Howell than he knew, and the more I elaborated, I knew he understood my predicament.

"And I suppose heading back to Larouche is not an option?" Father Caius hesitated and watched me, carefully.

"You're not serious! A priest would never endorse such a place!" I nearly scoffed, and he chuckled to himself. Artfully, he curled his fingers around his cup before he proceeded.

"You are trapped in quite a mess, Andrew," Father Caius said, staring at me with an odd twinkle in his eye. "Well, I'm here to tell you that I may have an answer for you... though I'm not sure it's one you're well prepared for."

With this, the priest stood up. He walked around the homely room and then stopped to look at me. In the apprehensive way that the priest regarded me, I knew it wouldn't be any simple solution. With some reluctance, I nodded.

"I think I should like to hear what you have to say," I spoke timidly. The priest nearly jumped from his skin, as he pulled out his chair and sat beside me.

"Excellent! I've been waiting for this day, Andrew Godfrey! This is the day when goodness makes its comeback, for I am here to tell you that the Hotel Larouche does not exist from hard work, brick, and stones alone."

"It was won in a bet, I was told," I said, recalling Patch's account of Larouche's history.

"Wrong!" he shouted. I looked at the priest, whose eyes grew wide, as they bore into my own. "Oh, Andrew! Your naiveté serves you well!"

He rushed to a wall and, from the ceiling, pulled down on a chain. Attached to it, a wide piece of parchment slowly began to unfold. I saw that it was a map of the interior of the Hotel Larouche and all its intricate rooms and passageways. The map itself was old, and a cloud of dust dispersed at its unraveling. Noticeably, I saw that a small brand, much like a ticket tag, marked the corner of it.

"*This* is one of the many souvenir maps found of the Hotel Larouche for travelers and residents alike. It's drawn on standard parchment and it sold for practically nothing," he said, watching me examine the map. He stood beside the map admiring it, then suddenly ripped it from its hook on the ceiling and slammed it against the table.

"*This* map, however, isn't the one everyone wants!" he said, staring at the map with disdain.

Admittedly, the wild look in his eyes frightened me. He wasn't the typical, reverent priest I'd met over the course of my life, and I wondered if he spoke the truth or nonsensical fantasy. Either way he spoke with great passion.

"Andrew, the Hotel Larouche runs on *magic* - used for dark and wicked purposes. If we find the magic, we can bring down the hotel and use its power for *good*."

Magic? The more he spoke, the more he lost me. "I don't understand," I began, "A million things have happened today and I find I can't keep up!"

"Listen, Andrew! It's simple. Nearly fifty years ago, a man riding on a half-dead horse came through the city of Roden. The man had wandered through our land alone, faced with death. He was starving Andrew, and all he wanted was a drink of water."

"A drink of water?" I asked quite perplexed, but the priest went on.

"Yes. Pay attention," he chided, "I hate to admit it, but no one offered him a drink. Lord knows how many people passed the man by, disgusted by his horrible smell and unsightly appearance. It was close to seven o'clock when I stumbled upon the unfortunate beggar. I was headed to a town hall meeting, hoping the grant for a new roof on this very chapel had been awarded to our parish. It was something I had been praying for, and finally I was to receive the answer!

"Seems silly now. My desire for a new roof had nearly caused me to miss the man lying on the edge of the road. I was in a hurry when I found the poor beggar lying beside his horse, pleading for water. I was torn, as I knew I would miss the beginning of the meeting if I went back to the church for some water for him. I knew they could possibly deny our little chapel the grant based upon my tardiness alone... but I couldn't leave him. I took the man back to the church, gave him clothes and a hot meal, and allowed him to rest here for the night," the priest reminisced.

"What happened to the man? Did you ever get the grant?" I asked, but the priest merely smiled.

"The church attained a new roof *eventually*, but not that night. The council deemed my absence as a sign of impropriety," he shrugged, "As for the man, I went to wake him for breakfast the next morning and found him gone. Not a trace of him to be found. The only thing he left behind was a thick roll of *hemp* on the bed with a note attached to it. The note read:

'*To be used only by one who is kind-hearted.*'

"Hemp, I knew, was a durable canvas used by painters, such as Rembrandt, to preserve their works through the centuries. Naturally, *I* had no idea what to do with such an odd gift, so I left it sitting in *that* closet for the longest time," he said, pointing to a tall narrow piece of furniture beside us. He continued, "I had no use for it, until one day, years later, I decided to draw a mural to accent one of the statues we have here - a backdrop that would enhance the alcove next to the altar. Simple flowers and sky, nothing elaborate. So, I went to the closet and brought out the hemp.

"Andrew, I painted on that hemp - nothing *stayed* on it! The more paint I used, the more that slid off the canvas and went soaring into the air - creating the most lifelike flowers and sky I had ever seen! Everything I painted on it became *real* and absolutely breathtaking. This was no *ordinary* canvas! With the hemp came powers that I knew I could never allow to fall into the wrong hands. So, that night I gathered up the sky, the flowers, and the *hemp* very carefully - unaware that I was being watched.

"There was an altar boy. The rebellious sort - he was frequently punished for his ill-tempered behavior. He spent his days angry at the world, Andrew, and I couldn't help him. I thought bringing him into the church would curb his wild nature, but things only grew worse.

"When I found my keys missing one evening, I feared the worst. A few chalices, money from the donation box, *and the hemp* were all gone - stolen! That it was the altar boy was confirmed to me by the only witness who saw the thief as he fled during the night - our dutiful groundskeeper Duncan Fellows - rest his soul."

Father Caius sighed, and then continued, "I never saw the boy again until years later, when he returned a *man,* boasting about his luxurious new hotel, hoping to persuade others to follow him in a wanton life of sinful pleasures."

"Larouche!" I gasped, and the priest nodded.

"Yes, *Meir Larouche* had done his damage to the world by creating the greatest haven for sin. He used the hemp, and painted us all into his fantasy, for us to unwittingly become his slaves. The patrons now wasted away with no hope for the future and Larouche and his assistant watched on...proud of what they'd created.

"Years after the hemp was stolen, I went to the hotel to aid your father who had reached out to me by letter. I saw, for the first time, that same temptation that every man saw. With the help of two blind clergymen who vowed to remove me from the place after every visit, I agreed to help your father. Temptation is difficult to resist, *even* for a priest. Only once, did I bump into Meir Larouche again, and it warmed my heart to see that he couldn't look me directly in the eye. With all his power, he could not remove the guilt from his heart.

"For years, I wanted to storm the hotel and reclaim the hemp, but no one would join me. One by one, people fell under the spell of Larouche's palace and never returned to their former world. My parish remained, but the parishioners didn't. It takes a strong person to resist such a place!" the priest said, looking me square in the eye. "And then, there's *you,* Andrew - the one human being I've stumbled across who I believe can enter the hotel with me, retrieve the map, and leave behind the deceptive life of Larouche. A wondrous boy who can save his brethren if he so chooses. A man who can save himself *and* his family."

I sat stunned and speechless. The priest had it all mapped out, but he simply couldn't execute his plan alone. The call to action was before me, plain as day. It was what I wanted and yet, I struggled taking that first step. Gripping my cup, I struggled to find the inner courage I needed, as I thought about the danger that faced me.

451

To confront Larouche, I knew, would be no easy task. To battle the residents who never wanted to lose their untroubled lifestyle would be a war in and of itself, and I wasn't sure I was the right person for the task. The way the priest looked at me, I saw that he whole-heartedly placed his faith in me. Why then, did *I* choose to doubt myself?

There were many questions I had for the man and his magic hemp, many questions about the sort of happiness it could bring. Would sickness cease to exist and death itself be a thing of the past? Would it restore love to Patch and would it be possible to - dare I think it - bring Matilda back?

To fight for this canvas, especially one with such power, didn't seem like a cause I could choose to forget. It seemed like something I was always meant to do. The priest continued, as he circled about me.

"You could, of course, choose to deny all this. We can part ways and you can build a life for yourself in some neighboring village. All would be well for you and life would be easy. I believe good things can come from the hemp, a betterment of mankind. Along with it, however, comes a great responsibility. We all know that is something you tried to run from, Andrew."

The words he spoke were true and I suddenly realized I did not want them to define me. "You're right. I've chosen the easy road before, Priest. I'm not sure I want to make that mistake again."

He smiled at my response and stepped toward a cabinet, taking out his keys and unlocking its door with great care. He then turned back toward me with a smile.

"Would you like to see my bit of sky then?" he asked, with a mystical look in his eyes.

I knew then that what I was about to see would change my life, or any sense of reality, as I knew it. Apprehensively, I stood and walked to the cabinet, as the priest looked on with great excitement. He held both doors open and I peered into the piece of furniture. In a split second, I was lost in the magic before me...

The sky! A piece of the sky was captured inside!

The magic found in the cabinet confirmed everything. There was work I had to complete - people who were relying on me. Certainly, I found a power - but it was a power I would use only for good. The feeling was unparalleled!

There was not a time before this that I felt whole. There was something always desperate or hungry, lonesome or selfish, within me... struggling to find my place in the world. Say what you will about my story, but we all try and we all fail. I say to you this:

Death is *not* the completion, for from it starts new life. She, now high above the clouds, flows through my veins. Her spirit leads me on, and I am forever indebted to her... for my life *began* with the death of Matilda Brew. I wasn't sure how, or when, but I knew I would find a way to see her again. I knew I'd find a way to carve out a future of hope *through a canvas*.

I turned back to the priest, with the courage I didn't have a year before, and spoke four certain words.

"I am with you."

END

Acknowledgements

This book has been a part of my life for about four years now. It's been a long time coming, but I really couldn't have come this far without a few people who really helped me bring this idea to life.

To my mother, for whom the book is dedicated. Thanks for your patience and support! Most of all, thank you for all of our late night coffee breaks and conversations. You always seem to put things into perspective!

To my boyfriend, who is *always* there to lend a helping hand. The song you composed for Matilda and her mirror is beyond perfect. You jumped into my life and took on a storm... I am very lucky to have met you.

To my brother, whose history lessons always provide great insight. You're a kid from the 21st century, but a *soul* from another time.

To my illustrator, Cihan Sesen. Wow! Your work always leaves me inspired, but you brought my vision to life with the beautiful cover you created. Safe travels, friend.

Finally, to Kathleen Adams, my lovely editor and friend. You put up with me! You really did! More than that, you were my teacher in all of this and I am a better writer thanks to you.

CANVAS CARVERS

FOLLOWING THE MAVEN

COMING SOON